"What's your favorite thing about Christmas?" Ben asked.

With any other woman, Ben would've been able to find a way to make her relax. Isabel wasn't just any woman, however. The fact that she disliked him made his task that much harder.

Her focus was on her gloved hands folded tightly together in her lap. "I like many things about this time of year. One of them is the renewed spirit of charity. People tend to treat each other better."

Her statement was a telling one. While he understood how it felt to live under the weight of a town's critical scrutiny, he hadn't grown up with a scandalous father like Isabel.

"Anything else?"

"I enjoy baking. This time of year has plenty of opportunities for that. My sisters and I spend extra time in the kitchen making treats for their friends."

"What about your friends?"

Her chin jutted out. "My sisters are my friends."

"Someday your sisters will marry and move away," he said gently. "What happens then, Isabel?"

Karen Kirst was born and raised in east Tennessee near the Great Smoky Mountains. She's a lifelong lover of books, but it wasn't until after college that she had the grand idea to write one herself. Now she divides her time between being a wife, homeschooling mom and romance writer. Her favorite pastimes are reading, visiting tearooms and watching romantic comedies.

Books by Karen Kirst

Love Inspired Historical

Smoky Mountain Matches

The Reluctant Outlaw
The Bridal Swap
The Gift of Family
"Smoky Mountain Christmas"
His Mountain Miss
The Husband Hunt
Married by Christmas
From Boss to Bridegroom
The Bachelor's Homecoming
Reclaiming His Past
The Sheriff's Christmas Twins
Wed by Necessity
The Engagement Charade
A Lawman for Christmas

Cowboy Creek

Bride by Arrangement

Visit the Author Profile page
at Harlequin.com for additional titles.

KAREN KIRST

A Lawman for Christmas

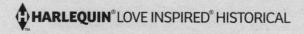

HARLEQUIN® LOVE INSPIRED® HISTORICAL

Recycling programs
for this product may
not exist in your area.

LOVE INSPIRED BOOKS

ISBN-13: 978-0-373-42546-4

A Lawman for Christmas

www.Harlequin.com

Printed in U.S.A.

And the King will answer and say to them, "Assuredly, I say to you, inasmuch as you did it to one of the least of these My brethren, you did it to Me."
—*Matthew* 25:40

To my husband, Marek, and our three boys

Chapter One

Gatlinburg, Tennessee
December 1887

Isabel Flores was face-to-face with a bank robber, and all she could think about were the disappointed children across Gatlinburg who'd receive no gifts and no Christmas goose—because this man had helped himself to others' hard-earned cash.

"You can't take that." Her hand tightening on the basket of merchandise she'd just purchased, she pointed to the bulging burlap sack tossed over his shoulder like Kris Kringle. "The Christmas season is upon us. Do you know how many families have scraped and saved the entire year in order to provide a happy holiday for their children?"

The black neckerchief the assailant used to mask his features had slipped below his chin, allowing her a clear view of his weathered face. His shaggy brows slammed down, and his mouth twisted in a scowl.

"Wrong place, wrong time, missy. Bawling brats missing their candy canes is the last thing you should be worried about." In two strides, he was before her, his fingers digging into her arm. "I'm not ready for my likeness to be plastered across Tennessee."

Her foolish behavior belatedly registered. Instead of confronting the criminal, she should've bolted. Should've screamed. Main Street was steps away from this darkened alley behind the bank. Most people were in their homes at this hour, enjoying a hot meal. There was a good chance someone was still at the livery, however.

She drew breath into her lungs.

He jerked her against him and clapped his hand over her mouth. "Don't do it," he growled as he tugged the mask back into place. The stench of unwashed hair invaded her nostrils. "What am I going to do with you, huh?"

Various scenarios pulsed through her mind, none of them good.

The distant click of a gun hammer echoed off the buildings, indicating a third person had joined them. Isabel found herself whirled about and locked against the thief's body. Her basket hit the ground with a thud, bright, fragrant oranges scattering in the dirt. Beneath the callused hand over her lips, she grimaced. The fruit hadn't been cheap.

"I'd welcome you to town," the newcomer drawled, "but you've already made yourself at home, I see."

Even without the fat moon's light washing over the alley, Isabel would've known the identity of her would-be rescuer. The deep, velvet voice resonated with lazy confidence. He was hatless, his dark red hair falling into his eyes, giving him a boyish air that didn't mesh with the grim determination etched on his handsome features.

Please, God, don't let Deputy Ben MacGregor's face be the last one I see.

He shifted, causing his coat lapels to fall open. The metal star pinned to his vest announced his occupation.

"I don't need a welcome from no lawman," the thief snarled. "I come and go as I please."

Cold metal pressed into her temple. Fear encased her, numbing her more than the winter temperatures stinging her cheeks. She made a low moan deep in her throat. Ben's gaze sharpened on her.

Why did it have to be *him* standing there? Why couldn't it have been the sheriff instead?

"Not with our citizens' hard-earned money, you don't. And certainly not with our women." His gun was as steady as his voice. "Release the lady, and then we'll discuss the bounty you're aiming to make off with."

"And lose my only ticket outta here? I don't think so." He shook his head. "Besides, she caught me without my disguise."

Using her body as a shield, he lowered the hammer. A muffled whimper escaped before she could stop it. Her sisters depended on her to run the gristmill. Sure, they were old enough to lead their own lives, but they weren't responsible with money, and Carmen would likely marry the first man who asked. Her mother had endured enough suffering for one lifetime. How would her fragile mind cope when she heard the news of her eldest daughter's death?

Ben lifted his other hand, palm up, and edged forward. "It's unlikely she got a clear view. Too dark." His gaze switched to Isabel, the flicker of concern heightening her unease. "Robbery's one thing. Trust me, you don't want murder charges brought against you."

"Too late."

Isabel registered multiple things at once. The hitch in Ben's measured approach, the slight compression of his lips, the almost imperceptible movement of the thief's finger.

She wasn't ready to die.

Lifting her foot, she brought her boot heel down on the

gunman's toe, then seized the hand over her mouth and sank her teeth into the dirty flesh. The thief howled in pain and jerked free. Isabel dived to the ground, knees protesting the hard jolt, and tried to scramble out of the way.

A piercing shot rang out. Someone grunted. A second bullet whizzed through the air.

A heavy thunk behind her registered, followed by the clink of coins. The money bag! Boots striking the hard-packed earth faded into nothingness.

A strong hand gripped her shoulder, and she flinched.

"Isabel, it's me." Hands and knees in the dirt, she slowly lifted her head. The deputy extended his hand. "You all right?"

"Fine." Her heart rattling in her chest, she allowed him to assist her up. Brushing the debris from her skirts, she said, "You've a fine sense of timing, Deputy. There wasn't a gun pointed to my head until you interfered."

"Your effusive gratitude is making me blush, Miss Flores," he said wryly. "I saved your life."

"I'm the one who distracted him." She squinted into the shadowed forest clinging to the hulking mountains flanking Gatlinburg. "Aren't you going to pursue him?"

He ambled over and hefted the large money sack. Faltering, he used the building's facade for support. "I don't think that's a wise idea."

Isabel had started to gather her belongings. All but one of the prized oranges had been spared. At the odd sigh in Ben's voice, she straightened and scrutinized him. He didn't look right.

"Why not?"

His eyes, which in daylight were the color of sunlight striking sea-green glass, gleamed in the darkness. "Because I'm likely to bleed out before I catch him."

He indicated his upper right arm.

"You've been shot?" Guilt punched a hole in her annoyance. Here she'd been berating him when he was in pain.

"Feels like a flesh wound." He inclined his head toward the bank. "Let me return this money to its rightful place, and I'll escort you home."

"You have to see Doc."

"Later." He disappeared inside the bank for a brief minute, then used his master keys to lock it up tight. When he reached her, he removed the neckerchief from around his throat. "Tie this off for me, will you?"

"I can get home by myself," she protested, concern for the Debonair Deputy at odds with her usual antipathy. "You need to get that wound cleaned and stitched."

"I happen to know that Doc Owens is out at the Barton farm, assisting in the delivery of their latest child. The sheriff has a steady hand and a cast-iron stomach, but he's taken Allison and the kids to Norfolk for the month. Besides, you heard the thief. You're a liability. Who's to say he's not lying in wait, intending on following you and making sure you can't talk?"

Suppressing a shudder, she seized the cloth and quickly wrapped it around Ben's thick biceps.

He grimaced. "A shame about the coat. My mother gave it to me before I took this job. It's kept me warm through four Tennessee winters."

"Our winters are typically mild."

He flashed a smile, the lopsided one that had slain countless hearts. "Not compared with my hometown in southern Georgia. Besides, according to the almanac, we're in for more snow than usual this year."

"So get it patched. Nicole Darling can have it repaired in less time than it takes you to make a girl swoon." Isabel snatched up a forgotten sachet of cloves.

"When was the last time that happened?" he challenged, laugh lines crinkling the corners of his eyes.

"I don't keep detailed records of your romantic exploits, but I seem to recall hearing about Edith Pulaski at the harvest festival. And Josie Strutin embarrassed herself during the annual August social."

"Edith fainted because she was ill with a fever. As for Josie, I choose to believe she was overwhelmed by the prospect of singing a solo in front of a crowd and not because I was nearby." He started for the boardwalk, his stride even and decisive, though he seemed to hold his injured arm close to his body. "Did you walk or ride?"

"I walked."

"You can ride with me, then."

She put her shaky legs in motion, unhappy with the prospect of spending any amount of time with him. Isabel went out of her way to avoid the shallow charmer. Ben MacGregor's reputation was a two-sided coin. While a respected lawman who'd committed his life to protecting Gatlinburg's citizens, he was also a confirmed bachelor who trifled with women's emotions. Isabel couldn't respect a man like that, not after living with the consequences of her father's repeated infidelities.

He led her to his grand sorrel horse whose copper-red coat mimicked Ben's hair. One of the most recognizable animals in town, his name was Blaze. Ben mounted first and, taking her basket, let her use his good arm to pull herself up behind him. During the first part of the slow journey, she utilized her leg muscles for balance. She soon tired, however.

"You can put your arms about my waist," he quipped over his shoulder. "I promise I won't get ideas."

"Like I'd ever be interested in you," she muttered.

His deep, husky laugh mocked her. "Every man in town is aware of your aversion to romance."

Isabel didn't care that she was considered a prude or that folks whispered she was destined to be an old maid. Better that than they think she shared her father's lack of morality.

The deserted lane on which they traveled crested a small incline. During the descent, Isabel had no choice but to use Ben as a support. He said nothing when she slid her arms around his waist. His body heat seeped into her, helping stave off the chill December air. Unaccustomed to this degree of closeness to a man, she became acutely aware of the play of muscles across his broad back, the solid leanness of his flanks and his flat stomach. He wasn't tall—average, really—but he had a stocky, honed build.

Thankfully, her family's property was situated only a mile from the heart of town. The gristmill and stream edged the woods to their left. A modest-size clearing surrounded by more woods contained the cabin, barn and outbuildings, space for a vegetable garden, and pasture for their livestock.

When he halted Blaze beside her porch, Isabel wasted no time scrambling to solid ground.

"Thank you for the ride." She stretched out her hand for the basket. "I'll take that."

An infuriating grin curved his generous mouth. He was well aware of her eagerness to be rid of him. "My pleasure."

The door banged open. Light spilled through the opening as her sisters, Honor and Carmen, emerged onto the porch and simpered over Ben's presence like every other ninny-headed female who fell prey to his outgoing personality and winning smile. When Honor noticed his injury, Isabel knew getting rid of him wouldn't be as easy as she'd thought.

* * *

Within a matter of minutes, Ben found himself seated at the Flores sisters' table while they gathered the necessary supplies to tend his wound. Trying to shut out the burning sensation engulfing his arm, he focused on his surroundings. Two years had passed since he'd been inside this cabin. He'd come the night Manuel Flores was murdered. Thankfully, his boss, Sheriff Shane Timmons, had shouldered the unenviable task of informing Manuel's wife and daughters of the events surrounding his passing.

Alma Flores had taken it the hardest, slumping to the ground and wailing as if her heart would never be mended. A mere month after the funeral, she'd gone to live with her sister in nearby Knoxville, leaving Isabel to care for her sisters and their small farm and gristmill.

His gaze sought her out, as it usually did whenever she was around. Unlike Honor and Carmen, who favored vibrant hues and rich fabrics, Isabel preferred somber, severe clothing. Ben surmised it was her way of trying to go unnoticed. He'd like to tell her the ploy was unsuccessful.

He tracked her movements about the central room as she lit multiple lamps. One she placed on the fireplace mantel, another on a squat table in between a pair of cushioned chairs. Still more she hung from pegs on either side of the door. Light flickered over her satin black hair, pulled away from her face in a thick, glossy French braid that curved around her slender neck and disappeared beneath her heather-gray fur-lined cloak.

All three Flores women were beautiful. Nineteen-year-old Honor was willowy and graceful, putting him in mind of a delicate bird. A year younger and the shortest of the three, Carmen had a healthy figure, and her round face was consistently animated. Isabel was different and, in Ben's estimation, without rival. She possessed noble features, her

Mexican heritage on proud display in her high forehead, distinct cheekbones, sleek jawline. Her olive skin was the perfect foil for arched dark brows, glittering black eyes and an apricot-hued mouth. His attention snagged there. Full and lush, her lips provided a soft counterpoint to her austere demeanor.

Ben sometimes contemplated different ways to provoke a smile from the elusive beauty. The usual methods wouldn't apply to her, however. She hadn't attempted to hide her disdain. He accepted how she felt about him. Understood her reasons.

She passed by his chair, Christmastime scents of cinnamon and other spices combined with tangy orange wafting over him.

"We'll have to cut off your sleeve." Hands on her hips, Honor considered his torn, bloodied shirt.

"As much as I'd love to stitch you up, I can't stand the sight of blood." Positioned beside her sister, Carmen's brown eyes were apologetic. The cloud of chocolate-brown hair tumbling about her shoulders quivered with the shake of her head. "I'd wind up a puddle at your feet."

"Not an uncommon occurrence where the deputy is concerned." Isabel unbuttoned her cloak and hung it on a coatrack. When she intercepted her sisters' disapproving stares, she shrugged. "What? It's true."

"You act as if it's his fault he's as handsome as they come," Carmen retorted, then blushed to her hairline.

Ben ducked his head to hide his smile.

Isabel made a shooing motion with her hands. "Off to your room, both of you. I'll see to the deputy's wound."

Their protests were met with a stern stare. "I won't be able to concentrate with the two of you fussing over him."

Grumbling to each other, they disappeared into a room on the far side of the cabin. Of modest size, their home boasted a cozy central space—the furniture arranged about a massive fireplace—a separate kitchen and two bedrooms. The sofa was, at best guess, two decades old. While the carved walnut frame was polished to a high shine, nothing could hide the sad state of the black-and-white upholstery. They'd placed brightly colored pillows along its length to mask the imperfections. Landscape paintings of winding rivers and fields dotted with bluebonnets and even one of a longhorn provided reminders of their home state of Texas. White, green and red paper chains hung from the mantel, a playful nod to the Christmas season.

"You own interesting artwork," he said, indicating the brick-red ceramic animal perched on the small desk in between the bedroom doors.

"That's a coatimundi."

"A what?"

"It's a raccoon-like animal that inhabits Central and South America. My great-grandmother brought it with her to Texas. That's how we acquired it."

There were other unique items harking back to their former home. There was a plate-size metal circle with a single star in the middle. Displayed on the coffee table was a hand-painted wooden bowl with brilliant blue, white and orange flowers on a black backdrop. Being in the Flores home was akin to being in a foreign marketplace surrounded by unique and interesting wares. He liked it.

Isabel picked up the scissors and moved beside him, close enough that her skirts whispered against his leg. Her fingers skimmed his shoulder in fleeting touches as she carefully cut away the sleeve.

Ben closed his eyes. He couldn't recall ever being this close to her.

"I have to remove the material," she warned. "I'll try to be gentle."

He opened his eyes and met hers, which unexpectedly mirrored concern. "The pain's manageable," he said.

"I haven't gotten to the hard part yet."

After discarding the tattered sleeve, she began washing the damaged area. Ben gritted his teeth and focused on his breathing.

He tilted his head back to get a better look at her. A tiny pleat had formed between her eyebrows as she worked, and her crisp plum-colored blouse whispered with her movements. Lace edging her cuffs and high collar was the only nod to whimsy. In spite of the late hour, her hair was tidy and neat, the glossy braid curving around to her front.

"You don't have to shop odd hours, you know."

"I prefer to shop in peace and relative quiet," she retorted. "I've found that the hour prior to closing time is perfectly suited for my purposes. Most folks are preparing supper then."

As the image of her at the thief's mercy resurged, he clenched his fists. "You should stick to daylight hours, Isabel. Safer that way."

Tossing the soiled washrag in the water bowl, she jammed one hand against her hip. "Are you implying it's my fault I happened upon a bank robber?"

"Stop being so prickly," he chided. "I'm simply doling out practical advice. It's my duty as a lawman."

Her frown deepening, she stepped around him and picked up a sewing needle.

He leaned the opposite direction. "I'm not sure I like the look in your eye. Maybe someone else should stitch me back together. Someone who doesn't see me coming and flee."

Isabel looked stunned he'd voiced what they both knew to be true. Her brows collided. "I would never intentionally hurt you. O-or anyone, for that matter."

He righted himself in the seat. "I suppose I'll have to trust you, seeing as how Honor is the only other option, and she was looking a bit green about the mouth."

"Like Carmen, she has a weak stomach, but she would never confess to it in front of you."

Her fingertips were cool and skittish against his skin as she took hold of his bare arm. Ben's mouth went dry. He mentally clung to that touch as she began the painful and tedious process of mending him. At long last, her hand fell away, and his eyes blinked open.

"All done?"

She studied her handiwork with a faint grimace. "It's not pretty, but as long as you keep it clean and dry, you should heal without any problems."

"Scars are a sign of manliness." He winked, then let out a slow, deep breath. "Now that you're finished wielding that needle, I can tell you I'll be sticking around until morning."

"You will *not* be spending this night or any other on my property!"

Isabel's hands, which had been steady throughout her task, began trembling. She washed and dried them and hid them in the folds of her skirt. Her rebellious gaze returned to his exposed limb. His skin was paler there, like rich cream, and incredibly pleasing to the touch, his flesh firm and warm.

Irritated with herself, she marched to the coatrack, retrieved his tattered coat and dropped it in his lap.

"You may have some bruising around the stitches. I advise you to have Doc Owens check it as soon as you're able."

"I'm confident you did a perfectly acceptable job."

Ben stood and eased his arm into the sleeve, wincing

as he did so. His color was good, she reassured herself. And he looked steady on his feet.

"He may have something to help dull the pain."

He deftly buttoned his coat, starting from the bottom and working up. Lamplight glinted off his dark red hair. Cut short around his ears and along his shirt collar, the front strands were slightly longer and slipped forward into his eyes. He might be too handsome for words, but Isabel was immune. Did it matter if his classic features could've graced any of the world's great sculptures? Or that his skin was smooth and sun-kissed, stretching over prominent cheekbones and chiseled jaw?

None of that mattered if his character was lacking.

"Pain will keep me alert tonight. I can stay in the warming hut," he said, referring to the structure near the gristmill where customers gathered to wait for their corn or wheat to be ground. "It's within view of the cabin. If our thief decides to pay you a visit, I'll be here to protect you."

"He doesn't know my name or where I live."

"I can't be one hundred percent positive he didn't follow us here."

"He's after the money, not me. Sleep in the bank."

His lips thinned. "You'd rather take your chances with a dangerous criminal than have me on your property?"

She sighed. "You want proof I can handle myself?"

Lowering one knee to the floor, she removed the small dagger from its sheaf below her calf and, with deadly accuracy, hurled it through the air. The pointed end dug into her bedroom door frame.

Ben shot her a disbelieving look before striding across the room to retrieve it. "You had this on you the whole time?"

"I would've utilized it if I'd had the chance."

"But I foiled everything by coming to your aid." Sarcasm

laced his voice. He bent his head and studied the carving in the wooden handle. "Expert craftsmanship." He tested the blade. "I wouldn't mind having one like it. Where did you get it?"

She extended her hand. He placed it in the center of her palm, curiosity making his eyes appear a shade lighter. Isabel was loath to reveal the truth, but she wasn't going to lie. "I made it."

His brow furrowed in disbelief. "You cut and carved the wood and forged the steel?"

"Why is that so hard to believe?"

"Not for the reason you're thinking," he said drily. "You can obviously do whatever you put your mind to. You've looked after your sisters' well-being and managed this farm, all while operating a gristmill. I simply haven't heard a whisper of your skills."

"That's because very few people know."

"I assure you, a man would pay a high price for one of those."

"I do sell them, just not in Gatlinburg." Returning to the table, she cleared her sewing supplies. "I knew when my mother left that I'd need additional income. My uncle, my mother's brother, is a blacksmith. He stayed with us for about a year when I was sixteen, and he taught me many things, the art of knife making among them. Papa hated the idea of one of his daughters learning a man's job." She smirked, remembering his tirades. "That's probably why Uncle Alejandro did it. They despised each other. Small wonder."

"You turned a valuable skill into a moneymaker."

"My knives are stocked in several stores, mostly in Maryville and Sevierville."

While she wrung out the cloth she'd used to clean his wound, he discarded the dirty water outside. The waft of cold air raised goose bumps on her arms. She put the kettle on to boil and debated whether or not to offer him coffee. It was the polite thing to do, especially after his valor tonight, but he wasn't the kind of man she wanted hanging around her home. Honor had a steady beau, but Carmen...the girl had nothing but fluff and romance between her ears.

He hovered in the kitchen doorway, his magnetic presence making her nerves skitter and scatter. Did he see the hole in the rug? Had he noticed the curtains were faded and needed to be replaced? She worked hard to provide for her sisters. God had met their basic needs—they had plenty of food, durable clothing, and their home was in decent shape—but there wasn't a lot of money for extras. Sometimes her many responsibilities threatened to overwhelm her. Maybe that's why the thought of the thief stealing from hardworking families had outraged her to the point she'd foolishly challenged him.

"Isabel, you shouldn't have to travel to a whole other town to sell your knives. And you shouldn't have to feel like you have to wait until almost closing time to shop. Your father's behavior doesn't reflect on you."

"Don't pretend to understand what I've been through," she retorted. "You haven't walked in my shoes, haven't felt the condemning stares or heard the whispers as you walk past."

Granted, not everyone in their mountain town had treated the Flores women as if they were morally tainted. There were those who'd treated them with respect and compassion. The situation might have improved with time, considering her parents were out of the picture, but past wounds ran deep. She preferred to spend much of her time on this farm. Her sisters' companionship was enough.

"I know what it's like to be the subject of gossip," he said gruffly.

She didn't attempt to hide her scorn. "You court speculation with your blatant flirting."

How anyone would willingly do such a thing was unfathomable. Isabel went out of her way to remain above approach, to avoid the stinging whip of judgment. She'd had enough of that throughout her childhood.

He held up his hand in defense. "I've made no secret of my decision to remain a bachelor. Everyone in this town from the age of sixteen to ninety-five is aware of my no-marriage policy. I'm not to blame if a girl chooses to believe she can change me."

"Such arrogance and flippant disregard for others' feelings! What would cause a man to go around kissing innocent women, I wonder, leading them on a merry dance that will only end in heartache?"

"Hold on, sugarplum." His laconic smile remained fixed, but his eyes glittered righteous fire. "Who said anything about kissing? That's crossing the line of friendship, something I would never do. That sort of behavior is reserved for serious romance."

"That's something, I suppose," she huffed, slapping a single mug on the counter.

"I was referring to a situation in Georgia. A scandal not of my making. It's the reason I ultimately found my way here."

She stirred the steaming water and coffee grounds together. "Let me guess, you trifled with the wrong girl, and her father ran you out of town."

Ben actually looked disappointed. His gaze rested on the mug then lifted to her face. "You have me pegged. Sure, that's *exactly* what happened."

He pivoted on his boot heel and headed for the door. "Thanks for patching me up."

Ignoring a pinch of guilt, she trailed after him. "You're going home, correct? Or the bank?"

"I won't stay here tonight," he said, his tone flat. "But I will be stopping by at odd times the next few days. Be alert to any suspicious activity. You know where to find me if you need me."

"I won't."

A muscle jumped in his jaw. "Let's hope you're right."

Chapter Two

Isabel couldn't shake the memories. The events outside the bank crowded in…the terror of the gun digging in her temple, the relief mixed with dread at seeing Ben at the end of that alley, more grave than she'd ever seen him. He'd looked like a lethal punisher of misdeeds as opposed to the usual congenial lothario.

You could've offered him coffee.

Isabel scowled as she carried a stack of one-pound sacks to the platform built around the millstones. She'd let her disdain for his reputation take precedence over common courtesy. The events to which he'd referred—his supposed brush with scandal—had grown into a perplexing mystery that had kept her awake. If his reasons for leaving Georgia hadn't involved a brokenhearted maiden and an irate father intent on revenge, what were they?

None of your business, Isabel. Your paths intersecting last night was a single event. No need to continue interacting with the troublesome man. Or letting thoughts of him prevent you from getting a good night's rest.

Her eyes felt gritty, her mind not as sharp as usual. She'd been operating their gristmill for so long she could do it in her sleep. Open every Friday and Saturday, the hours usually passed in a blur. Today she found little comfort in the familiar water wheel's whir and the muted grinding of the gears beneath the floor.

She was building a fire in the woodstove when Honor entered the mill, eyes bright and determined. This didn't bode well. The nineteen-year-old usually didn't make an appearance until lunch.

"Something the matter?"

Her long, wavy hair constrained with a bright red ribbon, she approached with a mug held out as an offering. "I've brought you hot cocoa."

Isabel brushed the wood bits from her hands. "What's the special occasion?"

"I thought you might need a bit of cheering up this morning. Not only was your life threatened, you were forced to spend time with the deputy."

Accepting the mug, Isabel sipped the somewhat bitter chocolate concoction and sighed in satisfaction. She didn't have the heart to scold her sister for dipping into their stores of the costly ingredient. Honor was attuned to others' feelings. It's why she was more concerned with lifting Isabel's spirits than the household finances.

"It's delicious." She dredged up a smile. "Thank you."

Honor claimed the lone chair and folded her hands in her lap. "Ben's a nice man, isn't he? There's no question he's as handsome as the day is long, but he's also got good character, don't you think? Does the fact he saved your life soften your opinion of him?"

"Your lack of subtlety amazes me." Drifting to the window that overlooked the homestead and their beloved mountains, she surveyed the wintry scene. "Just because you've found happiness with John doesn't mean everyone else must be in a relationship."

"I can't understand why you refuse to give any man a chance. Not everyone is like Papa."

"Repeating this conversation every few months won't change my view of the opposite sex. At their core, men are self-serving creatures. Why on earth would I subject myself to one?"

She would never be like her mother, who'd endured Manuel's indignities in silence. Alma's refusal to stand up for herself had formed a wedge between mother and daughter. How she could've lamented his passing was beyond Isabel.

Her sister's nose scrunched like a child's, dispelling her usual air of tranquility. "You're being unfair. And cynical."

"I'm realistic."

The first customer of the day arrived then, putting an end to the pointless exchange. Her sisters wouldn't succeed in convincing her to risk her independence on the slim chance she'd meet a man who'd treat her as a respected partner. As more customers filed in, a majority of them men, Isabel overheard countless conversations about the attempted bank robbery and how Ben's heroic actions had netted him even more female admirers. Hoping her disgust was well hidden, she took their corn and, after removing a one-eighth portion for herself, loaded the top hopper and waited for the fine meal to appear.

She kept expecting someone to interrogate her. The way they talked, she hadn't even been present! Resentment burned in her chest. Irrational, she knew, but wasn't it just like a man to take all the credit?

By midafternoon, her temper had reached a high simmer. The arrival of brothers Myron and Chester Gallatin—bullies, both of them—only inflamed her unhappy mood.

The men's father, Sal Gallatin, owned the lumberyard. They'd spent their whole lives working there and were built like stone mountains. Their nasty dispositions made them ugly.

"You thinking what I'm thinking, Chester?" Leering at Isabel, Myron elbowed his brother's ribs.

"What's that?"

"I'm thinking the miller's in a foul mood." He rubbed his massive hands together. "What do you say we try and fix that?"

Isabel ceased sanding the four-inch beech-wood handle that would pair nicely with a large blade. There'd been a lull in customers in the past hour, and she was currently alone. After last night's run-in, she was especially sensitive to the threat of trouble. She debated reaching for her dagger. While she had excellent aim, she only had one weapon at her disposal and two targets.

Chester lowered his buckets of shelled corn to the floor and grinned, revealing one missing front tooth. "Good idea."

Myron advanced, cruel mischief in his eyes. "Want to hear a funny story?"

Her muscles went rigid. "As you rightly pointed out, I'm not in the mood to chat."

He reached behind her, crowding her on purpose, and snagged the measuring container for her share of the corn. "That's a shame. It's guaranteed to entertain."

No doubt completely aware of her unease, Myron winked before scooping out the allotted amount and returning the container to the chest-high platform.

Squaring her shoulders, she started for the buckets. Chester's hand encircled her wrist.

"Stop right there, Miss Flores. These are heavier than usual. Allow me."

She jerked her hand free. In that moment, the door

creaked open and in strolled the deputy. Sharp relief cascaded through her.

"Deputy MacGregor, you're just the man I wanted to see."

The tension inside the building was unmistakable. The Gallatin brothers weren't fond of him. He'd taken them to task over multiple offenses, although nothing serious that would require jail time. The fact he was younger than both of them pricked their pride. Myron met Ben's gaze in silent challenge. Chester took a step back from Isabel.

Her outfit reflected the overcast day outside. The gray blouse she donned boasted pencil-thin navy stripes and was paired with a somber black skirt. A wide velvet belt accentuated her slender waist and the flare of her hips. Color heightened, midnight eyes churning with displeasure, he knew her greeting was too good to be true.

She clasped and unclasped her hands at her waist. "I need to speak to you about a private matter."

"Good thing I stopped in. I have business to discuss with you, as well."

Ben greeted the men, drawing them into a conversation about a big building project they were supplying lumber for in a neighboring town. With Myron and Chester distracted, Isabel was able to work unhindered. When the pair had taken their leave—though not before goading her with promises to return soon—she rounded on him.

"I should've known you'd play the role of valiant hero."

"And here I thought I was the man you desperately wanted to see." He flashed his most winning smile.

She didn't even blink. A sound between a sigh and groan escaped her. Spinning, she stalked to the corner, grabbed a broom and began sweeping the fine white dust that coated the mill's surfaces.

"Careful. You're going to whip up clouds of that stuff." He came as close as he dared. "Care to explain what's got you hot under the collar?"

Her knuckles were white on the handle. "You spun a yarn, Deputy. A pretty story that only hinted at the truth. It's like I wasn't even present in that alleyway."

"Ah, I see." Taking off his hat, he gestured to encompass the structure's spacious interior. "You're upset that this place isn't packed wall-to-wall with curious townspeople hankering for the gory details."

Her lips parted, and her spine lost some of its starch. "The reason you didn't include me was to shield me from gossip?" Her tone insinuated he was incapable of such insight.

"You despise being the center of attention. I figured you'd thank me." He adopted an innocent grin.

Her brow became pinched, and her chest expanded on a deep inhale. Apparently, his charms were ineffective where Isabel Flores was concerned. He didn't completely mind. It was refreshing to be in the company of a woman who wasn't trying to finagle a marriage proposal from him.

"That's not the only reason," he continued. "I figured leaving you out of the narrative would help in protecting you from our criminal."

"Hmm." Head bent, she began sweeping at a more sedate pace.

His expectations of gratitude evaporated. He peered out the window. "You haven't had any suspicious activity, have you?"

"None whatsoever."

"Good." Leaning against the window ledge, he cradled his sore arm against his chest and watched her work. "I sent telegrams to the surrounding towns. If anyone has information on our man, they'll contact us."

Sheriff Timmons deserved a holiday with his family. Still, Ben could've used some assistance in this matter. He respected the older, more experienced lawman and had patterned his methods after Shane since arriving in Gatlinburg.

"Did you pass the night on the bank floor?"

"In one of the leather chairs, actually. Much more comfortable."

She looked up, her dark gaze raking him from head to toe. Unlike others, she didn't gaze upon him with manufactured adoration. Isabel was incapable of false feeling. She was a straight shooter. He liked that about her.

You like many more things about her, a warning voice inside knelled.

He suppressed the pointed reminder that he wasn't meant for marriage and family. Dwelling on it only served to arouse dissatisfaction and, if not kept in check, regret that painted his days with a gray film. Better to focus on the many blessings God had bestowed upon him.

"And did you visit Doc Owens?"

"First thing this morning. He praised your handiwork, Nurse Flores, as I knew he would."

A becoming blush tinted her cheeks. "Just be sure to keep it clean and dry so you don't negate my efforts," she said pertly.

He pushed off the wall and inclined his head. "Yes, ma'am."

"Was there anything else?" She raised her eyebrows. "Because I have work to do."

"Do the Gallatins frequently give you trouble? When I walked in, you looked about five seconds away from wielding your dagger."

"They're more of an annoyance than anything." She lifted her chin. "Besides, I can take care of myself. My sisters and I have been on our own for nearly two years and have managed just fine."

"I admire your grit." He also admired her dogged commitment to her siblings and their livelihood. Her spunk. Plainspoken manner. Her courage. The list went on. "About what happened last night —"

"I'm fine, Deputy. Truly."

"That's what I thought after my first brush with violence. In the coming days and weeks, you may have nightmares. You might feel jumpy, even frightened for no reason at all. It's important you talk to someone." At the instant refusal forming on her lips, he wagged his index finger. "Doesn't have to be me. You could wait and speak to Shane when he returns next month. Or I could round up a woman who's experienced similar circumstances. The point is, you're not alone."

Her inner struggle was evident. "Thank you," she finally allowed. "I'll keep your advice in mind."

With no other excuse to linger, Ben bade her goodbye, his thoughts lingering on the beautiful miller for a long while after. He spent the afternoon informing Main Street's business owners of the need to be cautious. The thief had one of two choices, either accept his failure here and move on, or bide his time and try again. They had to be prepared for him to choose the latter.

Having been invited to dine with his good friends the Parkers, he arrived anticipating a pleasant evening in their company. A former US marshal, Grant Parker understood the rigors of Ben's profession. His wife, Jessica, was part of the O'Malley clan, two large families who'd resided in the Smoky Mountains for decades. The redheaded beauty was sharp as a tack and outspoken. She was one of a handful of women, including Shane's wife, Allison, and the Plum

Café owner's wife, Ellie, who openly took him to task over his heartbreaker reputation.

As soon as they welcomed him into their home, he sensed a charge in the atmosphere. The husband and wife tended to be affectionate. This night, however, there was an added significance to their exchanges. Ben shelved his curiosity until Jessica placed three hefty slices of dried blueberry cake drizzled with icing on the table.

As tempting as the dessert was, he didn't immediately reach for his fork. He folded his arms across his chest and winced when the stitches pulled the tender skin. "All right. Out with it."

Grant stopped chewing midbite, his blue gaze startled. Jessica's fork halted halfway to her mouth. Blushing to the roots of her hair, she lowered the utensil to the plate and took a sip of milk, not the coffee she typically enjoyed with her dessert.

"We should've known you'd guess something was amiss," she said.

Grant chased his cake with a long draw of coffee. Setting the mug down, he ran a hand over his short blond hair. "You're right. He's not one to miss details."

"Noticing details has helped preserve my life. In addition to God's protection, of course," he pointed out. "What's the big secret?"

Jessica found Grant's hand atop the table and threaded their fingers together. "We're not quite ready to share this news with anyone outside the family. However, you eat at our table often enough to be considered family." She shot him an arch smile.

Ben studied their faces, certain what was to come next. He braced himself. Visualized his cheerful response. It had to be a balance of enthusiasm and happiness for the deserving couple.

"We're having a baby."

Ben felt his mouth stretching into a smile—a convincing one, he hoped. "That's wonderful news."

Sliding his chair back, he moved to hug Jessica, who surreptitiously swiped at her eyes. Grant stood and accepted his bear hug and hearty pats on the back. Still gripping his friend's shoulders, Ben eased back. "I'm thrilled for you both."

A flicker of concern temporarily dampened Grant's expression. Before the other man could voice his thoughts, Ben returned to his seat.

"When's the bundle of joy set to arrive?"

"Midsummer." Grant held Jessica close. "Probably late July."

Wonder and excitement made her eyes shine. The couple had been married more than two years. They must've wondered if they'd be able to have children. It occurred to Ben that they'd been happy without children, but then, they hadn't entered the marriage aware that having a baby wasn't even a possibility. He couldn't think of a single woman who'd willingly agree to a childless union.

The summer before his twentieth birthday, he'd suffered a terrible illness that many had feared he'd succumb to. His parents and sisters, along with his fiancée, Marianne Ogden, had kept vigil at his bedside. And while he'd eventually recovered, it hadn't been without cost. The long bout of mumps had led to complications. Rare ones, his doctor had implied, but they did occur. Ben would not be able to father a child.

He dug into his cake with false enthusiasm. "You'll be pleased to know I'm available to be the official baby spoiler," he quipped, winking at Jessica.

"I imagine you'd take quite well to that task," she responded. "And one day, when the right woman lassoes your heart, I'll return the favor with your kids."

Grant grimaced. Ben shot him a quelling look. Of Gatlinburg's population, Grant Parker was the only soul who knew Ben's secret. And he was determined to keep it that way.

Chapter Three

Isabel was closing the mill the following evening when a male figure separated from the shadows.

"Evenin', sugarplum."

She jumped and would've screamed if her lantern light hadn't spilled over his all-too-familiar features.

"You again!" She pressed her hand to her throat. "This is becoming a habit."

An annoying one, at that.

"I apologize for frightening you."

Ben was dressed in his Sunday best, a black suit that enhanced his vibrant coloring. His hair was combed neatly off his forehead, and his lean cheeks had recently seen a razor blade. The suit jacket molded to his firm shoulders and hung straight to his hips, where the slight bulge of his weapon was noticeable. A navy-and-black plaid wool scarf was wrapped about his neck.

She resisted the urge to ask him where he was headed. Probably to some young lady's house to engage in what he did best—making women fall in love with him with very little effort.

"I have news to share." His breath created white clouds in the still air. "This afternoon, I received a response from the Pigeon Forge sheriff's office. One of their banks was hit in the wee hours of the morning. The perp's still in the area."

Freeing her braid from beneath her cloak, she set out for the cabin. Ben fell into step beside her.

"How can you be sure it's the same man?"

"I can't, not for sure. We haven't had any robberies of this type—attempted or otherwise—for nine months or so. However, given our town's proximity, I'm inclined to believe it is."

Ascending the stairs, she paused on the porch and curved her hand around the nearest post. "If I promise to be alert to any hint of danger, will you cease these unexpected visits?"

He'd remained on the bottom step, bringing them on an even level. Mild amusement danced over his features. "Come now, there's no use pretending you don't enjoy our exchanges."

For a moment, she put his incorrigible behavior toward women and her poor view of men in general out of her head. Take away those obstacles and she could *maybe* see his appeal. Not only was he pleasing to look upon—a girl could get lost in those sea-green eyes—he also had an affable personality. He was well liked and respected by many in the community.

"Surely you must know that a woman like me, whose own father engaged in flagrant indiscretions without a thought to what his behavior was doing to his wife and daughters, would never enjoy spending time with a man like you." She felt as jaded as she sounded.

His light mood vanished. Was that actual regret passing over his face?

She'd never get to hear his response, because it was cut off by her sisters' intrusion. Honor and Carmen were the epitome of Christmas cheer in their matching holly-red dresses. They'd each requested and received new fabric for their birthdays. They'd taken great pleasure in designing the outfits. Their excited chatter faltered at the sight of Ben.

"Deputy! What a pleasant surprise," Carmen gushed, testing the artificial flower tucked amid her brunette tresses. "Are you here to escort Isabel to the serenade?"

Adjusting the half cape covering her shoulders, Honor turned astonished eyes on her. "You've decided to attend after all?"

"Of course not."

Isabel eschewed most social gatherings. Why put herself at the mercy of others' harsh judgment? As the daughter of the infamous Manuel Flores, her presence drew whispers and speculation about her character. Her sisters argued that it was her reclusive nature that fanned the flames of curiosity. She should make more of an effort, they insisted, allow people to get to know her. Then they'd see she didn't have anything in common with Manuel besides his last name.

"You should hear Isabel singing around the house," Honor told Ben. "She has a lovely soprano voice."

"Is that so?" A new reserve held his charm in check.

She imagined his pride had been wounded by her bluntness. He was accustomed to silvery praise and unwavering adulation. Ben MacGregor wouldn't ever get that from her.

"You should convince her to come with us," Carmen exclaimed, clapping her hands. "The four of us can go together. It will be tremendous fun!"

"I'm not certain my opinion will hold much sway," he allowed, his enigmatic gaze locked on her. "You do work very hard, Isabel. How long has it been since you've done something out of the ordinary? An activity unconnected with this farm?"

A rebellious impulse reared its head. Even she had to admit her life was a cycle of ordered routine. "I'd planned on spending the evening before the fire with a good book."

Carmen rolled her eyes and groaned. "You do that every weekend night!"

Isabel refused to be embarrassed. It was no secret that she was a spinster by choice.

"We get hot cider at most of the homes we visit. If it's been a profitable year, Mr. Hatfield hands out sacks full of apples, oranges, peppermints and nuts. Laura Hatfield hinted this year's been a good one." Honor's dark eyes gleamed. "It's time for you to break out of your shell." Linking their arms, she tugged her toward the door. "You could do with a bit of Christmas spirit."

"I'll do your hair." Carmen's glee was undeniable. "You will wait for us, right, Deputy?"

Isabel silently willed him to refuse. His slow-growing smile dissolved her hopes.

"I wouldn't miss this for the world."

Isabel's mood plummeted. Not only would she be attending the serenade, but she'd be arriving with the most popular bachelor in these mountains. This night would be talked about for weeks, possibly months, to come. Her life's goal to avoid attention had been thwarted by her interfering sisters and one highly vexing lawman.

"What do you think, Deputy? Doesn't she look festive?"

Hands in his pockets, Ben turned from studying the somber family photograph on the mantel and caught his breath. Carmen urged Isabel forward while Honor trailed behind, checking their handiwork.

A dozen flowery compliments popped into his head. He suppressed them all. She would label whatever he said insincere, so he opted for a casual response. "Indeed, she does."

Her dress had been crafted of lush velvet, a deep green the color of a spruce bough. The snug bodice had a rounded neckline trimmed with ribbon and gave way to a swath of material falling in graceful folds to kiss the floorboards. Isabel's hair had been swept off her neck and coiled into an elegant style. She was the epitome of feminine sophistication.

Her sisters looked disappointed by his low-key reaction. Isabel avoided his gaze as she circumvented the furniture in a swish of skirts.

"Are we riding or walking?"

"I readied the wagon," Ben said, joining her at the coatrack. While she tugged on her gloves, he retrieved her wool cloak and held it open for her. "I hope you don't mind."

Isabel pursed her lips and, after the slightest hesitation, stood still and allowed him to drape the heavy garment over her shoulders. He took the liberty of fastening the clasps, taking a moment to breathe in her unique, feminine scent, a blend of spices and orange.

Her gaze pinned his. "We're going to create a spectacle, arriving with you."

"Yes, we will," he concurred with a grin. "I'll be the envy of every man there."

She brushed his hands aside and took a step back. "And we will be unpopular with the women."

"Only the ones without beaux," Carmen inserted with a straight face.

At the Johnson farm, the serenade's starting point, he assisted the Flores sisters from the wagon and looked up to find a veritable sea of shocked countenances. Three wagons fitted with hay squares would take the group around to the appointed residences. Already some of the young people had found seats. Others conversed in clusters about the yard.

Beside him, Isabel stood as stiff as a mannequin, braced for flaming arrows to descend. He could almost see her hatching an escape route.

"Everyone's staring."

He dipped his head close. "That's because they're as in awe of your beauty as I am."

Her dark gaze swerved to his in instant irritation. "Don't start."

"Oh, look, there's John." Carmen nudged Honor.

John Littleton separated himself from his friends. Taller than most, the dark-headed farmer was easy to pick out in a crowd. His gray eyes glowed with pride as he put his arm around Honor and kissed her cheek.

To Ben's knowledge, the couple had been together for more than a year and were obviously crazy about each other. He wondered why they hadn't already set a wedding date. The Littleton family had a thriving farm on the west side of town. John's older sister had already married and moved away, leaving a starter cabin uninhabited.

"Good evening, ladies. Deputy." Smiling, he raised his brows at Isabel. "I'm surprised to see you here. What did your sisters have to do to convince you?"

"They didn't give me much of a choice." Though her tone was disgruntled, Isabel's expression had softened somewhat. "How is that knife working out for your father?"

"He's been showing it off to his friends, so I'd say he's very satisfied. They're pestering him to divulge where he got it."

"He won't, will he?" Isabel asked, worried.

"John said he would need one for himself in order to continue keeping your secret." Honor snuggled close to his side and grinned cheekily up at him.

"Don't believe her." He chuckled. "She's simply stumped as to what to get me for Christmas."

Reaching up, she straightened his tie. "That's not true. I've actually already decided on a gift, and it has nothing to do with weapons."

He snapped his fingers. "A shame."

John brought out a sassy side in the quiet girl. Glancing at Isabel, Ben was shocked to witness her open approval. Apparently her dislike of men didn't extend to her sister's beau. How had John managed to get in her good graces?

"Virgil and Timothy have saved us a spot in their wagon," John said. "Would you like to sit with us?"

"No, thanks." Carmen waved to a cluster of girls her age. "I'm going over to talk to Rosa and the others. I'll meet up with you later."

As she hurried off, Honor peered toward said wagon and frowned. "John, it's already filling up. Looks like there's only enough room beside Virgil for the two of us."

John looked apologetic. "We could sit in that last one—"

"No, that's okay," Isabel intervened. "The deputy and I will find our own spots."

When the couple had gone, Ben guided her to the rear wagon, the least occupied of the three. "What does a man have to do to obtain one of your knives?"

Caught off guard, her brows pulled together. "I didn't realize you wanted one."

"I—"

"Ben!" The Smith sisters, both brunette, petite and hazel eyed, blocked their way. "We've been waiting ages for you to arrive." The eldest by eighteen months, Laila gifted him with a sunny smile. "We've saved a seat for you in the second wagon."

"Tommy Hatfield's driving," Lynette told him in a confidential tone. "He avoids the ruts and dips, ensuring a smooth ride."

Ben liked the girls well enough. When they weren't hinting about what great wives they'd make, Laila and Lynette were pleasant company. He often spent Sunday evenings in the Smith home, more for their father's company than anything else. Allen Smith reminded Ben of his own pa, whom he didn't get to see often. He had a feeling the sisters wouldn't be thrilled with that bit of insight.

"That was thoughtful of you, ladies, but we're taking the third one. I like to observe what's up ahead."

Squinting at their driver, a rotund man in overalls, Lynette uttered a disapproving noise. "Ollie's got night blindness. He almost ran a group into the woods last year."

Ben choked on a laugh. "We'll take our chances, right, Isabel?"

Laila's countenance lost some its brilliance. "I didn't realize you and the deputy were close acquaintances."

"We're not." She silently implored him to concur.

He shrugged. "I happened to be in the vicinity of the Flores property at the appropriate time. Made sense to come together."

Mr. Johnson let loose a shrill whistle and announced they'd set out in five minutes.

"Time to find a seat." He leaped into the bed and, after pointing Isabel to the sturdy footstool that had been provided, offered her a hand up.

The Smith sisters debated what to do. Ultimately, they trudged off. Their dejection wasn't lost on Isabel, who shot him an arch look. She'd accused him of disregarding others' feelings. Could she be right? He hated to think he might've inflicted emotional wounds, especially considering how he'd suffered at the hands of his former fiancée. Maybe his stated vow to remain a bachelor wasn't enough.

Maybe his single female acquaintances considered it his way of throwing down the gauntlet.

Ben led her to a spot behind Ollie. The seats around them filled up quickly. Carmen and her friends reached the wagon too late to sit close. She mouthed her regrets. Isabel shrugged and offered a false smile.

Crushed as they were, their shoulders wedged together, Ben didn't have to tilt his head very far to whisper in her ear. "I know you're putting on a brave face for your sisters' sakes. Are you sorry you agreed to come? Or sorry you got stuck with me?"

She twisted slightly to meet his gaze. "I should be sitting with them. You and me together like this gives everyone the wrong idea."

"A single man and woman can't talk in this town as friends?"

"You're not just any man," she retorted in a stilted voice. "You're the Debonair Deputy."

"I'm a confirmed bachelor," he countered.

"Didn't you notice the way Lynette was ogling you? As if you'd accomplished great feats worthy of being recorded in history books?"

"Who says I haven't?" he teased.

Her mouth tightened. "Don't do that."

"Do what?"

"Smile and twinkle your eyes at me."

He gave a disbelieving laugh. "I'm not allowed to smile at you?"

"Not in public," she said. "I'm a dedicated spinster. Everyone will think you've charmed me off my farm and are even now filling my head with thoughts of wedding bells."

"Why does it matter what anyone else thinks?"

"You know why." She turned her head. "Oh, but look, there's another of your crestfallen admirers."

Ben spotted Veronica Patton right away. The last to embark, she stared at him and Isabel with obvious disdain. His wave was met with a halfhearted response. He hid a frown. The sense that he'd made a grave error assailed him. His interactions with the elegant blonde weren't like those with the Smith sisters. He'd spent time alone with her, apart from her family. A couple of meals at the Plum. One stroll about town. And while he'd been a perfect gentleman, he was beginning to suspect Veronica viewed their association in a very different light.

He could thank Isabel Flores for this new, disturbing sensitivity regarding the women he occasionally spent time with.

"Everyone ready?" Ollie hollered over his shoulder. "Hold on to your hats, gents. Your sweethearts, too."

Laughter rumbled through the wagon as they lurched into motion. Ben pushed the troubling thoughts aside. This was likely his one and only shot at seeing that Isabel enjoyed herself. He wouldn't get another chance. With any other woman, Ben would've been able to find a way to make her relax. Isabel wasn't just any woman, however. The fact that she disliked him made his task that much harder.

"What's your favorite thing about Christmas?" When she hesitated, he murmured, "Is talking to you forbidden, as well?"

Her focus was on her gloved hands, folded tightly together in her lap. "I like many things about this time of year. One of them is the renewed spirit of charity. People tend to treat each other better."

Her statement was a telling one. While he understood how it felt to live under the weight of a town's critical scrutiny, it had been for a brief time and in another state. He hadn't grown up with a scandalous father.

"Anything else?"

"I enjoy baking. This time of year has plenty of opportunities for that. My sisters and I spend extra time in the kitchen, making treats for their friends."

"What about your friends?"

Her chin jutted. "My sisters are my friends."

"Someday your sisters will marry and move away," he said gently. "What happens then, Isabel?"

Isabel didn't wish to contemplate the future. Too soon, her sisters would marry and move on, leaving her alone. Honor wasn't too far from that reality, in fact. She wouldn't begrudge them their happiness. When the time came, she'd celebrate their blessings.

The wagons rolled into the first dwelling's yard and, once at a full stop, the postmaster's son led everyone in a heartfelt rendition of "O Come, O Come, Emmanuel." It was one of her favorites.

Trying to ignore Ben's nearness and his pleasant tenor voice, she lifted her face to the sky and studied the patterns of twinkling lights in the black velvet expanse. She imagined God in all His glory, who'd crafted those stars and knew their exact number, listening to their voices. Was He pleased?

The words trailed off. Clapping startled her out of her reverie. The family, who'd come onto the porch, wore happy smiles. The youngest sons carried baskets of cookies and doled them out to the carolers.

"You have a delightful voice." Ben's warm breath teased the tendrils about her ear, and she shivered.

Amazing. Despite being fully aware of his reputation, she was still affected by him.

"You have an endless supply of false flattery, Deputy. Save it for someone gullible enough to believe you."

"And you, Miss Flores, have a peculiar inability to accept praise."

Their conveyance jerked into motion, knocking them into one another. Isabel gritted her teeth. The wagon's occupants sneaked glances at them, no doubt cataloging their every exchange to dissect later. Ben had no inkling the amount of speculation they were drawing, because he was immune. He evidently didn't care what others thought of him. For a brief instant, she envied him that.

They reached the next home within ten minutes. This time they sang "Silent Night," a song that put Isabel in mind of Jesus's earthly parents and the events leading up to His birth. If anyone knew how it felt to be talked about and judged, it had been Mary. How had she endured the speculation and accusations? Had she lived her life as usual while awaiting the Savior's birth? Or had she perhaps sequestered herself, seeing only her family and Joseph?

When the song ended, they disembarked and gathered around a table with mugs of fragrant, spice-laced cider. Veronica swooped in with eagle-like accuracy.

"I apologize for arriving late." Slipping her arm through Ben's, she regarded Isabel with a brittle smile. "I would've gladly kept him entertained in your place. Everyone's aware you detest having to associate with your peers."

Veronica Patton actually thought she had something to fear from Isabel? A classic beauty, with long golden hair, crystal-blue eyes and creamy skin, she was popular, poised and perfect. And her family name didn't have a single blemish.

Ben's brows descended. "Veronica—"

"I'm the one who should apologize," Isabel said with as much equanimity as she could muster. "I shouldn't have monopolized the deputy's attention. I'll give you the privacy you crave."

Before Ben could respond, Isabel pivoted on her heel and joined Carmen and her friends near the well. They huddled together to ward off the cold, their mugs cradled close, the welcome steam warming their faces.

"I'm glad you came, Isabel," Rosa said kindly. "Are you enjoying yourself?"

Sipping the liquid, she savored the apple flavor and tried to steady her nerves. "It's been a while since I've gotten to sing Christmas carols."

Sharp-eyed Samantha Rogers studied her over the rim of her cup. "I didn't think you'd ever join Ben MacGregor's gaggle of admirers, Isabel. What changed?"

Carmen elbowed the girl.

Isabel's stomach knotted. "I'm afraid you've gotten the wrong impression."

"Appears I'm not the only one."

Glancing around, she noticed the pointed stares bouncing between her and Veronica. What did they expect? An actual altercation to break out? Oh, wouldn't Ben love that, she fumed, two women fighting over him?

Ignoring her nudging conscience that protested she was being unfair, she bade the girls goodbye and pulled Carmen aside.

"I'm going home."

"What? Why?"

"This was a mistake." She shook her head. "I shouldn't have come."

Carmen's round face wrinkled with distress. "You don't have to leave. Sit with me and the girls."

"I'd rather be alone." She snagged Carmen's hand and gently squeezed. "Tell Honor I'll see you both at home."

"Shouldn't we tell Ben?" She bit her lip. "It's a long walk, and it's dark. What if he's right about that bank robber?"

"He's preoccupied at the moment," she said, wincing at the note of bitterness in her voice. She didn't care that he and the gorgeous blonde were locked in a private conversation. She *didn't*. "He's making a bigger deal about the threat than he needs to." Dragging her gaze away, she gave a brief wave. "Have fun, and I'll see you later."

Isabel left the yard, passing the annoying Gallatin brothers on her way. Myron smirked at her and nudged Chester. If they hadn't been engaged in obvious flirtation with a pair of young women, she was certain they would've made trouble.

Soon the lights and laughter faded. Darkness closed around her, the deserted lane lit by infrequent patches of moonlight. At first, her relief at escaping Ben's frustrating presence and too many prying eyes bolstered her along, without a thought to her surroundings. Gradually, though, she became aware of her isolation. Every snap and rustle in the night forest startled her. The memory of being held captive by the unkempt thief resurfaced, along with Ben's warnings.

Was he out there, hiding in the shadows, poised to strike?

Isabel increased her pace. By the time she arrived at her cabin, her heart threatened to beat right out of her chest. Her trepidation was compounded when she climbed the porch steps and noticed the door ajar.

Chilled to the bone, her exposed skin stinging, she stopped and stared. Had one of the girls failed to latch it? Or was someone inside awaiting her return?

Retrieving her dagger, she prayed for God's protection as she forced her feet forward.

Chapter Four

Where was Isabel?

Ben scanned the crowd, frustrated when he saw no sign of her.

"Ben?" Veronica pressed her palm against his cheek. "You didn't hear a word I said, did you?"

The gesture struck him as intimate. He shifted out of reach. "I'm afraid not. What were you saying?"

"I asked about your injury."

"It wasn't serious. A mere flesh wound."

Her blue eyes bore evidence of real distress. "I was so very frightened when I heard the account of your ordeal. The thought of you facing that madman alone has tortured me ever since." She shivered.

He hadn't been alone, though. Burying that crucial information would help keep Isabel safe, but he felt as if he were cheating her somehow. She'd displayed true heroism that night.

Veronica gripped his arm. "I wish I'd been there while Doc stitched you up. I would've held your hand."

Ben strangled on a cough. He doubted she'd be so swift to offer comfort if she knew who'd actually tended him. "A sweet sentiment, Veronica."

"It must've been difficult to return home to your empty cabin after such an ordeal."

Something in her tone set off a warning bell inside. "I'm used to living alone."

She licked her lips. "Don't you get lonely? P-perhaps you've underestimated the advantages of having a wife. A companion who's always on hand to comfort and cheer you."

Ben fell back a step. He was well acquainted with the advantages of a loving relationship. He'd seen the evidence in his own parents' union, as well as his friends' marriages. A fluke illness had robbed him of that chance. God had allowed it. He'd stopped asking why, because the obvious conclusion—that he was unfit to be a father—was too painful.

Why was Veronica suddenly venturing into these waters? She'd never dared before. Was it because he'd arrived with Isabel?

"My thoughts on marriage haven't changed," he told her in a gentle but firm voice. "My solitary path is set."

"Of course, I didn't intend to suggest otherwise," she rushed out, her brows forming a deep V.

Ben's attention wandered to the refreshment table, where Carmen and Honor were engaged in a heated discussion. He craned his neck and scanned the crowd, straining for a glimpse of raven hair and a proud profile.

"What do you say, Ben? Will you join us?"

Ben dragged his gaze back to Veronica, who was waiting for his answer. Not about to be caught woolgathering a second time in the space of five minutes, he nodded. "Um, sure. I'd like that."

Her mouth curved into a bright smile. "Wonderful."

He inwardly cringed. What had he agreed to?

"Excuse me." Carmen rushed to their side. "I'm sorry to interrupt. Ben, can I steal you away for a moment?"

His thoughts leaping to Isabel, he made his excuses to Veronica.

"What's happened?"

"Isabel left. I tried to convince her to stay, but she wouldn't listen."

"Alone?"

Carmen winced and nodded.

Worry mingled with anger. She knew the danger, yet had forged ahead anyway. "How long ago was this?"

"About fifteen minutes."

"I'll go right away."

"Honor and I are coming with you."

"Are you decent, Isabel?" Carmen was speaking as she breezed through the door. "Ben accompanied us home and…" Spying her in the rocking chair, she stopped suddenly, causing Honor to bump into her. "Whatever's the matter? You look as if you've seen a ghost."

Unwilling for them to guess how afraid she'd been, Isabel hid the dagger in her skirt folds. "Who was the last one out tonight? Do either of you remember latching the door?"

"It was me," Honor said, her eyes apprehensive. "I distinctly remember latching it. Why? Was someone here?"

"The door was open when I got home."

Carmen rushed over and knelt at her feet. "Are you all right? I warned you not to come alone."

"I'm fine."

"Ben needs to hear about this."

Ducking outside before Isabel could stop her, Honor explained the dilemma. The deputy followed her inside and quickly inventoried the cabin. His intent gaze came to rest on her in somber assessment.

"Did you see anything unusual? Any of your belongings out of place or missing?"

"No. Nothing. I didn't check the bedrooms closely, however."

Carmen stood and grasped Honor's hand. "Let's check them together."

Honor nodded and, with a final glance at Isabel, went off to search both rooms. Their subdued conversation competed with the popping and hissing of the fireplace logs. After hanging his hat on the stand, Ben positioned a footstool near her rocker and sank onto it. Then he latched his hands together and examined her features with an intensity that made her self-conscious.

"Why did you leave without telling me? I would've gladly escorted you home."

"I wished to be alone."

"And what if our thief had been waiting for you?" Concern darkened his eyes to sage green.

It wasn't personal, she reminded herself. His duty to the townspeople was of paramount importance.

Isabel removed her dagger from its concealment. "I'm not completely helpless."

Ben sighed and, rising to his feet, motioned for her to do the same. Baffled, she stood and immediately regretted it. In a blink, he'd seized her dagger and waggled it midair.

"The thief has your weapon," he challenged, jaw twitching. "Now what?"

Isabel stared up at him, a shiver of admiration rippling through her. She'd never get used to this side of the Debonair Deputy, the justice-wielding, deadly serious lawman.

"I wasn't expecting you to act. You haven't proven anything."

"Let's try again then." He handed her the dagger. "Pretend I'm an outlaw intent on silencing you."

Unease settled in the pit of her stomach. Ben didn't tower over her, but he was one hundred percent solid muscle.

"This is ridiculous."

"Is it?" He leaned close. "You wouldn't think so if your sisters had come home to find you wounded—or worse."

Images of their faces, stricken in horror as they knelt over her prone body, flooded her mind. Causing them sorrow was the last thing she wanted to do.

His hand encircled her wrist like an iron manacle. She resisted, but he was far too strong. Ben had the dagger pried from her fingers in no time flat.

He waved it in front of her nose. "Care to try a third time?"

Anger sparked into a smoldering flame. Why was he doing this?

"You didn't give me proper warning," she gritted out.

"And you think a lawbreaker bent on doing you harm would?" he retorted, color etching his cheeks. "You're an intelligent lady, Isabel. Don't be stubborn because I'm involved. If the sheriff was here in my place, would you brush his warnings off as easily as you do mine?"

Floorboards creaked in the girls' bedroom. Isabel snatched her weapon and replaced it in her sheath, all the while mulling over his accusation. She didn't want to acknowledge the truth.

"Isabel." He reached out and stroked her cheek. His fingers were cold, his touch a complete shock, and she flinched. Ben assumed she'd reacted out of disgust, for he grimaced and dropped his arm to his side. "Don't let your dislike of me jeopardize your safety."

The girls emerged then. Turning toward them, Isabel surreptitiously pressed her palm against her cheek in the spot where he'd touched her. What had possessed him to do it?

"Everything looks in order as far as we can tell," Honor announced, her fingers plucking at the ribbons encircling her sleeves.

Ben retrieved his hat. "I'll take a look around outside."

"Be careful." The words were out before she could stop them. At his look of surprise, she said, "I don't want to have to stitch you up again."

"Yes, ma'am."

Carmen brought over a small brown sack. "Mr. Hatfield was indeed generous this year. When I told him we had to leave early, he gave us our bags, including one for you."

"Forget about food for a minute, will you?" Honor reprimanded. "Isa's had a fright. Someone's been inside our home."

Carmen jammed her fists on her generous hips. "We can't know that for sure. You might've pulled the door closed but failed to latch it."

"I distinctly remember doing it, Carmen."

"We were all aflutter over the deputy's arrival and in a rush to prepare Isa."

"No matter what actually transpired, I believe we have to take the threat seriously." Isabel wasn't convinced the man would go to such trouble to find her. It would be far easier to flee the area and take his chances elsewhere. She couldn't risk her sisters' safety on a hunch, however. "We're all going to have to be on our guards."

"You should've seen Ben's face when I told him you'd left." Carmen's gaze was troubled. "He was visibly upset."

Her heart tripped over itself. "I can't imagine why. He had plenty of girls vying for his attention, Veronica in particular." Of all the girls who'd cast their nets for Ben, she seemed the most likely candidate to lead him to the altar.

"Perhaps *your* company is what he truly wants."

She sliced the air with her hand. "Impossible."

"Haven't you noticed he treats you differently?" Carmen said. "He's more serious around you."

Isabel went to the kitchen and deposited the bag's contents in a festive china bowl with green holly patterns, a hand-me-down from their *abuela*. "The only reason Ben doesn't flirt with me is because he knows I'm immune to his charm." Another thought occurred to her. "Or maybe I'm not the type of woman he'd be interested in."

There was no reason to be offended, she reasoned, busying her hands with arranging the unblemished fruit. So why then did the thought suddenly irk her?

"Of course he'd be interested in you!" Carmen added her bounty to the bowl. "You're beautiful and capable and wise. The deputy's a fair man. I'm certain he'd overlook your tendency to be bossy and hardheaded."

Honor released a long-suffering sigh. "Carmen, don't you ever think before you speak?"

Isabel patted Carmen's hand. "I appreciate what you're trying to say, but it hardly matters what he thinks."

"That's odd."

"What is?"

"You care what everyone in Gatlinburg thinks about you *except* for Ben MacGregor." Carmen twisted to look at Honor. "Don't you think that's peculiar?"

Isabel was grateful Ben chose that moment to return to spare her from answering. His cheeks and hands were ruddy from exposure. The impulse to lead him to the fire and ease his discomfort took her unawares.

"I assume you didn't encounter any outlaws in our barn?" she said, ignoring her sisters' curious gazes.

"Just a few cows and a friendly feline." He good-naturedly brushed orange cat hair from his pants.

"That's reassuring." *If* there'd been someone poking

around their property, he was long gone. "Would you like a cup of coffee before you head home?"

"Coffee sounds wonderful. As for heading home, I won't be doing that until morning. I aim to stay in the warming hut."

Ben braced himself for an argument that never materialized.

"I'll gather the proper bedding."

As Isabel started for her bedroom, the younger sisters exchanged a dubious look. Like him, they must've expected her to protest once again.

"It's barely nine o'clock," Carmen objected. "Far too early for the deputy to retire. Isn't that right?"

Isabel wouldn't relish putting up with him any longer than was necessary, but he wasn't sleepy, and hot coffee would go far in chasing the chill from his bones. Besides, he couldn't pass up this rare opportunity to spend more time in the feisty miller's presence, no matter that a relationship with her was out of the question.

"You're quite right." He began to unbutton his coat. "I'd be a fool to turn down an opportunity to spend an evening with three of the most captivating ladies in these mountains."

Carmen blushed to her hairline. Honor laughed. Isabel wore an indignant frown. Good. The more he riled her, the less likely he'd do something stupid. He couldn't afford to forget his reasons for not getting serious. Isabel was the one woman who could make him forget, and she deserved a man who could give her what every woman dreamed about…a house full of children to love and nurture.

Her irritation was clear in the way she bustled about the kitchen, thumping cups and plates on the counter. She was entrancing, even in her annoyance, and Ben had to consciously work to keep his gaze averted. In contrast, Honor and Carmen were gracious hostesses. They spoke of upcoming Christmas festivities and encouraged him to indulge in the snack Isabel provided, airy yeast rolls slathered with creamy butter and tart blackberry preserves washed down with cinnamon-laced coffee, a traditional drink recipe passed down from their *abuela*.

As soon as the clock struck ten, Isabel fetched the bedding and insisted on accompanying him to the hut. Positioned several yards from the gristmill and stream, the soundly built structure contained a single chair and a woodstove. It was large enough to hold about five or six people comfortably. One tiny, bare window gave the occupants a view of the mill.

While Isabel rolled out the woolen blanket and quilts that would serve for his makeshift bed, Ben retrieved kindling from the box in the corner and focused on building a fire.

"You probably won't be comfortable, but you'll be warm."

Ben glanced over his shoulder. Kneeling on the floor, her cloak a cloud about her crouched form, she plumped the pillow she'd brought for him.

She caught him looking and shrugged. "It's a tight space. Won't take much to heat it."

"It'll be fine. I've slept in worse places."

Curiosity leaped to life on her expressive face, but she didn't put voice to it. Standing, she folded her hands primly. "Thank you for staying. My sisters are unnerved by what's happened."

"I have three sisters of my own. I know what it's like to want to protect them."

Her brows inched up. "Are you the oldest?"

He nodded. "There are two years between me and my next youngest sister, Tabitha."

She opened her mouth to say something, then bit her lip to halt the words.

Pushing to his feet, he brushed his hands against his trousers. "You've had no problem speaking your mind in the past. Go ahead and say whatever you're thinking."

The firelight flickered over her noble features and made her eyes gleam like coals. "I find it difficult to reconcile the fact you were raised in a house full of females with your cavalier treatment of the local ladies. I would think you'd be sensitive to their feelings. You speak of protecting your sisters. Why doesn't that sentiment extend to those outside your family?"

Ben slouched against the wall and crossed his arms. "I don't see how the term *cavalier* applies to me. Am I friends with a number of marriageable women? Certainly. Have I given any of them reason to believe I've a serious interest in courting them? Absolutely not."

The Smith sisters' disappointment mocked his claims, as did Veronica's surprising mention of marriage. Uncertainty took up residence inside him.

"You're a shameless flirt."

"I like to think of it as harmless teasing." Everyone knew he wasn't looking for commitment. He'd made sure that bit of gossip rode the grapevines as soon as he relocated here.

But what if that wasn't enough?

"Harmless?" She shifted her stance, her cloak's hem swaying around her boots. "You call dashing hopes and breaking hearts harmless?"

"I'm a game to them," he countered. "It's a competition, and they view me as some sort of lofty prize. I promise you not one of them would rejoice if they actually won me."

She gaped at him. "And I thought *I* was the cynical one. What happened to set you against commitment? Were your parents unhappy? Did your father indulge in indiscretions?"

"On the contrary, my parents are the best of friends."

"You were in love with someone, then. She spurned you. Or worse, deceived you."

Wistfulness clawed at him, regret and helplessness over his plight on its heels. He hoped the indistinct lighting hid those tumultuous emotions from her. She was perilously close to the truth. Marianne had indeed spurned him the moment she learned his diagnosis. His overwrought fiancée had sputtered words that hadn't yet lost their potency. Words like *damaged* and *useless* and *abnormal. What good are you to me?* she'd railed. *Indeed, to any woman?*

Until that confrontation with Marianne, he'd had a flicker of hope that she'd be able to come to terms with his new reality. "Why must there be a reason? Why can't I simply desire to be free and independent, like you?"

She narrowed her eyes, studying every inch of his face. What did she see? The push and pull of denial and acceptance he wrestled with on his weaker days?

He surged off the wall and would've paced if there'd been enough space. The curious impulse to divulge his secret to Isabel threw him. She was the last person he should share his most private disappointment with.

"It's been my experience that infatuations shift as often as the weather. The girls here are no different than the ones back home. Sally Hatcher is a prime example. Mere weeks ago, she claimed to be in love with me. Didn't take her long to take up with someone new once she figured out where we stood."

Isabel snapped her mouth shut. If she felt the tiniest bit sorry for him, she didn't show it. He wished he could've foreseen how quickly she would develop a full-on infatuation. He'd truly enjoyed spending time with Sally—as friends.

A thud on the stoop vibrated the door. Immediately on alert, Ben maneuvered Isabel behind him and reached for his gun.

Chapter Five

Shielded by Ben's strong, muscular body, Isabel's only thought was that he was going to be shot again because of her. Her heartbeat drummed in her ears. They were trapped in this tiny building, which meant they'd have to shoot their way out. The curious sadness she'd glimpsed in Ben moments earlier faded from her mind.

Had he been right all along? Had the frustrated robber tracked her here in order to silence her?

"Stay behind me," he ordered.

Weapon drawn, he edged forward and eased the latch open. His tension leached into the air around her. From her limited view, she saw the cords of his neck stiffen, and his jaw was locked in steely determination. She didn't doubt his ability to keep her safe. Ben MacGregor was many things—a coward wasn't one of them. He'd lay down his life to protect her. Hadn't he already taken one bullet for her?

Isabel offered up a fervent plea for his safety.

The door's hinges groaned as he inched it open. In a sudden movement that had her gasping aloud, Ben pivoted into the opening, his finger on the trigger.

No rash of gunfire rained down on them. No ambush from a vengeful outlaw.

Instead, the water's familiar music, trickling over the wheel in a full spin and gently splashing back into the stream below, greeted their ears. Then came an unusual sound, out of place on the Flores farm—a child crying.

Isabel pressed close to Ben's back and gripped his arms. He stilled and angled a glance over his shoulder.

"Are you hearing the same thing I am?" he whispered.

Pushing past him, she ignored his hushed objection and rushed onto the porch. Unrelenting darkness cloaked the countryside. The hut, positioned between the gristmill and cabin, blocked what little light might be shining from the windows.

Ben's hand clamped on her waist. He would've pulled her back into the hut if she hadn't locked on his fingers and squeezed.

"Wait! Listen."

She heard the plaintive cry again, a heart-wrenching sob that filled her with urgency and the need to soothe hurts. She left the cover of the stoop and tiptoed around the corner. Ben was right behind her, so close she could feel his breath on her nape.

They spotted the small form huddled against the hut's foundation at the same time. The small boy ceased sobbing and started to scramble in the opposite direction.

Masking her consternation, Isabel crouched to his level and spoke in a soft, gentle tone. "Hello. My name's Isabel. I live in the cabin over there with my sisters. What's your name?"

His attempt at escape abandoned, the boy stared at her without speaking. She could tell little about him besides the fact he was very young and had short, tousled dark hair.

"I'll get a lamp." The air stirred as Ben dashed back inside.

"My, um, friend Ben, he's going to get an oil lamp so you can see us better. I don't like the dark, do you?"

The boy's negative head shake was almost imperceptible. Isabel couldn't comprehend where this child had come from or where his parents might be. Her instinct was to pull him into her arms and hug him until he felt safe.

Ben soon returned, the lamp emitting enough light to show his concern-ravaged features as his gaze met Isabel's. He assumed the same position as her, his knee bumping hers as he steadied himself.

"I was just telling our visitor that your name is Ben."

"That's right. I'm Ben MacGregor." He spoke in an upbeat tone. "What's your name?"

The boy's pointed chin wobbled. He was a pretty child, with pale skin, large cornflower-blue eyes and hair the color of syrup. Judging by the dirt smudges on his face and hands and the stains on his clothing, he hadn't seen a bath for some time.

"I want Happy."

"Is Happy your dog?" Ben said.

He shook his head.

Ben cut her a look. "Is he your cat?"

"Don't have a cat."

Isabel noticed his shirtsleeves were too short, and his trousers had been patched multiple times. "Is your mother or father around?" She gestured to the forest. "Did you get separated from them?"

His lower lip quivered, and a fresh surge of tears brimmed in his eyes. "My mama's dead."

She heard Ben's sharp inhale. "I'm right sorry to hear that, little man."

The sorrow this child was suffering, and indeed his

current plight, weighed heavily on Isabel. "What about your pa?"

"Don't got one." He toyed with his shirt buttons. "I want Happy."

Ben gestured to the hut. "I have a peppermint stick in my bag. Would you like to have it?"

Isabel held her breath while the child considered them both with a heavy dose of distrust. Finally, he nodded.

Some of the rigidness in Ben's body receded. He slowly stood and held out his hand. "What do you say we go inside where it's warm? You can eat the candy in front of the stove."

The boy popped up. Instead of taking Ben's hand, however, he edged in Isabel's direction. She offered him a reassuring smile. "I like peppermint, too, but my favorite is horehound."

"Horehound?" Ben said in mock horror. "I can't stomach the stuff. Peppermint is the best, and lemon is a close second. Do you like lemon, little man?"

"I never tried it." His high, childish voice held a note of longing.

"Is that so? Well, that's a problem I'll have to remedy. Every boy must try lemon drops at least once."

Ben started for the hut entrance, chatting about other sweets and acting as if finding a lost child was an everyday occurrence. Isabel beckoned for the boy to follow her. He did so, reluctantly, his suspicion unusual for a child his age, which she guessed to be around three or four.

By the time they reached the threshold, Ben had retrieved the promised candy and removed a single stick from a small brown sack.

"There's only one thing I ask in return for this," he began, his expression serious. "I'd like to know your name."

Isabel watched the boy's wide gaze roam the hut's interior before settling on Ben and the treat at hand. He was waif thin, and his curly hair needed combing. Whoever had been caring for him hadn't done a good job.

"Eli."

Ben held out the stick. "A strong name suited to a sturdy boy like yourself. You know your last name?"

Eli snatched the peppermint and sucked on it greedily. When had he last eaten?

He shrugged. Isabel dragged the chair closer to the stove and patted the seat. "Why don't you sit here? We need to close the door to keep the warm air inside."

When Eli had climbed onto the chair, Ben said quietly, "Isabel? A word."

She met him at the door.

"I'm going to take a look around outside. You should take him to the cabin. It's too late to find him other lodgings. He could probably use something more substantial than a piece of candy, too."

"What are you expecting to find?"

He kneaded the back of his neck. "Whoever's had charge of him has to be around somewhere. Boys his age don't simply wander the woods alone. I suspect something dire has happened."

"You'll be careful?"

A ghost of a smile graced his mouth. "For someone who claims to dislike me, you issue that warning quite often."

Heat flooded her cheeks. "That's because I—"

"Don't want to stitch me up again. I know."

He ducked outside and headed for the mill. She watched his confident stride, troubled by her deepening interest in the lawman's welfare.

He found nothing. Saw nothing. Ben had no answers for Isabel. After his search the boy was as big a mystery as he'd been an hour ago. His ears stinging and nose numb, he rapped on the Flores cabin door.

Isabel greeted him with a cautionary finger to her lips. Admitting him into her home, made toasty by the crackling fire in the hearth, she waved him over to the sofa. Eli slept beneath a maroon knitted blanket. His small hands were clasped together beneath his cheek as if in prayer, his forehead puckered in disquiet that had followed him into his dreams. Ben reached out his hand to smooth the mop of curls from his face before catching the action. He sank it deep in his pocket.

There could be no room for tenderness in this case, no personal attachment. Work involving children was tricky, full of emotional pitfalls, and Ben would have to be vigilant in order to remain detached. The sooner he reunited Eli with his guardian, the better for everyone.

Isabel regarded the child with open concern. "He seemed nervous with my sisters around, so they retired early. I fed him enough for three children his size. He was ravenous."

A lump formed in his throat. Ben couldn't abide the thought of anyone going hungry, much less an innocent child.

"Once his stomach was full, he got droopy eyed. I would've liked to give him a thorough washing, but it will have to wait until morning."

"Thank you, Isabel." He peered deep into her eyes. "Right after breakfast, I'll interview the neighbors. It's possible his family was traveling through the area, and he got separated. It may take a few days to locate them. In the meantime, he can stay with one of the O'Malleys."

"I see no reason to move him. He obviously has a hard time trusting new people."

He rested his hands on the sofa's scrolled wooden edge.

"You've got a point. But if I can't reunite him with his folks in the next day or two, I'll find a more permanent place for him."

While she didn't look happy with the pronouncement, she didn't argue.

"Would you like for me sleep in here?" he said, indicating the rug beside the hearth.

"That's not necessary. I can sleep here in case he wakes in the middle of the night."

"I noticed he kept his distance from me."

"To a four-year-old boy, a lawman like yourself must present an intimidating figure."

"Did he tell you his age?"

"That was the only tidbit of new information I coaxed out of him."

"Not a chatty little guy, is he?"

Her gaze clouded over. "Who knows how recent his mother's passing was or what his current situation is like. The state he's in…he didn't accumulate this amount of filth by exploring the woods for an hour or two."

"He's awfully thin. In my experience, kids his age resemble cherubs with full cheeks and chubby hands and legs."

"I'll make certain he eats well," she said, a fierceness to her tone.

As much as he yearned to linger, he chose the wiser course of action. "I'm off to my sleeping quarters for the night, then. Try to get some rest."

"You, too, Deputy."

"This deputy has a name, you know."

She arched a brow. "Good night, Ben."

"Good night, sugarplum."

Seeing her protest brewing, Ben ducked through the door. He passed a fitful night in the hut, his mind alert to danger and not fully allowing his body to rest. At daybreak, he saddled Blaze and paid a visit to the Floreses' immediate neighbors. No one had any useful information to share about the boy. Dissatisfied with his venture, he returned to the cabin eager to see how both Isabel and Eli had fared during the night.

She greeted him with disheveled hair—her braid was untidy, stray tendrils trailing her cheeks—and flour dusting her mauve blouse.

"Am I glad to see you." Seizing hold of his coat sleeve, Isabel tugged him inside.

"What disaster has occurred that you'd say such a thing to me?" he uttered, nonplussed.

"That one right there."

She jerked a finger toward the kitchen, where Eli was gleefully stirring the contents of a bowl, uncaring that some of the liquid was splashing over the rim. Eggshells oozing with remnants of whites littered the makeshift counter built into the wall. Milk puddled on the floorboards beneath the chair on which he was perched.

"I've never had a child in my kitchen before," she whispered desperately. "You have to help me."

Ben couldn't stop a grin from forming. Isabel was a strong, independent woman. To see her unsettled by a tiny human filled him with mirth.

"Your sisters haven't ever made messes?"

"I'm only three years older than Honor. I don't remember the three of us in the kitchen together. Mama allowed only one of us to help at a time, and she had high standards of cleanliness."

"Hmm. What will you give me in exchange?"

Her lips compressed. "I'll grind your corn for free."

"Have you ever known me to patronize your mill?" He

laughed, tugging off his buckskin gloves and laying them on the hutch. "I don't cook."

"That's right. You enjoy the generosity of the citizens your work for, mostly families who have eligible daughters."

He chafed his hands together. "Don't think I haven't noticed the lack of an invitation from you."

"Are you angling for one?"

Ceramic thudding against the wooden floor was followed by a guilt-ridden *uh-oh*.

They both turned to see Eli's bent head as he contemplated the batter oozing onto the floor.

"I don't handle messes well." Isabel put a weary hand to her forehead.

"I'll clean it up if you promise to cook for me."

"Fine. I was in the process of preparing breakfast anyway."

"Doesn't count. Has to be a full evening meal."

She glowered at him. "Served on my best dishes, I suppose?"

"As long as it includes dessert, you can use whatever dishes you want."

Chapter Six

Isabel's sisters were aware of her preference for neatness, even in the midst of a task such as preparing flapjacks. If Eli's circumstances had been different, she would've had no qualms guiding his attempts to help. But he was motherless and lost, stuck with strangers mere weeks before Christmas—the most special time of year for any child. He'd tossed and turned during the long night, at times calling out for his mama. How could she manage a single stern word to this hurting child?

As Ben approached, Eli pressed flat against the counter, apprehension in his thickly lashed blue eyes.

"Are you angry?"

"Angry? No, sir. Accidents happen." Ben indicated the chair. "I promised Miss Isabel I'd clean this up, though. Once that's done, how about we watch her make breakfast and later, after we've eaten, you can help me wash the dishes?"

Eli looked to Isabel for confirmation. She nodded in encouragement.

"Okay."

"Good. Mind if I help you down from there?"

Without waiting for an answer, Ben picked him up and

deposited him beside the doorway, close to where Isabel stood watching them. Eli toyed with his hair, knotting it further. Somehow she was going to have to coax him into the bath.

As Ben hunted for a clean washrag, she couldn't help noticing his bedraggled allure. Auburn-tinted whiskers shadowed his jaw, and his hair refused to stay out of his eyes. He'd divested himself of the suit jacket, and his shirt and pants were slightly creased from sleeping in them. Even so, his shirt's pale green fabric added a rich sheen to his hair and deepened the sea-glass hue of his eyes.

If anyone had suggested she'd be fixing breakfast in the company of Ben MacGregor, she'd have marked it off as an insane notion. She glanced at Eli and, resisting the impulse to tidy his out-of-control curls, admitted she was grateful for Ben's company.

"Where's Honor and Carmen?" he asked.

"In the barn tending our animals." They shared her curiosity and concern about Eli, but sensing his shy nature, had decided not to crowd him. "We divide the chores. I'm responsible for breakfast and supper, and Honor fixes the noon meal."

"Carmen doesn't cook?"

"You don't want her to cook, believe me."

Wiping the floorboards clean, he said, "With my ma and three sisters in the house, I didn't see the need to learn. I could use the skill now, though."

"Are any of them married?"

"Anne's married with one child. According to Ma, the other two are enjoying the attentions of multiple beaus."

"They've learned from your example."

His gaze enigmatic, he lifted one shoulder. "Or I've learned from them."

The girls returned then, glad to find Ben in their home.

They chatted with him as if they were a group of old chums. Isabel prepared another bowl of batter while Honor set the table and Carmen poured coffee for the adults and milk for Eli. Content to quietly absorb the activity around him, Eli remained close to watch Isabel cook.

When the meal was ready, Honor and Carmen abandoned their usual spots in order to accommodate their guests. That put Isabel between Eli and Ben. Squelching the complaint springing to mind, she busied herself tucking a cloth into Eli's collar.

"Is that necessary?" Carmen smoothed her napkin on her lap. Her bright yellow blouse, combined with her tanned skin and flashing brown eyes, put Isabel in mind of summer and sunflowers. "Extra stains on that shirt will hardly be visible."

"Carmen," Honor said in exasperation, "don't be rude."

"When will you stop chiding me as if I'm eight years old?"

Isabel caught Ben's sparkling gaze upon her. "I miss this."

"What? Constant squabbling?"

"Family," he said simply.

She averted her eyes. Never had she thought of the deputy as lonely. He had enough admirers to keep him entertained during his nonworking hours. She envisioned her fragile mother and the many moments over the past months when Isabel had wished she was around. And while her siblings sometimes annoyed her, she couldn't imagine living an entire day's journey away.

"When was the last time you saw your family?" Carmen shifted the molasses closer to her plate.

"I spent a couple of weeks in Georgia last summer. My father's not one for traveling, so if I want to see them, I have to go out there."

Impatient, Eli ambled onto his knees and reached for the topmost flapjack.

"We haven't said grace yet, Eli."

She placed her hand on his back, compassion and consternation mingling when she felt his leanness. He could be part of a destitute family with a guardian who struggled to put food in the children's bellies. Or he could be in the care of someone who put their selfish desires above his welfare. Isabel found herself hoping he'd stay with her long enough to see him gain weight.

"Who's Grace?" Eli said.

Carmen snickered. Honor shot her a quelling glance.

Seated around the corner from Isabel, Ben's forehead pleated in dismay. "Saying grace means we pray to God and thank Him for the blessings He's given us," he explained.

"Oh."

Honor asked Ben to say the blessing. Isabel placed her hand in his outstretched palm, tingles scrabbling up her arm when his fingers closed over hers. Her pulse leaped. His skin was smooth in places and callused in others. She'd never held hands with a man...the contact was wondrous and oddly comforting. His gaze locked onto hers, and he swallowed hard.

Eli tapped her other arm. "Do I hold your hand, too?"

Glad for the distraction, she smiled down at the boy. "It's customary to hold hands while we pray, at least in our home."

His thin face far too serious, he laid his hand atop hers. "Like that?"

Her heart squeezed with a foreign ache. "Yes, sweetie. Exactly like that."

As Ben's husky, velvet voice washed over her, she was struck by the fact that this was the first time a man had sat at the Flores table and offered thanks to God above. Manuel hadn't been a churchgoer. He'd allowed his wife and daughters to attend, but he hadn't wanted to be confronted with the evidence of their faith. No praying before meals. Scripture reading had to be done in the privacy of their rooms, out of sight.

Growing up, Isabel had observed the church's congregants and wondered what it would be like to have a father who loved Jesus. Zeroing in on the sensation of Ben's strong yet gentle hold, her thoughts turned to marriage and the blessing of a God-fearing husband.

She withdrew from his intoxicating touch as soon as the prayer concluded. The conversation buzzed around her as she concentrated on cutting Eli's flapjack and dusting his eggs with salt. She sensed Ben's attention returning to her from time to time but didn't engage. How disheartening to discover she wasn't as immune to him as she'd thought.

When everyone's appetites were sated, it was decided that Honor and Carmen would attend services while Isabel remained home with Eli. She could hardly take him to church in his current state.

Ben began clearing the dishes. "I'll stay with you."

Isabel's heart stuttered in her chest. She was ready for him to leave—already he'd far outstayed his welcome. A return to their former distant lives would reestablish her mental boundaries. The words that would spur him to do so refused to materialize, however. Instead, she nodded her acquiescence.

Isabel studied the small boy licking syrup from his fingers. The sooner they reunited him with his caretaker, the sooner she'd be rid of the deputy. But what if that wasn't best for Eli?

* * *

"Time for you to get clean, little man."

Eli eyed the basin filled with steaming water and scowled. "I ain't never washed in nothing like that."

Isabel lowered the stack of folded towels to the cushioned chair nearest her. "Did you bathe in a stream?"

"Sometimes."

Ben crouched to the boy's level. "Want to know a secret?"

"What secret?"

"Isabel, cover your ears."

She arched a brow at him but did as he'd bidden.

He cast his voice in a conspiratorial whisper. "Ladies like it when us men smell nice. Did you know that?"

Eli lifted his arm to his nose and sniffed. "I don't smell too good."

Ben masked a smile. "Miss Isabel has agreed to let you borrow her good soap."

The boy tipped his head up to regard Isabel, who was gamely still covering her ears. She bestowed Eli with a sweet, encouraging smile that made Ben's chest seize with longing. Isabel should smile more often. It softened her features and warmed her brown-black eyes to pools of melted chocolate. Her smile invited him in, this confounding woman who was adept at keeping men, especially him, at a fixed and uncrossable distance.

Stop this foolishness. She's not smiling at you, Mac-Gregor. She's smiling at the child.

Eli looked at Ben again. "After the bath, can I go find Happy?"

Ben gestured for Isabel to listen in. "Is Happy your toy? A stuffed bunny, perhaps?"

His nose wrinkled. "No."

Isabel sank onto the footstool. Before her sisters departed, she'd ducked into her room, brushed her hair and restrained the heavy mass with a wide ribbon. A pair of dainty black-and-white cameo earrings adorned her earlobes. Her beauty nearly stole his breath away.

"Is Happy your friend?"

His head bobbed up and down. "He takes care of me."

"After you're clean, would you like to draw a picture of Happy? That way Ben and I will know what he looks like."

"Good idea," Ben said.

Once Eli was submerged, Isabel held up the soiled clothing and sighed. "I'm not sure these can be salvaged. The mercantile's closed today. I'll send the girls first thing tomorrow morning. Quinn Darling typically has a good selection of ready-made clothes for adults. I hope he has something for children."

"Have him put the expense on my tab."

"That's kind of you, but—"

He rested a hand on her forearm, the cotton sleeve soft from many washings. "You have your sisters to provide for. I have no one. My expenses are few. Let me do this."

She quickly disengaged from his touch. Funny, she hadn't seemed to mind holding his hand at breakfast.

"I can afford to buy him an outfit."

"I'm not suggesting you can't." He motioned for her to join him beside the desk. "He's not your responsibility, Isabel. Or at least, he shouldn't be. I, on the other hand, have a duty to the townspeople and those who pass through our borders, even temporarily."

"I don't have the energy to argue, so we'll do it your way."

He skimmed the ridge of her cheekbone with his fingertip. "You lost sleep last night."

Her apricot-tinted lips parted on a breath. "I'm fine." After glancing over her shoulder, she leaned close and whispered, "Stop flirting, will you? I know it's become second nature to you, but I refuse to play your game."

Ben mentally cringed. He had no one but himself to blame for Isabel's low opinion. Intent on hiding his true reason for avoiding marriage, he'd crafted this footloose and fancy-free persona and played it with a finesse that had fooled everyone. Since others' opinions about his romantic interests weren't important, he was able to brush off any censure he incurred. Until Isabel.

"I apologize for daring to touch you, my lady." He sketched a deep bow. "I'll do my best to restrain my untoward impulses around you."

His anger directed at his unfortunate circumstances, he spied a comb amid the supplies she'd gathered and snatched it up. Forcing a lightness into his voice that he didn't feel, he said, "Eli, my boy, have you ever seen a dog with burrs twisting his fur?"

Eli ceased his splashing.

"I hate to say it, but that's what your hair looks like." He waggled the comb. "We're going to get rid of those knots, all right? And then you'll not only smell nice for Miss Isabel and her sisters, you'll look presentable."

When the boy appeared uncertain, Ben said, "I promise I'll be gentle. I've had plenty of practice. I was often responsible for dressing my three younger sisters' hair."

Isabel excused herself to go in search of an article of clothing for Eli. Using a cup she'd provided, Ben scooped up small amounts of water and wet the boy's curls. As he washed the grit from his scalp, he asked, "Do you have any sisters, Eli?"

"My mama had a baby."

Ben rested his arm on the copper basin's long edge. "And that baby was you?"

"Not me. I'm a big boy."

"That you are." His mind whirling, he continued his task. Had the boy's mother died in childbirth?

"I want Mama back." His lower lip trembled.

Ben had little experience comforting children. The lawman in him wanted to pepper the boy with questions, but he couldn't treat Eli like a suspect in an investigation. He reached out and awkwardly patted the boy's shoulder.

"What was her name?"

"Annie."

"Pretty name. Did she have dark curls like you?"

Shaking his head, he manipulated the soap bar around the tub like a boat. "Mama had long hair the color of corn."

"Eli, I'd like to find your guardian. You said your pa isn't around?"

"Mama said he was a bad man." His eyes reflected a hint of worry.

Isabel had entered the room. At these words, she frowned. Was she thinking the same as he? That the timing of the attempted robbery and Eli's arrival might not be coincidental? He tried to make sense of a connection between Eli and the man who'd threatened Isabel but couldn't.

She neared the tub, her skirts making soft swishing noises. "You're safe here, Eli. Ben's a lawman. A deputy, in fact."

Eli didn't look impressed. "Can I get out?"

Ben smiled and winked. "I'm almost done with your hair. Just a few minutes longer."

When they'd gotten him dried and dressed in a white shirt that swallowed him whole, he scowled down at it.

"Since we weren't able to attend church this morning," Ben suggested, "I could read the account of Jesus's birth."

Isabel looked stunned. "You wouldn't mind?"

"It'd be my pleasure."

As she went to her room to retrieve her Bible, he settled

on the sofa and patted the middle spot. "You can sit between us, little man."

Eli clambered onto the cushions, his soapy-clean scent a huge improvement from before. His curls flopped over his forehead and skimmed his brows. He could do with a trim.

When Isabel handed Ben the revered book, he flipped to Luke, the worn pages a sign that it wasn't a dust collector.

"What's a Bible?" Eli said.

Isabel's clasped hands tightened on her lap. He shared her concern.

"This is God's Word," he said. "Did anyone ever tell you about Jesus?"

Eli shook his head. A great weight settled on his soul. So this was what it felt like to be a father, he realized, with the privilege of telling his children about the Creator of the world and His Son, Jesus Christ, sent to spare humankind from eternal condemnation. What an awesome responsibility.

Ben wouldn't have a son or daughter to share the good news with, but God had granted him the opportunity to tell Eli.

Praying for guidance, he searched for a way to relate what he knew in terms a child could understand. Then he read the Holy Scriptures, his heart swelling anew at the miracle of Christ's birth.

Out of the corner of his eye, he noticed Isabel dashing tears from her cheeks. He was fervently thankful it was her sitting here with him, sharing this moment, and not some starry-eyed girl who'd duped herself into thinking he'd make a fabulous husband.

He looked at Eli, who was absorbing everything with wide-eyed innocence, and vowed to use whatever time they had together to point him toward the Lord.

Closing the book, he headed for the coatrack. "I'm going to the church. As soon as services conclude, I'll make an announcement. Maybe someone will have information that will benefit us."

Isabel followed, her misgivings clear. "I'm not convinced returning him is a wise idea. He clearly hasn't had the best of care." Hugging herself, she whispered, "Ben, he's never even heard the true reason for Christmas."

He agreed with her, but he had a duty to uphold the law. "He doesn't belong to us, Isabel. We have a legal obligation to search for his guardian. At first, he said he didn't have a father. Just now he indicated his mother had spoken of him. I get the impression he's not a law-abiding citizen."

She searched his countenance with dawning concern. "You believe our bank robber is connected to Eli somehow?"

"The timing is suspicious." He tied his new neckerchief around his throat. "As far as we know, no one's been looking for him."

"Which would indicate a person who doesn't truly care."

"We need to learn more about this Happy person he keeps mentioning."

"I'll get out pencils and paper right away." She regarded Eli with obvious anxiety.

"Isabel."

"Hmm?"

"I don't want you to get hurt."

She refocused on him. "I won't."

"If there are no developments today, we should place him elsewhere."

"You don't think I'm up to the challenge of caring for a small child?"

"That's not it." He thumped his hat against his thigh. How was he supposed to explain his reservations? "I'm worried you'll get attached in a way that a married couple with children of their own might not."

She folded her arms over her chest. "Your worry is for

naught. I've resigned myself to a life without a husband and, therefore, no children."

Ben felt as if an arrow had pierced his heart. The dream of a large family had been ripped from him. He couldn't fathom anyone deliberately making such a choice.

"You have a lot to offer a child," he rasped. "Be sure you're making the right decision. Regret makes for cold company."

Chapter Seven

Ben's public announcement was met with surprise and expressions of pity. What he didn't receive was insight into how Eli had come to be in their town. Like Isabel, he found it odd that no one was frantically searching for the boy. The reverend and his wife, along with several others, offered to assist his investigation in any way they could.

In the crowd of people pouring out of the church, he found the post office operator and convinced him to delay his noon meal so that Ben could send telegrams to the surrounding communities. He'd thanked the man for his time and was strolling along the spruced-up boardwalk, the sharp scent of evergreens filling his senses, when Grant hailed him from the mercantile across the street.

His friend quickly traversed the wide dirt street and joined Ben in front of the Plum Café.

"I'm glad I caught up to you," he said, his gaze penetrating. "How are the Flores sisters coping? Is there anything we can do to help?"

"Thanks for the offer. Right now, we're focusing on finding answers."

"Not easy when you're dealing with a four-year-old. I imagine he's scared out of his wits."

"He's doing okay, all things considered." Ben unwound his horse's reins from the hitching post. "He's taken a shine to Isabel."

Grant made a considering noise. "That's the piece of the puzzle I can't figure out."

"What puzzle?"

"I heard you showed up at the serenade with her. Were you at her place when she found the boy?"

A sigh gusted out of him. "You're not a marshal anymore, remember?"

Grant's grin did nothing to diminish his intensity. He wouldn't stop until his curiosity had been appeased. "I find it interesting that two people who go out of their way to avoid sharing the same air are suddenly in each other's pockets."

"Isabel avoids men on principle." He thought about her reaction to his Scripture reading. To his knowledge, Manuel Flores hadn't darkened the door of a church since moving to Tennessee. The man had failed in his responsibility to his family on more than one front.

"You more than others," Grant retorted. "I notice these things."

"Yes, I know you do."

Stuffing his boot in the stirrup, Ben grabbed the saddle horn and hauled himself onto Blaze's back. Grant stepped close and patted the animal's neck.

"Out with it, MacGregor." His blue gaze was relentless. "I've proved I can keep my mouth shut when I need to."

Ben shifted in the saddle, hearing what his friend hadn't said. Grant wasn't in the habit of keeping secrets from his wife, yet he hadn't breathed a word of Ben's condition to her.

He scanned Main Street and the churchyard, now empty save for one remaining couple rounding up their kids and urging them into their wagon. The sun hadn't made an appearance today. Behind the soaring steeple, winter fog blanketed the hollows between rounded mountain ridges. On days like these, the majestic mountains assumed a navy blue hue.

"Three nights ago, Isabel interrupted the bank robbery. I happened to be walking home when I noticed movement in the alley behind the bank. I made my presence known, and the blackguard put a gun to her head."

"That's how you wound up getting shot." After smoothing Blaze's golden mane, Grant lowered his arm. "Why did you keep her role secret?"

"She would've hated the extra scrutiny."

He scraped his hand over his jaw. "Yeah, makes sense."

"The man knows she can identify him." Ben related her experience after the serenade. "I didn't want to take any chances, so I insisted on staying in the warming hut. Before I retired for the night, we discovered Eli."

"And suddenly you're spending time with the beautiful miller."

"It's not as if I'm courting her." She'd never allow it, anyway.

"You like her."

"I respect and admire her. That's it." He couldn't permit it to be more.

Grant shifted on his feet, uncertainty touching his features. "We didn't get a chance to talk after our announcement the other night. I apologize for bombarding you like that."

"Don't you dare apologize. I'm thrilled for you and Jess."

"I know. I'd planned to tell you alone, though. It's a sensitive subject."

"Not that sensitive," he denied, not wanting the other

man to feel an ounce of guilt. Grant deserved to celebrate his impending fatherhood without worrying about Ben's feelings. "I've been living with this knowledge since I was nineteen."

"What if your doctor was wrong?"

"Dr. Powell's a respected physician in our part of Georgia, in possession of a keen intellect. He showed me the cases he'd studied to support his conclusions." The burden of those memories settled on his chest, an intangible weight pulling him down. "There is a chance he was wrong, but I couldn't bring myself to enter marriage knowing the odds are against me."

"I respect a man's right to make his own decisions," Grant declared. "That being said, what about adoption? It worked out for Jessica's sister Megan."

Megan and Lucian Beaumont had a large, loving family. After years of trying for a child, they'd adopted a little girl from Lucian's hometown of New Orleans. Not long after that, teen siblings Patrick and Lillian had come into their lives and, most recently, a two-year-old boy named Artie.

"For Shane and Allison, too," Ben agreed. Their twins were a seamless part of their brood, as was the older girl, Matilda. For those unaware of their background, they'd assume all three were the couple's natural-born children. "Those situations are different. Megan and Lucian fell in love and married *before* discovering they couldn't have kids. I'm not convinced any woman would willingly shackle herself to a man like me. It wouldn't be fair."

"You're making assumptions, Ben, as well as underestimating love. I'd have married Jessica no matter what. I wouldn't have let anything stand in our way."

Frustration welled inside him. "What are you suggesting? That I court someone in earnest and wait until she hopefully falls in love with me before springing the terrible news on her?"

Blaze fidgeted beneath him, his long tail whipping from side to side.

"I'm suggesting you revisit the matter. You were young when you were handed this verdict. It's been, what? Six years? Pray about it. You never know. God may be leading you to a different conclusion."

While Ben appreciated Grant's intentions, he couldn't allow himself to entertain a different future for himself. He'd accepted his lot. To dream of something other than his solitary journey would only lead to deeper disappointment.

"I'll keep your advice in mind. Right now, I have to focus on protecting Isabel from a possible attack and returning a motherless boy to his guardian."

Eli's big blue eyes reflected wonder as Isabel grouped the oranges on the table along with an assortment of fragrant spices.

He picked a whole clove from the bowl and smelled it. "What's this?"

"Those are cloves." She picked up a short nail. "We're going to make pomanders. I'll make patterns on the fruit with this nail, and you can help me by sticking the cloves in the holes. Would you like that?"

Carmen swept past with a bunch of pinecones and several sprigs of greenery. She made a work space out of the coffee table. "I'll arrange these items in a bowl, and we'll put the pomanders on top. They freshen the air and look pretty, too."

She'd returned from church alone—Honor had gone to John's for the afternoon—with a full report of Ben's announcement and the aftermath. Isabel had tried to shove the frustrating lawman from her mind and had failed miserably. He'd gotten into the habit of surprising her at every turn and crumbling her preconceived notions about him. Who could've guessed Ben MacGregor had a way with kids? Or that beneath his frivolous banter beat a heart that revered God's precious Word?

He'd been gentle and patient with Eli, qualities she greatly admired. The way he'd responded to the child's lack of knowledge about Jesus—with tenderness and compassion—had revived a part of her heart that had grown cold with bitterness. The flash of frustration he'd shown her before ducking out the door had evoked more questions about what went on behind those green eyes and flippant smile.

"Soon we'll gather enough evergreens to adorn the mantel and drape over the windows and door frame," Carmen told Eli, her eyes alight with anticipation. "Closer to Christmas, we'll cut down a tree and decorate it with strings of cranberries and popcorn."

Isabel picked up the first orange and started making shallow holes in a circular pattern. Following Papa's death and Mama's move, she'd committed herself to making the season special for her sisters. They'd engaged in new traditions and created happy memories.

"Can I help with your tree?"

At Eli's hopeful expression, Isabel's heart squeezed. "We'd love for you to help, Eli. But don't you want to spend Christmas in your own home?"

"I don't stay there anymore." He frowned, tapping the table with the clove. "I stay with Happy."

"Is he a family friend? Or a neighbor?"

He lifted a thin shoulder. "Is it time to put the cloves in now?"

"Almost." Not wanting to push the boy for answers, she focused on her task and handed him the orange. "Hold it over the table, all right? And don't squeeze too hard. We don't want juice dripping out."

"Okay, Miss Isabel."

It was the first time he'd called her by name. Watching him attack his task with grave seriousness, his brows furrowed and his small pink tongue protruding, she recalled Ben's warning. He was worried she'd become too attached to this precious child. What she wouldn't confess was that he was right to worry. While she was resigned to a life without a husband—her mother's disgrace and unhappiness had cured her of romantic notions—the abstract concept of going childless troubled her. Spending time with Eli was opening her eyes to the joys of motherhood.

Carmen started humming "We Three Kings," and Isabel sang the words. Eli seemed to enjoy this, so they continued with more songs, some slow and reverent, some silly. When all the oranges were embellished with reddish-brown swirls, she showed him how to dust them with ground cinnamon and nutmeg.

Ben returned just as they were washing their hands and storing the leftover spices. He smiled at Eli's enthusiastic explanation of what they'd done. When he gently ruffled the boy's curls, Isabel forced her gaze away. She couldn't start viewing the lawman as anything other than a player of hearts.

"Want to help me arrange the oranges in my bowl?" Carmen beckoned Eli, who grabbed one in each hand.

Ben held his Stetson in both hands over his chest and leveled those intense eyes at her.

"Did the drawing help?"

She plucked it from the hutch. "What do you think?"

He grimaced. "Looks more like a marionette doll than a man."

"It was worth a try. I did learn that he's staying with

this person. Maybe Eli lived in another town and, once his mother died, came to live with a relative or friend here?"

Ben tugged on the ends of his scarf. His whiskers were gone and his wavy hair tamed. Beneath his coat—the hole where the bullet pierced had been patched—he wore a fresh change of clothes. This outfit was more casual, more in line with his profession. He'd paired a blue-and-white-striped shirt with a tan vest. Dusky trousers hid most of his work-worn leather boots.

"It's not that cold out today," he said. "We could ask him to retrace his steps."

"It was dark when we found him."

He observed Carmen and Eli, who were on their knees at the short table. "Considering his age, I suppose it'd be a lot to expect him to remember his surroundings."

"Did you learn anything else while you were out?"

"No." He held up a finger. "I do have a surprise, however."

Picking up a leather satchel he'd brought inside, he placed it on one of the chairs and pulled out a bundle of clothing. "I swung by Sam and Mary O'Malley's place. You know their sons Josh and Caleb, along with their families, live on the property. Between the lot of them, I was able to procure a couple of pairs of pants and three shirts for Eli."

Thrilled, Isabel inspected each article. "This is wonderful, Ben. Thank you. He'll be much more comfortable in these." There were also undergarments, socks and a single pair of shoes.

At his tender smile, her gullible heart flipped over.

"I think he'll like this even better." He produced another item.

Isabel skimmed the miniature wooden rocking horse painted in festive green and red hues. "It's darling," she breathed. "Did Josh make it?"

A renowned woodworker, Josh O'Malley owned a store on Main Street where he sold the furniture he crafted.

"This is actually store-bought."

"The mercantile's closed today."

"I purchased this last week and was going to mail it to Tabitha for Christmas. She has a son about Eli's age."

Gently nudging his arm down, she said, "I'm sure it cost a fair amount of wages. Keep it for your nephew. We've done all right keeping Eli entertained without toys."

"I want to do this, Isabel. Besides, I already told you I don't have a lot of expenses. I can afford to purchase a different gift for Xavier." His forehead furrowed. "I'd guess Eli doesn't have many toys."

"I'd have to agree with you."

Mischief sparkled in the green depths. "There's a rare occurrence."

"Better savor the moment." Tossing her head, she claimed a spot on the sofa. Carmen sent her a curious look. Then, noticing what was in Ben's hands, she tapped Eli's shoulder. "I believe Christmas has come early for someone."

Eli lifted his head. With a gasp of delight, he dropped the orange and rushed over to Ben. He stopped short of actually touching the horse, however.

"Who's it for?"

Crouching to his level, Ben held it out. "For you, if you want it."

He gingerly explored the white hair made of yarn. "I can keep it? Forever?"

Ben chuckled and ruffled the boy's hair again. "You sure can, little man."

Eli gleefully accepted the gift and, plopping down on the hearth rug, admired it from every angle. Isabel was reminded why she treasured this time of year. Giving to others, whether it was a material gift or a sacrifice of time or talents, evoked a sense of joy that couldn't be matched.

A familiar New Testament verse sprang to mind— *Every good gift and every perfect gift is from above, and cometh down from the Father of lights, with whom is no variableness, neither shadow of turning.*

Isabel turned her head and glimpsed Ben's solemn expression, one she had trouble interpreting. He didn't look like a carefree bachelor. He looked like a man in mourning...but for what?

Chapter Eight

Ben noticed her assessment. His features shuttering, he plastered on a smile. This time, Isabel recognized it as fake.

"My mother makes these." He tapped an orange. "But she uses apples."

"We'll have to try that next year," Carmen said from her spot on the floor. She propped her elbows on the table and gazed up at him. "What were holidays like in the Mac-Gregor household?"

"Loud. How could it not be with three boisterous sisters?" His eyes softened with an affection that belied his dry tone. Balancing against the sofa arm, he folded his arms over his broad chest. "We didn't have much, but my mother did her best to make the holidays festive. We used nature's bounty to decorate the house." He nodded toward their mantel. "My sisters and I spent hours making paper chains like yours."

"That's part of the fun," Carmen piped up. "Isabel usually left that task to Honor and me. She preferred to be in the kitchen with Mama baking special goodies."

"I remember the entire month of December, our house smelled like a bakery. I snuck cookies whenever I could.

My favorites were the almond cookies and lemon-flavored meringues, which my ma called kisses." His grin widened, white teeth flashing. "Ma knew what I was doing but never scolded me for it."

"One of the perks of being the only boy?" Isabel queried, intrigued despite herself.

"My sisters would argue that point, I'm certain."

"Did you have a huge Christmas feast?" Carmen said.

"Yes. Every year, my mother and father invited people in the community to join us. Widows. Single mothers or fathers. Anyone without family around who'd otherwise spend Christmas alone."

"Don't you miss spending the holidays with them?" Isabel said.

"I do. But I have good friends here. Shane and Allison are like family. I've gotten to know Alexander and Ellie better in recent weeks. I spent Thanksgiving with them."

"Both couples are out of town, though." Carmen jumped up and clapped her hands. "I have a marvelous idea. Why don't you spend Christmas with us this year?"

Ben slid a glance at Isabel. "That's kind of you to offer, but I'm sure your sister has plans that don't include me."

"Nonsense. Your company is sure to liven up our modest celebration. Right, Isa?"

"Um…" She struggled to find the right response. It was just like her youngest sibling to blurt out an invitation without thinking it through. The deputy was the last person Isabel had envisioned sharing the most special day of the year with.

Ben rescued her. "Christmas is several weeks away. For now, I have a suggestion. Why don't we all gather evergreens? My poor cabin could use some, and those paper chains would look even prettier against a backdrop of holly."

Carmen loved the idea, of course, but Eli preferred to play with his new treasure.

"You two go on ahead." Carmen shooed them toward the door. "I'll stay and keep Eli company."

Isabel balked. Traipsing through the forest as a group was one thing. The prospect of a solo outing with Ben put her nerves on edge. "Shouldn't we wait for Honor?"

"She won't mind. She's too distracted by thoughts of John and whether or not he's going to propose."

She froze. "Truly?"

"She overheard John and his pa talking right after Thanksgiving. She didn't linger—eavesdropping is not what a lady does, she said—but heard enough to believe he's making plans for their future."

This was news to her. Honor hadn't breathed a word. Was she afraid how Isabel might react?

"What do you want to do, Isabel?" There was a subtle challenge in his tone, a clear question in his eyes.

He expected her to refuse. She did the opposite.

"The house could use some Christmas cheer." She marched to the coatrack and gathered her own outerwear. "Let's gather some evergreens."

His lips curving into a boyish grin, he opened the door with a flourish. "After you, my lady."

They could've been the only two people in the world.

The higher their horses climbed, the denser the forest and the more serene their surroundings. Isabel obviously didn't feel the need to fill the silence with inane chatter. Instead, she quietly soaked in the flora and fauna characteristic of the higher elevation.

Contentment suffused Ben. He didn't have to try with Isabel, didn't have to pretend that he lived a charmed life unblemished by difficulties. Playing his part of the Debonair Deputy took up an increasing amount of energy. He was growing weary of it.

"Is that where we're headed?"

Isabel pointed to a stand of Fraser firs beneath the summit. The stately blue-green pines lent a bit of cheer to the gray day.

"Yes, ma'am." Tugging gently on the reins, he guided Blaze to a stop and nodded to the valley spread out below. Mountain ridges marched toward the horizon in all directions. "Will you look at that view?"

She took a moment to appreciate it, a slight smile curving her lips. "God's creation is a wonder. I don't often get a chance to stop and appreciate it, especially from this angle."

"You're fortunate to have grown up here."

"My parents moved here from Texas six months before I was born. A terrible drought drove them from the only home they'd ever known." Sitting tall and regal in the saddle, her soft gray cloak spread out around her like a queen's cape, she patted her mount's neck. A gray scarf shot through with purple matched her mauve blouse. "I'd like to visit their former home someday."

"Do you have family there?"

"Aunts, uncles and cousins. I know them by name only. Papa didn't see the need to take us for a visit."

"Why don't you plan a trip?"

She nudged her roan to continue. "I can't afford to close the mill for the amount of time we'd need. Besides, I'm not sure Honor would be willing to be apart from John."

Ben's horse pulled abreast of hers. He noticed her fleeting consternation.

"You aren't ready for her to leave the nest, are you?"

"John's a good man. If I didn't think he'd treat her right, I would've discouraged the courtship. They love and respect each other." Her lips turned down. "I confess the thought of her not being around every day is difficult to accept, however."

"You'll still have Carmen."

Her features relaxed. "Carmen has a zest for life. She has the ability to delight in the smallest things. She's spontaneous and loving. It will take a special man to complement her personality."

"I commend you, Isabel. You were, what, twenty when you assumed responsibility for your sisters?"

She looked uncomfortable with the praise. "I didn't have a choice. Besides, they were sixteen and seventeen years old, hardly children."

"You could've insisted they live with your mother and aunt. You could've sold the place and moved with them."

"I'm not cut out for city life."

"It would've been the easier path. You could've started fresh without Manuel's reputation shadowing you." A pair of birds, one larger than the other, burst from the trees and engaged in a game of chase. When their squawks had ceased, he continued. "I'm getting the sense you don't often take the easy way out."

She halted her roan mare, aptly named Honey, and dismounted. She indicated the fir trees yards ahead. "How long do you think this will take?"

Ben followed suit, walking around to where she stood. "Tired of my company already?" he jibed.

A hawk's cry pierced the silence, but it did nothing to detract from the fact they were alone on this mountain with no one else around for miles. She backed up a step. Her gaze had trouble holding his.

"We've spent more time in each other's pockets the past three days than in the four years you've lived here," she retorted. "It is getting a bit tiresome."

He wasn't sure he believed her. "I'm enjoying your company. Very much."

Her head reared back. "But I don't treat you like a beloved prince."

"Exactly."

He fished his shears from the saddlebag and led his sorrel farther up the incline. Releasing the reins, he ducked beneath the full branches and examined the trees. He filled his lungs with the pungent scent.

"Smells like Christmas." When she didn't join him, he called to her. "Come point out which ones you want."

She complied, her demeanor cautious. His admission must've spooked her. "They look alike to me. You pick."

"Easy enough."

He cut through the first branch, and Isabel dragged it out of the copse. She returned with a scowl.

"What's the matter?"

She'd removed her gloves. "My glove got snared on the wood and ripped."

Ben laid the shears on the ground and tugged his off. "Here. Wear mine."

"No." She clasped her hands behind her back. "You'll get resin on your skin."

"Better me than you." Advancing, he did a give-me motion. "Hand them over."

"Your fingers will get cold."

"I'm used to being in the elements." He lowered his face to within a breath of hers. "Humor me, sugar—"

She pressed her smooth, bare fingers to his mouth, effectively cutting off his words. Ben willed his body to remain motionless as the effects of her bold touch rocked him to the core.

Her face was so very close, her eyes big and dark, her inky eyelashes lush and curving downward. The cold air had brushed her cheekbones with a hint of pink. Despite the thick scent of pine and sap permeating the mountaintop, her unique spice-and-orange scent still teased him.

"Why do you call me that?" she whispered.

"Because—" At the movement of his lips, her attention slipped to his mouth and her hand still covering it. Her eyes widened. To his instant disappointment, she snatched her hand away.

His head fuzzy with yearning, he cleared his throat. "You, ah, tend to wear shades of purple. When you stitched up my arm, you were wearing a plum-colored blouse. Put me in mind of sugarplums."

"Oh."

He reached out and adjusted her scarf, his knuckles skimming the underside of her chin.

"It's a nice color on you."

She shivered. "T-thank you."

"See? Isn't it easy?"

"What?" She seemed somewhat dazed.

"Accepting compliments at face value."

Her features cleared, and the familiar suspicion with which she so often regarded him reared its ugly head. She slapped her ruined gloves against his chest. "You want to forgo your comfort for mine, fine. If you get frostbite, don't expect me to play nurse again."

"Too bad," he mourned. "You're an excellent one."

Tucking her torn gloves into his pocket, he watched to make sure she put his on before setting about cutting enough branches for both their cabins. Since he only wanted one for his mantel and one for his front door, it didn't take long to amass the necessary amount. Once he had them bundled and tied securely with twine, he hefted equal portions into the two oversize canvas satchels attached on opposite sides of his saddle.

"Ready?"

Isabel seized his wrist and inspected his hand. The air whooshed from his lungs. "As I warned, you're covered with resin. You'll have a time getting this off."

"A worthy price considering your cabin will reflect the season's bounty. Eli will enjoy helping you decorate."

Releasing him, she nodded. "I have a feeling he's missed out on a lot. I'll include him in our preparations as much as possible."

They both knew the boy's time with them was tenuous. While they were no closer to finding his guardian, who knew what the next day might bring?

Halfway down the mountain, Ben heard male voices. He slowed his horse and lifted a hand to indicate she do the same. Unable to make out their conversation, he slipped out of the saddle.

"Stay here."

Her posture going rigid, she gripped the reins more tightly. Ben shifted his coat for easy access to his weapon. His hands were numb from the cold and sticky, but that wouldn't prevent him from pulling the trigger if he had to. Walking up and over the knoll, he quickly cataloged the scene, recognizing farmers who owned property not far from this spot. One of their horses was in dire trouble.

A thin stream that originated higher up the mountain pooled where the ground leveled off. The unfortunate horse must've fallen and was now stuck in the mud and muck surrounding the shallow pond. The animal was on her side, her head thrashing and eyes wild.

The men's faces reflected relief the instant Ben made his presence known. After promising to assist them, he hurried back to Isabel.

"There's a horse in need of rescue," he explained, his fingers clumsy as he gathered the rope attached to his saddle. "I have to help." The slide of metal against leather sounded. "Take my gun. I don't foresee any problems, but you'll have protection in case you need it. Shouldn't take you another twenty minutes to get home."

Isabel stared at him, his gun and the knoll. "I'm staying."

Before he could protest, she was out of the saddle and in possession of both horses' reins. "Lead the way, Deputy."

Chapter Nine

Seeing the resolve settle over Ben's features was like watching a soldier prepare himself for battle. When she returned his gloves to him, he accepted them without question, his mind already on the difficult task ahead. This was the no-nonsense lawman she'd glimpsed in the alley days ago.

She waited near the base of the knoll with Blaze and Honey as Ben discussed the best course of action. After the elderly men related what happened, he slowly crouched and, speaking in a soothing voice, stroked the incapacitated mare's neck. He checked her pulse first, then inspected her gums.

"Healthy pink color," he murmured. "That's good." He ran his hands over her legs. "I can't feel any signs of fractures. Her muscles aren't seizing up, so I don't think she's in shock. How long has she been like this?"

"About an hour. She's been struggling to free herself, but her movements slowed about ten minutes ago."

Ben frowned. "The water's ice-cold. We need to act fast." Working carefully so as not to spook her, he attempted to slide the rope beneath the mare's body.

The horse, whose name was Wishbone, thrashed and

quivered. Isabel's heart went out to her. The farmers did nothing to ease her distress. Either the thought didn't cross their minds or they weren't keen on getting too close to the spooked mare.

Her mind made up, Isabel led Blaze and Honey to a nearby tree and tied them to low-slung branches. She approached on Ben's right side in clear view of Wishbone.

"Let me hold her head while you secure the rope."

On his knees in the muck, the deputy shifted to regard her with surprise. He'd tossed his hat in the grass, leaving his hair to flop into his eyes. "Sure you want to do that? The water's freezing, and I can't promise you'll be able to wash this mud from your skirts."

In answer, she knelt on the ground beside him, hiding her wince at the cold shock of moisture seeping through her layers of clothing. "I'll work on keeping her calm."

Admiration flashed in his eyes. "I appreciate the assistance, and I'm sure Wishbone does, too."

"Say, ain't that one of the Flores girls?" The thin, bald-headed man standing several feet away nudged his portly friend. "Pretty thing, ain't she?"

"Couldn't say. I forgot my spectacles at home."

"With a good-for-nothing pa, she could be as pretty as a newborn foal and still not catch herself a respectable husband."

Humiliation scalded her. She'd heard this and much worse over the years, but having Ben witness it added an extra layer of embarrassment.

"Enough." Ben scowled at them both. "No more comments like that if you want our help, got it?"

The thin one shrugged. "Just statin' facts, Deputy."

Ben dipped his head to catch her gaze. "Ignore them."

Lips compressed into a thin line, she nodded and focused on Wishbone. Ben shifted to the side to allow her room. The water was several inches deep here. She prayed the mare wouldn't suffer any adverse effects.

"Hello there, sweet lady," she crooned, lightly rubbing between her ears. "The deputy here is going to get you out of this mess real soon."

"Thanks for the vote of confidence," he said on a strained laugh.

Funny, Isabel didn't doubt Ben's abilities, whether it was saving her from a thief, seeing to the needs of a scared little boy or rescuing a trapped horse. He was a man of many talents.

It took multiple attempts, but he was able to tie a bowline knot around her girth.

He lumbered to his feet. His pants were wet from the knees down, and little clumps of mud marred his coat. "Let's see if we can't convince Wishbone to abandon her watery bed."

With a parting word of support to the mare, Isabel pushed upright and moved out of the way. Her legs were shaky. One glance at her mud-caked skirt confirmed she would most likely have to discard it.

"Isabel, you hold on to her lead rope. Wilbur, you and Cary come and stand behind me. It's going to take our combined strength to get her upright."

On Ben's count, they tugged and coaxed and tugged some more. The mare was tired and cold and not budging. After half an hour passed, Isabel's uneasiness grew. Wishbone had given up. Ben's jaw was locked tight, perspiration dotting his forehead. Belatedly, she remembered his injured arm. With all the effort he'd been expending, she wouldn't be surprised if he'd popped one or more stitches. For certain he must be experiencing discomfort.

"I can't pull no more." Cary released the rope and lifted his arms in surrender.

Wilbur mopped his bald head. "I'm afraid we're gonna have to let her go, Deputy."

Ben's gaze flashed fire. "I'm not ready to give up." Dropping the rope, he returned to Wishbone and patted her side. "We're going to try something else, okay, girl? I know you're exhausted, but this is our last shot."

Shifting on his haunches, his gaze met theirs. "Here's the plan. We're going to roll her onto her other side, give her a chance to use a different set of muscles."

Isabel rested her hand on his shoulder. "What do you want me to do?"

His mouth softening in silent gratitude, he gave her instructions. Their eyes locked, and it was as if they were connected somehow—they shared the same mind, the same purpose.

He acquired ropes from the farmers and tied them to Wishbone's legs. It took some convincing, but Cary and Wilbur finally agreed to help once more. With the four of them working together, they were able to gently roll the mare. The new position had her angled downhill. Isabel held her breath. Somehow, her hand found Ben's. His tight hold was reassuring as Wishbone flailed and, with a great heave, finally hobbled onto her shaky legs.

A whoop escaped Ben. Seconds later, his arms closed around Isabel's waist, and he whirled her in a circle.

Isabel laughed as he set her back on her feet. Steadying her with both hands firmly gripping her waist, he beamed at her, his eyes sparkling with triumph. The air between them shimmered with anticipation. The lightheartedness vanished. Ben's gaze lowered to her mouth and darkened with want. Just like on the mountaintop, Isabel experienced a magnetic pull that chased away rational arguments. It was as if they were linked by an invisible tether that was shrinking with every second that passed, urging them closer.

He swallowed hard and released her, turning away to examine Wishbone.

What had just happened? And why did she feel disappointed that the moment had passed?

"Tell me the story of the horse again?"

Isabel tucked the thick covers around Eli's chest, leaving his arms free. He refused to part with the rocking horse, despite her reassurances it would be safe on the bedside stand.

She couldn't resist finger combing his springy curls away from his brow. "It's late. I promise to tell you over breakfast."

Carmen and Eli had been agog at her and Ben's filthy state hours earlier. While Isabel had intended on helping him remove the resin from his hands, he'd declined her offer and returned to his cabin. Amid the barrage of questions from her sister and young charge, she'd forgotten to ask after his wounded arm, and now worry festered.

He's a grown man, Isabel. If he requires medical attention, he'll visit Doc.

He yawned widely. "I hope Wishbone's okay."

Shifting on the edge of her bed, she said, "I'm sure she's doing fine."

The farmers had promised to bathe Wishbone with warm water and give her a clean, dry place to pass the night. Ben planned to visit her the following day. Isabel would like to accompany him, but she doubted the wisdom of spending even more time in the handsome lawman's company. That charged moment between them, the feeling of his strong hands cupping her waist, replayed in her mind, releasing a thousand butterflies in her middle.

She'd *liked* having him close.

Averting her face, she squeezed her eyes tight. *I will not develop an infatuation for the Debonair Deputy!*

"Will we go to the mercantile tomorrow like Ben promised?"

The heavy dose of doubt in Eli's voice produced a frown. What had the adults in his life done to engender this mistrust?

"He didn't promise, remember?" she pointed out gently. "Ben said that if at all possible, he'd take you to town. He's our deputy, and the sheriff's spending Christmas in Virginia. That means he's in charge. Whatever problems arise, he has to see to them."

She'd developed a newfound respect for him. Ben's willing spirit to help man or beast—without complaint—was a rare thing.

Eli thought about that for a minute. "You're coming with us, too. Aren't you?"

"I don't know," she hedged. "I have chores to tend to."

His face reflected his inner turmoil, and Isabel patted his hand. "You can trust Ben. He's a good man."

When he continued to fiddle with the toy, she said, "Is Happy a good man, Eli?"

His blue eyes lifted to hers, and he nodded against the pillow. "He's nice to me."

Relief surged through her. "I'm glad to hear that."

"Why did he leave me here?"

She stiffened. Keeping her voice even, she said, "Happy brought you to my home?"

"He picked it 'cause there are three girls here." He tried to hold up three fingers. "He said you'd take care of me."

Could this be true? A stranger had chosen to abandon a four-year-old boy on their doorstep with the assumption they were decent people and would care for him?

Bewildered, she debated whether or not to ride over to Ben's. This news was huge.

"Your friend was right. You're safe here, Eli." She stroked his arm. "Did you know this has been my room since I was your age? Actually, my sisters and I shared this room." She pointed to the opposite corner where the wardrobe now stood. "Their bed used to be over there."

When their mother left, Honor and Carmen claimed their parents' old room. Isabel relished having a bedroom to herself. She'd chosen an elegant fabric for the windows— a blend of plum and dove gray that coordinated with the quilt atop her bed. A single painting hung on the wall, a gift from her uncle, depicting a rural scene near Mexico City.

Tucked against the wall opposite her bed, a chest-high mahogany dresser contained her clothes that didn't need to be hung in the wardrobe. A jagged groove marred the topmost drawer. She and Carmen had been wrestling over a pair of scissors. While fortunate neither of them got injured, their papa's punishment had been almost as bad. Those days were best forgotten, however. Manuel's oppressive personality no longer darkened their home. Isabel and her sisters had created a cozy haven to suit their tastes. Finally, they knew freedom and peace. If she did entertain fleeting thoughts of married life from time to time, she quickly squelched them. The wrong choice of husband could land her right back in daily upheaval.

Those exquisite, confusing moments with Ben resurfaced. He'd spent time here, shared meals with them and even washed their dishes. Not once had his presence detracted from what she and her sisters had created, an atmosphere of love, tranquility and acceptance. He made her nervous, yes. Sometimes he annoyed her. But he never, ever demeaned or disrespected her. He was, beneath the playful grins and disarming endearments, an honorable man.

Isabel refocused on the task at hand. "Our *abuela*—that's Spanish for grandmother—she used to come in at bedtime every night and pray with us. Would you like for me to do that?"

Eli nodded, so she bowed her head and offered a short, simple prayer thanking God for His protection and guidance. When she'd finished, she leaned over and lowered the lamplight.

"Good night, Eli."

His droopy gaze tracked her to the door. "I'm scared."

Isabel remembered her and her sisters' ploys to postpone going to sleep—they were thirsty or their nightclothes were itchy; something was making strange noises beneath the bed. This was only Eli's second night here. He'd apparently been dumped by his guardian…and for what reason?

She couldn't bring herself to leave him in this room, frightened and alone.

"How about I tell you a story?"

"What kind of story?"

Resuming her seat, she folded her hands in her lap. "A story about a Christmas mouse who was far from home."

"Like me."

Her chest felt tight. "Maybe a little like you."

Isabel wove the tale, drawing from her long-ago experience of comforting her younger sisters when they'd burrowed in her bed during their parents' arguments. Eventually, Eli drifted off to sleep. She listened to his even breathing and watched his lips tremble with each exhale. He was precious, this boy. Although she'd only known him a short while, she couldn't imagine leaving him to the mercy of strangers.

Gingerly removing the toy from his limp grasp, she propped it on the stand and bent to kiss his cheek. She gazed down at his innocent face and finally acknowledged that she'd been foolish to dismiss motherhood out of hand.

Leaving the door slightly ajar, she left the bedroom. The lights had been dimmed in the living room. Heat from the fire made it comfortable. Honor emerged from the kitchen cradling a delicate aqua-colored teacup. Already in her nightclothes, a thick white gown with baby blue flounces, her hair hung in rippling waves past her shoulders.

"Is he asleep?" She padded to the sofa and curled into the far edge.

Isabel assumed the opposite end and hugged a pillow to her stomach. "He was exhausted. Carmen kept him busy the entire day."

Honor laughed softly. "She wore herself out right along with him. She's already snoring in there."

"Are you sure you're all right with him staying? I have no idea how long he'll be with us."

She ignored the part of her that hoped it would be a long time, maybe even permanent.

"Of course, Isa." Her sister's dark eyes were earnest. "Eli's a sweet boy. He's certainly attached himself to you. Carmen said that in those moments he wasn't occupied, he'd dart to the window and watch for you. She thinks he was worried you wouldn't come back."

"Because of his guardian's actions." She related what he'd told her, and Honor was understandably shocked.

"I want to speak to Ben as soon as possible," Isabel said, gazing unhappily in the flames. "It will have to wait until morning, I suppose."

"I haven't seen any lights in the hut. He didn't say whether or not he'd be back tonight?"

"There's no reason for him to stay. Eli's guardian doesn't pose a threat, and there's no evidence our would-be thief stuck around."

Honor gave her a considering look. "Have your feelings for Ben undergone any changes?"

"Forget the deputy," she retorted, desperate to evade the subject. "I'd much rather discuss the conversation you overheard between John and his father. Do you truly expect a proposal soon?"

Honor sipped her tea and nestled the cup in its saucer. "I was going to tell you—"

"But you were afraid how I'd react, I know. Sweetie, I didn't expect you to live here forever. Life is all about change. John makes you happy, which in turn makes me happy."

Moisture glistened in her eyes. She placed her cup on the coffee table in order to give Isabel a tearful hug. Isabel wrestled with her own emotions.

"It's not as if you're going far," she said lightly. "I'll still see you, just not every day."

Honor pulled back and dashed the moisture from the corners of her eyes. "He hasn't proposed yet," she cautioned. "It could be spring. Summer, even."

"You've been courting a full year. I think he'll propose this month and ask you to set a spring date for the wedding."

Hope brightened her features. "I admit I'm impatient to become his wife."

Isabel smiled. "Gauging from the way he looks at you, you're not the only one who's impatient."

Honor grabbed Isabel's hand. "I want you to have a good man in your life, too, Isa. One who wouldn't be intimidated by your independent spirit and who'd love you to distraction."

Ben's expression when she'd stopped him from calling her that pet name surged into her mind. His lips had been incredibly firm and warm, despite the exposure to winter elements. She'd found herself imagining what they'd feel like against hers.

"No."

She didn't realize she'd spoken aloud until Honor's expression registered.

Bolting upright, she knotted her fingers together and paced before the fire. "I mean, I'm not sure it's a possibility...to find a man I respect and trust. Papa ruined my perceptions of marriage. I'm grateful you and Carmen weren't affected the same way. He didn't destroy your optimism."

Honor sighed. "You must find a way to forgive him, *hermana*."

She whirled from the fire to gape at her. "Forgive him? He's not sorry for how he treated Mama or us!"

"When God commanded us to forgive others, He didn't say anything about their remorse being a requirement. You're allowing Papa's horrid behavior to dictate your choices."

Isabel stared at the oval rug beneath her feet, her heart and mind in turmoil. She was well acquainted with God's views on forgiveness. However, the thought of releasing the bitterness and resentment that had become such an integral part of her was overwhelming. Holding on to those feelings had made her feel in control, somehow, at a time when she hadn't had any control over her life. She'd been helpless in an untenable situation, unable to alleviate her mother's sadness or guard her sisters from hurtful gossip. She hadn't been able to stop her father from betraying his marriage vows and breaking their family apart bit by bit.

"I know this is difficult to hear," Honor said softly. "But it pains me to think of you spending your life alone." When Isabel opened her mouth to speak, she held up her hand. "If you are truly content on your own, I will respect that. But I know you, and I don't believe you would be for very long."

Isabel thought about Eli and the new, surprising feelings he stirred inside her. And her reaction to Ben's touch. Until now, she'd been content with her life. Things were changing so fast she couldn't get her bearings.

"You're a good sister," she said at last. "No matter what happens, we'll always be close."

To Isabel's immense relief, her sister let the matter drop. The conversation progressed to their Christmas preparations, but thoughts of her future intruded. Spending it alone on this farm didn't hold the appeal it once did.

Chapter Ten

Ben followed the sound of metal striking metal to a small shed-like structure located between the barn and the smokehouse. The double doors had been propped open with rocks, allowing him a clear view of Isabel working over a portable forge. He stopped a couple of yards out to observe her in action.

Clad in black, she'd exchanged her cloak for a short men's-style coat. A leather apron protected her skirt. Leather gloves extending past her wrists protected her skin from stray embers. Her focus was intense as she shaped the steel.

It was unusual to see a woman in a predominately male profession. Out of all the women in these mountains, he'd be surprised if even two knew the blacksmith's trade. Same for her gristmill work. Ben hadn't met another woman like her. Isabel was an intriguing mix of bold beauty and independent stubbornness, with a compassionate heart buried beneath a cynical shell. If he wasn't very careful, he'd find himself in dangerous territory.

Isabel heated the blade's end until it glowed red, then inserted it into a horn handle, which was secured in a vise.

Unwilling to break her concentration, he remained quiet until she balanced the tongs in the glowing coals.

"Good morning, Isabel."

Her head whipped up. "You're here early."

"I spent the night in the hut. I was on my way to the cabin when I heard the noise. There's something I need to tell you."

"I need to discuss something with you, as well. If I'd known you were coming back last night, I would've waited up." She pulled off her gloves. "I hate to think of you passing another uncomfortable night in the hut when there's no need. You could've been at home in your own bed."

"After what happened after sunset, I felt it necessary. Quinn Darling interrupted an attempt to rob his store."

Unease rippled across her features. "What happened, exactly? Do you have this person in custody?"

He propped one hand against the door frame and shook his head. "Quinn had left for the night but returned when he realized he'd forgotten to check if the office lanterns were extinguished. He entered through the front and discovered a man behind the sales counter. Quinn pursued him, but he escaped out the rear exit."

"Did he get a good look at him?"

"Unfortunately, no. It was dark inside the store. Outside, Quinn was hindered by his dash down those steep stairs. He was only able to ascertain that the man was of medium height and weight."

"You think it's the same man."

He nodded. "I'm inclined to, yes. The bank was targeted four days ago, a reasonable amount of time for our suspect to hang around the area and plan his next move."

She sucked in a shaky breath. "What now?"

"I'm waiting for responses from the area sheriffs. If

anyone has seen a man of his description, they'll let us know. In the meantime, we stay vigilant."

Clearly distracted, she noticed the flames getting low and used the forge arm to get the blower wheel moving.

"Is everything okay with Eli?" He pushed off the frame. "Did he sleep well last night?"

"He's fine." Her mood lightened a little. "I told him a story at bedtime, which put him to sleep. He awoke once during the night, disoriented and asking for his ma. It didn't take long to soothe his fears, however." She worried her lower lip. "I wanted to tell you what he said. According to Eli, his guardian deliberately left him with us."

"What?" Disbelief barreled through him. "I assumed he'd gotten lost."

In his line of work, he should know better than to make assumptions. He'd gotten sloppy. Because Isabel was involved?

"It was the logical conclusion. I get the feeling this Happy person studied us before deciding to leave Eli with us. Why would he do that? And does he mean to come back for him?"

"I wish I knew. In my line of work, the search for answers isn't always straightforward." He kneaded his stiff neck. "If it gets to be too much, let me know and I'll find another place for Eli."

"It won't." She jutted her chin. "I like having him around."

Ben clamped his mouth shut against the urge to reiterate his prior warnings. Isabel wouldn't appreciate it.

He gestured to the unfinished project. "That's a lot larger than the gambler's dagger you carry."

She looked at first surprised, then amused. "I haven't heard it called that before. This one's a bowie knife. It's for a Christmas order that I have until Friday to ship out."

When she started to untie her apron, he jerked his thumb over his shoulder. "If you need to continue working, I don't mind helping your sisters with Eli."

She cocked her head. "Are you angling for a breakfast invitation, Deputy?"

He chuckled. "I'm more interested in that dinner you owe me."

"What about this Saturday evening?"

Taken aback by her ready offer, he repeated, "*This* Saturday?"

She raised a well-shaped eyebrow. "Unless you have a prior commitment."

"No, ma'am. My schedule is open. I'd be honored to accept."

Hanging her apron on a protruding nail and slapping her gloves on her tool bench, she joined him. "Would you mind waking Eli while I start the biscuits?"

"Not at all."

She paused before climbing the porch steps. "How's your arm?"

"A little sore." That she entertained even a drop of concern for him filled him with joy. "Worried about me?"

She tried to shrug it off. "You wrangled with Wishbone yesterday. I thought you might have aggravated the injury."

"I checked it last night. Your handiwork remains intact."

The childish chatter that greeted their entrance signaled the boy was already awake. A rumpled-looking Carmen met them at the door and held up an empty basket. "Eli is clamoring for his breakfast. I think he has a hollow leg. I'm off to gather the eggs. Morning, Ben."

She clomped outside. Her unbound hair had obviously not yet seen a hairbrush. That Isabel's little sister felt comfortable around him pleased him. It also made him miss his own sisters.

Eli rushed over and threw his arms around Isabel's legs. "Tell me about the horse stuck in the mud again!"

A tender smile transformed Isabel's face as she reached down and smoothed the child's curls. Ben's heart climbed into his throat. Her fierce guard had slipped, revealing a breathtaking gentleness that called to him.

"Why don't you ask Ben to tell you his version of events?"

Still holding tight to Isabel, Eli turned his face toward Ben and blinked up at him.

He offered the boy a friendly smile. "Wishbone had a rough time. I'm supposed to go and see her today."

Eli dropped his arms to his sides. "Can I come, too?"

"We could all three go." Ben shot a questioning glance at Isabel. "If Miss Isabel is free."

"Yes, I would like to see her."

"Afterward, I have to go to the jail and catch up on paperwork."

He hadn't spent much time in the office these past few days, causing folks to wonder about his whereabouts. It wouldn't do for certain gossipmongers to learn he'd mostly been at the Flores farm.

It was decided that after breakfast, he, Isabel and Eli would stop by the mercantile—Honor had insisted they have one spool of red ribbon and one of gold before hanging the greenery—and then pay a visit to Wishbone.

Typically, Ben ate breakfast alone, scouring the local newspapers and occasionally ones from back home that his mother sent him. Starting the day with the lively Flores sisters was a treat. Like all sisters, they irked one another at times, but their bond was undeniable. He felt honored to be afforded this glimpse into their lives. A week ago, he wouldn't have dreamed he'd be sitting across the table from the elusive Isabel Flores.

This isn't going to last. It could be tomorrow or the next day or a week from today, but sooner or later you'll have no reason to be included.

A pang of denial struck him. When his gaze encountered Isabel's, he felt a jolt of longing. He liked her. He wouldn't delude himself into thinking they could be friends. She wouldn't want that. In fact, she was merely putting up with his intrusion. She was biding her time, impatient to be rid of him.

He ducked his head and focused on his meal. This Christmas had the potential to be the best he'd ever experienced. Or the worst.

Walking along the boardwalk with Ben, Eli between them and holding each of their hands, Isabel felt as if she was in school again, giving a speech in front of a mostly condescending group of kids. The humiliation she'd endured, the knowledge that they pegged her as unworthy, was like an old friend come to call. Since her father's death at the hand of a vengeful husband, she'd worked hard to live beyond reproach, to do nothing to call attention to herself and invite judgment. Yet here she was, keeping company with the popular deputy—and with an abandoned child, no less!

Isabel refused to let her unease show. She kept her head high and pretended to be riveted by the newly hung decorations. Main Street was draped in Christmas cheer, transformed by festive spruce and pinecone wreaths on every shop door and garlands adorning posts and pillars. Wide cherry-red ribbons lent pops of color to the wooden structures. The window displays bore evidence of the season— fruits shipped in from warmer locales, assortments of nuts and boxes of expensive chocolates. There were toys, too— miniature metal trains, wooden whistles and china dolls.

Eli's blue eyes were huge, his jaw sagging. If she could be granted one wish, it would be for the chance to give him an exceptional Christmas.

Stationed on the bench outside the mercantile entrance, a trio of wizened men gawked at them.

"Mornin', Deputy. Who's the kid?"

Ben smiled down at Eli. "This is my new friend Eli."

Eli said hello. The man who'd spoken peered at him, tobacco juice dribbling out of the side of his mouth. He wiped it with his sleeve. "He's a funny-lookin' one, ain't he?"

Tightening her grasp on Eli's hand, Isabel glared down her nose at the rude man. "Not at all. He's as handsome as a child could hope to be."

Jerking open the entrance door, she swept inside with Eli at her side. The bell above her head clanged, drawing curious gazes their way. The shoppers' faces reflected instant interest. Isabel didn't make a habit of patronizing the mercantile at this time of day, especially not with a child no one had ever met. Wonderful.

She assumed what she hoped was a forbidding expression. There'd be no more comments like that one, if she could help it.

A gentle hand forestalled her. "Whoa, mama bear," Ben murmured in her ear. "I doubt the boy will be unduly harmed by a clueless old man's observation."

"I know what it's like to endure unwarranted criticism," she said in a controlled voice, "and I will not allow him to be subjected to any sort of ridicule."

Eli tugged on her skirt. "Look! Cookies!"

Beside the sales counter, where a noticeboard served as a community news center, Quinn and his wife, Nicole, had set up a square table with a platter of cookies and an urn that dispensed tangy apple cider. Every year during the month of December, the couple offered the complimentary treats to their patrons.

"Can I have one? Please?"

Isabel ordered herself to relax and offered him a smile. "Yes, you may have one."

Together, they moved to the refreshment table. Ben doled out the cookies as if they were precious gems. Indeed, they were buttery rounds of melt-in-your-mouth goodness, boasting a hint of almond flavor. To her astonishment, Eli's enjoyment couldn't match Ben's, who closed his eyes and hummed as he chewed. Isabel's gaze became riveted on his handsome face. His auburn-tinted eyelashes were thick and spiky, his mouth framed by light stubble that glinted red in the morning light.

What would it feel like to trace his brow, his cheekbones, his chin with her fingers? How would it feel to be free to bestow affection and receive it in return? To share a genuine bond with this man, a relationship deeper and more intense than any other she'd ever experienced?

Ben slowly opened his eyes, twin pools of iridescent green locked on her. She gulped. Could he guess her wayward thoughts? Could anyone else? Glancing about to make sure no one had caught her mooning over him like a lovesick calf, she resolved to be more careful.

"Can I have a second one?"

Isabel absentmindedly dusted a crumb from Eli's borrowed shirt. "We don't want to ruin your lunch." At his crestfallen expression, she pointed to the jars along the counter containing rainbow-hued candies. "You may choose a penny's worth of candy to take home, if you'd like."

His eyes lit up. While she was waiting for him to make his choices, identical twins Jessica and Jane arrived, along with their sister Megan Beaumont and her daughter Lillian.

Members of the extensive O'Malley clan, they had always been kind to Isabel and her sisters. She introduced them to Eli, and Megan encouraged her to bring him to a special Christmas-themed story time that Friday evening. The kindhearted woman lived in a spacious Victorian home with her husband, Lucian, and regularly invited the town's children and their parents to book readings and refreshments.

Ben offered to accompany them, and Isabel could hardly refuse. If she were completely honest, she didn't want to refuse. She couldn't have guessed that having him around would lend her confidence where Eli was concerned.

They resumed their shopping. Isabel quickly located the ribbon Honor had to have, but she couldn't find it in her to rush Eli from the aisles. He craned his neck to take in every single item, those suspended from the rafters and stuffed in barrels and lined on shelves.

"He acts like he's never been in a general store," Ben observed. "I'd be surprised to learn he's from a big city."

"Good point."

When she'd paid for her purchases, they emerged from the store as Veronica Patton and her mother, Patricia, were on their way inside. Fetching in a petal-pink vest and pink-and-white-striped high-collared blouse, her blond hair arranged in a sleek style, Veronica did not look at all pleased to see Isabel in Ben's company. Her nostrils flared, and jealousy glimmered in her eyes.

As soon as the greetings were dispensed with, she regarded him with slight reproach. "I've stopped by the jail several times this past week, but you weren't there. I even brought you the roast quail and potatoes you like so much."

"I'm sorry I missed it," he said smoothly. "I've been busy of late, what with Shane's absence and all."

"Yes," she sniffed, glancing dubiously at Eli. "I can see that."

"We'll make up for it on Saturday," Patricia inserted.

Ben scraped a hand over his jaw. "Saturday?"

Veronica's pale brows crashed together. "You agreed to dine with us, remember? We spoke about it last week at the serenade."

Ben shifted his weight from one foot to the other, his gaze shooting to Isabel. "I, ah, hate to admit it, but the dinner slipped my mind."

Isabel experienced a flare of anger at her own stupidity. These past days with him—mostly isolated on her farm—had lulled her into a false sense of companionship. He wasn't spending time with her because he found her fascinating or because he wished to lure her into joining his group of admirers. He was with her because it was his job to protect all the citizens of Gatlinburg. Ben believed her safety was threatened, so he'd stayed. And now he had the task of locating Eli's guardian.

"I made other plans—"

"You know what?" Isabel interrupted, schooling her expression to indifference. "You agreed to have dinner with the Pattons first. You should honor that."

Mother and daughter exchanged glances.

What looked like very real distress settled on his features. "But—"

Addressing the other women, she shrugged. "I had planned to fix the deputy a meal—along with my sisters, of course—in order to thank him for helping us with Eli. But I wouldn't dream of standing in the way of your special time together. I apologize for taking up so much of his time," she said to Veronica. "I'm certain he's missed you."

The blonde's lips parted in blatant hope while Ben's mouth pressed into a thin line of displeasure.

Holding up her sack, Isabel indicated the bustling boardwalk. "Good day, ladies. Deputy."

Her insides aflame with heightened emotion, she led Eli away.

"Aren't we going to see Wishbone?" he said, dragging his feet.

At the bridge suspended above the Little Pigeon River, Isabel slowed her pace. "I'm afraid we will have to see Wishbone another time."

"You promised!"

Releasing his hand, she squatted to his level. "Eli, I know we made plans to visit her, and I understand why you're upset. But she's not going anywhere. We can try another day this week."

He searched her face and, seeming to take her at her word, said, "Can I take her a carrot?"

The question was so unexpected that she smiled. "That's a fine idea. We have an assortment of root vegetables stored in the tater hole behind the house. You can help me pick one."

Eli was quiet the remainder of the walk home, which gave Isabel ample opportunity to scold herself for forgetting her fleeting role in Ben's life.

At home, Honor and Carmen noticed her ill mood and questioned her. She evaded their questions and, leaving Eli in their care, spent an hour and a half in her shed finishing the knife she'd started that morning. The work consumed her, her quest for quality craftsmanship demanding her full concentration. There was no time to dwell on thoughts of Ben and Veronica.

By the time she'd secured the blade to the handle, she had herself in hand. She rejoined the others and spent the rest of the afternoon reading to Eli and incorporating his aid in preparing supper. When everyone had had their fill, she got out the evergreen boughs and ribbons.

"Aren't we going to wait for Ben?" Honor asked, watching her closely.

Isabel cast a quick glance at Eli, who was helping Carmen carry the dirty dishes into the adjacent kitchen.

"Ben isn't part of this family. There's no reason to include him in our holiday preparations."

Honor lifted the platter of leftover tortillas. "Did something happen today? You two seemed to be getting along rather well this morning."

That's because she'd succumbed to temporary blindness.

"Let's just say I remembered why he's been hanging around, and it's not because he's eager to be our friend. He's lived here for four years. Not once did he seek us out."

"Perhaps that's because our paths didn't have occasion to cross." Honor's face was solemn. "Maybe God brought him into our lives at this moment for a specific reason."

"If that's the case, the reason is Eli. As soon as we reunite him with his guardian, Ben will be gone."

Chapter Eleven

The day that had started off on a promising note had soured.

Slouched in his desk chair, he crumpled the letter he'd been attempting to write and tossed it in the waste bin. The vacant desk situated at an angle from his own mocked him. If Shane were here, he'd have a few words to say about Ben's current predicament—namely, that he'd brought it on himself.

Dropping his head in his hands, he moaned. "What an idiot."

He couldn't get Isabel's proud bearing—or the glittering mortification in her brown-black eyes—out of his mind. How could he have forgotten Veronica's dinner invitation? Easy. Isabel. Ever since he'd interrupted that robbery, he hadn't been able to think of anyone else.

Whatever ground he'd gained with her was lost now. *Why, God? Why push us together when nothing can come from it?*

Grant's advice lingered, taunting him. He dismissed it. Isabel was the only woman he could see himself seriously pursuing, and ironically she had zero interest in him. There was no reason to ponder if she'd accept a life without children.

And his friendship with Veronica? That would have to end. Isabel's accusations had removed the blinders. Whether or not the signs had been there before, today he'd seen evidence that Veronica viewed him as a suitor, not a mere friend. The possessiveness in her blue eyes had been the first clue. Her treatment of Isabel—as a rival for his affections—had been the second.

This upcoming dinner with the Pattons would be his last. He hoped Veronica could forgive him for fueling false hopes.

He'd set pen to paper again when the banker, Claude Jenkins, came to see him.

"How are you faring without Shane?" He swiveled one of the wooden chairs to face Ben's desk and made himself comfortable, lacing his hands over his protruding middle. "Not that I think you're incapable of taking care of things, mind you. I simply wanted to see if you needed anything."

"I appreciate the offer, Claude. I'll be sure to let you know if I can use your assistance." He twirled the pencil in slow circles. "And I'll come to you as soon as I know something about our would-be thief."

"Scary business, that." His gaze got squinty. "I heard about your shopping trip this afternoon. Have you learned anything more about the boy's origins?"

Ben related the latest information, apprehension tightening his gut.

"I see." Claude shifted in his chair, his mood pensive. "There's a good chance he'll need a permanent home. I'm sure the Flores sisters are doing their best, but it will be easier for everyone involved if we go ahead and place him with a couple who are interested in caring for him long term. Possibly even adopting him."

Ben's pencil clattered to the desk. He reined in his indignation and buried it deep. "Does this suggestion have anything to do with the stigma of the Flores sisters having an unrepentant adulterer for a father?"

"Of course not," the older man denied. The way his eyes shifted to the side told a different story. "I'm simply looking out for the boy's best interests."

"Isabel, Honor and Carmen are fine, upstanding women. Eli couldn't be in better hands."

Claude unlatched his hands and leaned forward, his vest buttons straining. "But for how long? Is it fair to let him develop a bond with them, only to later move him to a new home?"

Ben scraped his chair back and stalked to the window. He had no argument—he'd already expressed these same sentiments to Isabel—but the thought of removing the boy from the Flores home unsettled him .

He heard the creak of Claude's knees as he stood. "I agree that the girls are above reproach. That's not the issue. They're unwed. The youngest one's barely eighteen. And I may not be aware of the exact state of their finances, but I know they don't have an abundance of resources. Providing for a child could very well put a strain on what they do have."

His chest squeezed with unhappiness. "Do you have anyone specific in mind?"

"I do, but I haven't spoken to them yet."

Ben twisted around and leveled a stern look at the banker. "I'd advise against it until I speak with Isabel."

Claude inclined his head. "I'll wait to hear from you."

Once he'd bidden him good evening, Ben fisted his hands and let his forehead fall against the windowpane. He released a slow, shuddering breath. If Isabel hadn't liked him before, after this she was going to hate him.

* * *

Something was bothering Ben. Or maybe he was preoccupied by his upcoming dinner with Veronica. Three days had passed since their shopping excursion. Isabel had expected him to seek her out and try to worm his way into her good graces. That hadn't happened.

He hadn't come to the cabin Monday night, and his spot at the breakfast table the next morning had remained unclaimed. Honor and Carmen had seen a light in the hut, evidence that he'd stayed, but when Carmen had taken a plate of food out to him, he was gone. He'd finally made an appearance Wednesday evening. Isabel's wayward heart expanded with pleasure, as if greeting a long-lost friend. Even Eli had acted pleased to see him. The teasing light in Ben's eyes hadn't materialized, however, and his mood had been somber. She'd managed to restrain the impulse to question him, to reassure herself that all was well in his world.

Yet again she had to remind herself that they weren't friends. His life, his worries and his problems were none of her business. And someday he would cease to be his. Where that would leave Eli, she didn't wish to ponder.

"Thank you for your business." She smiled and nodded at the single mother who was her last customer of the day.

Hazel cradled her sack of cornmeal to her chest. "I'll see you this time next week."

"Take care."

Reentering the mill, she grabbed the broom in the corner and started the tedious job of sweeping the floorboards. The spot between her shoulder blades ached from hefting countless bundles of corn into the hopper. Her arms were sore, and her lower back muscles were stiff. Her fatigue couldn't detract from a solid day of business, though. Impatient to see Eli, she pushed herself to work faster. He'd spent an hour with her before and after lunch. She smiled, remembering his enthusiasm as he'd explored the mill. The gears beneath this floor, visible through gaps in the platform, had mesmerized him.

"What are you smiling about?"

Isabel yelped and almost dropped her broom. "Ben. I didn't hear you come in."

Plunging his hands in his pockets, he sauntered to the platform and peered at the gears like Eli had. His profile revealed his subdued mood lingered.

"I didn't see the Closed sign, and the door was unlocked…" He turned to face her, his gaze hooded. "Was business steady today?"

"Busier than usual, actually."

He glanced at the high ceiling, the hopper, the even stack of empty sacks. "Does the mill bring in enough income to provide for your family's needs?"

"That's a personal matter."

"I'm not asking for an amount," he said evenly. "I'm just curious if it's profitable and if you sell your knives because you have to supplement."

"You're meddling, and I don't like it." Isabel had no intention of supplying him with answers. "You're in a strange mood. You have been since our shopping excursion. Care to explain why?"

Ben pulled his hands from his pockets. He walked to where she stood in the far corner and curved his hands around hers where she held the broom handle. Her pulse became erratic. His heat seeped into her skin, and she found she liked the contact.

"W-what are you doing?"

"I'm going to finish sweeping while you go and change." His husky voice enveloped her like a quilted blanket on a wintry night.

Isabel's thoughts were muddled by his nearness and the ever-expanding circle of warm tingles his hands on hers generated. She wiggled free of his hold.

"Why should I?" She noticed the stiff white collar at his neck, the black silk puff tie with minute red stripes and the straight line of his suit jacket lapels disappearing beneath the buttons of his overcoat. "Why are you dressed up?" A suspicion hit her. "I hope you don't think I'm cooking for you tonight because of your prior engagement tomorrow. Your mix-up with Veronica has nothing to do with me."

His auburn brows wrinkled. "That's not why I'm here. Isabel, I am sorry I ruined our plans. I would much rather spend the evening with you."

Isabel hardened her heart against the earnest appeal in his eyes. "Veronica would be crushed to hear you say that."

"I'm sure you're right," he admitted sheepishly. "To be honest, I was preoccupied with locating you during the serenade when she issued the invitation. I didn't wish to be rude, so I accepted without realizing the nature of her question. I've come to grips with a hard truth, thanks to you." Gripping the broom handle, he became fixated on the floor beneath their feet. The tips of his ears burned red. "You were right. I arrogantly assumed the ladies I spent time with wanted the same thing as me—simple companionship."

Speechless, she stood rooted to the floor. He had as good as admitted he'd been wrong. What did that mean for the Debonair Deputy?

What does it mean for you?

Nothing. It means nothing. Didn't you hear him? You can't be like the others and disregard his bulldog adherence to single life.

"I don't know what to say."

Lifting one shoulder in a partial shrug, he began sweeping in short, jerky strokes. "I don't expect you to say anything. I wanted you to know that now I've seen my error, I'm going to fix things."

Wonderment burgeoned in her chest, along with a heady wave of respect. Admitting mistakes, humbling oneself, wasn't easy.

"We're going to be late if you don't change soon," he said without looking up.

"Late for what?"

"We agreed to take Eli to Megan's story time."

She'd completely forgotten Megan's invitation. "You could take him yourself."

He slowly lifted those piercing eyes to hers. "I could, but I don't think he'd have as good a time without you there. He's still reticent with me."

As much as she hated to admit it, Ben was right. "I think his mother instilled fear of authorities in him. We have no way of knowing what type of person she was, especially if his father lives outside the law, as he's suggested."

His handsome face revealed nothing of his thoughts. "Could be."

Isabel considered suggesting Carmen accompany him, but she didn't want to miss out on this experience with Eli. As she hurried into the cold evening alone, she acknowledged that, despite her best efforts to the contrary, she was starting to care about the deputy. A most unfortunate development.

At the cabin, she asked Honor to help Eli put on clean clothes while she changed into the green dress she'd worn to the serenade. She would've left her hair in a braid, but Carmen insisted on brushing out her long locks and arranging it in a more sophisticated upswept style.

"Let's hope they have mistletoe there." She winked at Isabel's reflection in the mirror.

"If they do, I'll stay clear of it," she stated with emphasis. "I haven't been to the Beaumont house before."

Carmen didn't blink at the change in subject. "I've heard it's lovely. They apparently have papered walls and crystal chandeliers." She chose a pair of earrings from the jewelry box and handed them to Isabel. "The gardens are rumored to be the finest in the area."

Isabel studied her reflection, her fingers trembling as she smoothed a hand over her middle, the stiff bodice stifling her ability to breathe. Or maybe it was the sound of the cabin door opening and closing and the rich tones of Ben's voice as he greeted Honor and Eli.

"Time for Cinderella to go to the ball," Carmen declared, enjoying this way too much.

"This isn't a ball," Isabel reminded her sister pertly. "This event is for the children."

"Relax, *hermana*. You do know it's okay to have fun once in a while, right?"

Isabel had forgotten what it was like to be lighthearted and free the day she'd learned what her papa was truly like.

They joined the others. Ben rose from where he'd crouched before Eli and scanned her from head to toe, his expression like a closed book. Was he feeling awkward after his admission? Ignoring the nervousness in the pit of her stomach, she went to gather her cloak. She struggling with a pair of older, smaller gloves she'd unearthed in her dresser when a small package appeared in her line of vision.

"Maybe this will help."

Isabel studied the plain wrapping before angling toward Ben. His gaze unreadable, he motioned for her to take it.

Her pulse tripped. "What's this?"

"Open it and see."

Isabel peeled the paper away and uttered a surprised

sigh. He'd gotten her gloves. Not just any pair, either. She tested the supple leather and soft wool lining.

"I used your ruined ones to gauge the size," he explained. "They should fit."

Eli bounced on his toes. "Mr. Ben brought you an early Christmas present, too."

"You're right, he did."

She didn't have to look at her sister to see her reaction. Carmen would read this as a romantic gesture. It was hardly that, she reassured herself. He felt bad about the ruined gloves and, even though it hadn't been his fault, had decided to be practical and replace them. She tried them on, inwardly groaning at the comfort and warmth they imparted. Every time she put them on, she'd think of him. And their charged exchange beneath the evergreen trees...the embrace that never was and never could be.

"I'm not sure I should accept them," she murmured, waggling her fingers. "They couldn't have been cheap."

Carmen marched over and patted Ben's arm. "You'll have to forgive my sister's awkward social graces. What she really means to say is you have wonderful taste and your thoughtfulness has scattered her wits."

Isabel felt heat climbing into her cheeks. Shooting a glare at her impertinent sibling, she forced herself to look at Ben and smile, although it was surely a discomfited one. "She's right, of course. Your gift was well chosen. Thank you."

He nodded. "You're welcome."

When they'd said goodbye to her sisters and it was just the three of them in the yard, Eli hopped between brown patches of grass. "Will there be a Christmas tree like the one in the mercantile?"

He looked spiffy in his borrowed clothes, his curls

somewhat tamed and his face shiny from a recent washing. His eyes got big as Ben boosted him atop Blaze.

"There might be," Isabel told him. "I know for a fact there will be refreshments."

"What are refwesh—" He gripped the saddle horn, his nose scrunching. "Refwesh—"

"Refreshments?" Ben said, a smile in his voice. "It's a fancy word for good food."

"Oh."

Isabel approached Honey. Ben had already saddled her. He hauled himself up behind Eli in one graceful move.

"Did you see the decorations?" Eli pointed to the wreaths on the door and windows. "I got to put the ribbons on."

As he got comfortable in the saddle, Ben admired the greenery. "You did a fine job, little man."

"I thought you were gonna help, but Isabel said you were too busy."

Her face felt hot as the deputy's gaze settled on her. "I would've liked to pitch in," he said slowly, "but she's right. I have been occupied this week with town business."

Nudging his horse into a walk, Ben regaled Eli with a few funny accounts of his law-keeping adventures. Isabel held her horse to a slower pace. *No reason to feel bad for excluding him. You have to protect yourself. He's well versed in male-female relationships and proficient at keeping his heart indifferent. You aren't.*

She was a spinster by choice. Her reasoning was sound. Logical. She couldn't allow this time with Ben to make her forget, even for a second, that marriage wasn't in her future.

Chapter Twelve

He hadn't told Isabel the whole truth. Admitting he'd been careless and self-absorbed had been difficult, the decision to do so born of the moment and the need to quell an extraordinary attraction. Alone with her in the mill, Ben had been tempted to kiss her. Since that would've been crossing a line he himself had drawn, he'd confessed to the error of his ways.

However, what he hadn't divulged was the deeper reason he couldn't continue spending time with Veronica or anyone else—that Isabel had encroached upon his fortified heart to the point he dreamed about surrender. Surrendering his secrets and his pride didn't strike him as quite so daunting when he considered the possibility of a future with Isabel.

Old hurts stood in his way. The memory of Marianne's scorn, the shock of her ready dismissal of him and their future, was never far from his thoughts. He'd believed she loved him enough to stick by him no matter what. He'd been a fool. The scandal she'd incited, the one that had provided the impetus for his ultimate move to Gatlinburg, had only added to his despair.

Glancing over at Isabel, Ben accepted that telling her

wasn't an option. Not now, at least, when the matter of Eli's living arrangements demanded attention. Maybe not ever.

Eli squirmed and fidgeted in the saddle. Ben kept a firm hold on the boy as the horses traveled the winding tree-edged lanes. Dull orange leaves littered the uneven forest floor, an autumn carpet from which thick gray trees grew, their wispy branches like spindly broom ends framed by the off-white sky.

After riding in silence for many minutes, they rounded a bend and the grand yellow Victorian planted atop a rise came into view. The spacious home had once belonged to Lucian Beaumont's grandfather, who'd been a close friend of Megan's before his death. Both avid readers, they'd utilized the ample space and vast assortment of books to entertain the local children. Shane had conveyed to Ben that Lucian had arrived in Gatlinburg ready to sell the house, but that he'd wound up falling for Megan before he could.

"Is that a castle?" Eli twisted his head to peer up at Ben. "Happy told me about dragons and castles."

The boy had a bright, active mind. "To my knowledge, castles are made of stone and have turrets and drawbridges. Our nation is too young, but there are many in Europe."

"Are we going to hear a story about a castle?"

Ben maneuvered his horse past multiple conveyances lining the drive. He glanced over at Isabel, whose smile was solely for Eli's sake. "I'd guess Miss Megan is planning to read a book about Christmas."

Eli's shoulders sagged. Ben patted his knee. "Maybe she has a book about knights and castles she'd let you borrow."

The boy's excitement lit up his face. His resiliency amazed Ben. Here he was, without parents or home, and he was doing okay. He was interacting with them and his surroundings with the natural curiosity of any boy his age.

"Will you read it to me?" Eli asked Isabel.

"I'd love to."

The fondness stamped on her face pricked Ben's conscience. A knot of dread formed behind his sternum. He couldn't delay another day. Claude Jenkins hadn't been the only one to express his thoughts on the subject of Eli's placement. Reluctant to hurt Isabel, not to mention upset the boy, he'd postponed the conversation. A cowardly act unbecoming of an experienced lawman.

They left the animals with the stable boy and climbed the wide white steps to the door inlaid with fancy scrolled glass. Eli stayed between them, clutching both their hands…like they were a genuine family unit. Yearning for the impossible robbed Ben of breath.

As they were relieved of their coats and ushered into the lushly appointed parlor where mothers and fathers gathered with their children, Ben realized that attending a children's event hadn't been his wisest idea. He didn't belong here.

"Ben. Isabel. I'm so glad you came." Megan greeted them with a bright smile. Arrayed in an ice-blue ball gown shot through with silver threads, her moonlight curls piled atop her head and adorned with sparkling jewels, she looked like a fairy-tale character come to life. Eli's mouth was agape as he stared at her in wonder.

"Well, hello, Eli," she said cheerfully. "We're about to start. Would you like to come and sit with the other children?"

Instead of answering, he inched closer to Isabel.

A slim, delicate young woman with hair almost the same color as Megan's crossed the room to join them. Lillian and her brother Patrick had been living with the Beaumonts for five years, ever since they'd fled from their cruel stepfather and hidden in an abandoned shack for many weeks. A temporary stay with the Beaumonts had become permanent.

Pretty and shy, Lillian was a natural with kids of any age. On her hip, she carried the Beaumonts' latest addition, a two-year-old boy whose parents had dumped him on their town's church steps when they'd learned he was deaf. Anger burned inside Ben every time he thought about the heartless act. What he wouldn't give for a child, no matter what challenges he or she faced.

"Eli, this is my daughter Lillian." Megan bussed the blond boy's cheek. "And this is my son Arthur. We call him Artie for short." Glancing over her shoulder, she pointed to a young girl arrayed in a blue confection similar to Megan's. "And that's Rose, our other daughter."

Lillian greeted Eli, a kind light in her eyes. "Do you like gingerbread men, Eli?"

He nodded.

"My mother's going to read a book about gingerbread soldiers who defend the candy castle from gumdrop wolves. And afterward, we're going to eat gingerbread-man cookies that my aunt Jessica baked. How does that sound?"

"I like castles," he said in a small voice.

A husky laugh slipped out of Isabel, and she lovingly smoothed his curls. Did she realize how often she did that? "I suppose I was wrong," she told him, her brown eyes dancing. "You will get to hear about castles, after all."

Lillian gestured toward the large printed rug where children of all ages had found spots. "Would you like to sit with me and Artie?"

Eli considered her offer, then he released his death grip on Isabel and went with Lillian, glancing back over his shoulder to be sure they hadn't moved from beside the fireplace.

"Deputy, it's good to have you here. And you as well, Miss Flores." Lucian greeted Ben and Isabel with a firm handshake. The New Orleans native spoke with a slight French accent. His inky gaze was friendly as he took up position on Isabel's other side. "Good-looking boy." He indicated Eli. "It's a kind thing you're doing for him."

"He's a precious child," Isabel said quietly. "We're the ones who've been blessed by his presence in our home."

Lucian's gaze strayed to his wife and children. "I understand exactly what you mean. I can give you the name of my lawyer when you're ready. He's handled our adoptions."

The start of surprise Ben felt mirrored Isabel's.

"I didn't say anything about adopting Eli," she said.

Lucian's expression turned knowing. "You didn't have to."

Another gentleman waved Lucian over. Once he'd excused himself, Ben touched Isabel's sleeve. "Is he correct? Are you considering making Eli a permanent part of your family?"

Her brow creasing, she was about to respond when Merilee Jenkins intruded upon their conversation. Trepidation barreled through him. He hadn't known the banker's wife would be in attendance.

"Miss Flores," she exclaimed, twirling a gold and black lace fan, "am I glad I ran into you."

Isabel looked confused. "Oh?"

Ben cleared his throat. "I didn't expect to see you tonight, Merilee."

"I brought my granddaughters. My daughter-in-law wasn't able to bring them, so I volunteered. They adore Megan and get such a kick out of her costumes." Tapping Isabel's arm with her folded fan, she leaned forward as if to divulge a secret. "Claude has spoken with the Watsons about Eli, and they're eager to meet him. As soon as Ben made the announcement about a found boy, they saw an opportunity to finally have a son. You know they have six girls." She shook her head and made a tsking sound. "*Six* girls to marry off, and not one boy to carry on their legacy. Can you imagine?"

Isabel blanched. "I'm afraid I don't understand."

Merilee's lips pursed in disapproval. "I see Ben has failed to do his duty. He was supposed to have told you days ago. The Watsons are willing to take Eli into their fold. They wish to meet him as soon as possible."

The look Isabel served him, as if he'd delivered a fatal wound, made him feel ill.

"Isabel," he started.

She was visibly shaking. "What did you do?"

He'd betrayed her.

Somewhere along the line, she'd come to regard Eli as her responsibility and no one else's. She'd prepared his meals, entertained him and tucked him in bed every night. She'd included him in her Christmas plans, had even decided to ask the schoolteacher for recommendations when to start teaching him to read and write. The thought of him living with someone else hurt more deeply than she could've imagined.

Afraid of the maelstrom brewing inside her, Isabel escaped onto the porch and dragged in lungfuls of frigid air.

Ben's heavy tread sounded behind her. "Isabel, please—"

"Stop." Whirling on him, she wrapped her arms around her middle and tried very hard not to notice the urgency gripping his features. "I let you into my life. I started seeing you as a friend. *Me.* The outcast spinster who doesn't make friends!"

"I was going to tell you." His voice was thin with strain. "I didn't want to upset you. I—"

"I trusted you, Ben. In this, I trusted you." She dug her

fingertips into the stiff structure of her bodice. "You repaid me by going behind my back and arranging for another family to take Eli!"

That he hadn't respected her enough to consult her wishes felt like molten iron branding her skin.

Ben glanced at the door and, before she knew what he was about, took hold of both her shoulders. "I *am* your friend, Isabel." His eyes blazed with silent appeal. "Please, hear me out."

Voices filtered through a nearby window. Ben slid his hands down her arms and cupped her elbows. Through the material, his palms blazed red-hot, whereas the rest of her body was as cold as an icy pond.

"Come with me where we can talk without being overheard."

"Eli will worry."

"The story has just begun, and afterward, they'll be treated to refreshments. Lillian will keep him company."

Isabel lowered her arms, and he took the opportunity to grasp her hand in his larger, rougher one. "Please, Isa?"

Her compulsion to avoid gossip at all costs spurred her to agree. There was no way to know who else besides the banker's wife had seen Isabel's mad dash from the parlor. If anyone were to discover her and Ben arguing on the Beaumonts' porch, there'd be no end to the speculation.

"Fine." She jerked free of his hold. "I can walk without you guiding me, though."

Tension emanating from him, he gave a clipped nod and descended the stairs ahead of her. Once in the shadowed yard below, they rounded the house and, passing the deserted veranda overlooking the rear property, entered the darkened gardens. Waist-high hedges lined the gravel path, whispering against her skirt hem. In the distance, water trickled from a fountain. Isabel stopped beside a stone bench beneath a rose arbor that would be magnificent come spring.

"I'm not going any farther," she said to his broad, suit-clad back.

He pivoted on his boot heel and retraced his steps, careful not to crowd her. The realization that she'd forgotten her cloak registered at the same moment a shiver racked her. Ben shed his suit jacket and draped it over her shoulders, pulling the lapels together over her collarbone. He hesitated. With only the lights blazing from the house windows to see by, she couldn't decipher his exact expression.

Isabel considered shoving him away. Instead, she jerked her chin up. "Tell me what you brought me out here to say so I can return to the party."

He released the lapels. "I'm sorry. I should've come to you as soon as Claude paid me a visit Monday evening. He said he had someone in mind to take Eli."

"Because a confirmed spinster and daughter of a notorious marriage wrecker isn't good enough to raise a child, right?" Bitterness laced her words.

"No, that's not it." He thrust his fingers through his hair. "It's true your single status factors into Claude's reasoning. You're already supporting yourself and your sisters. He's concerned that Eli's continued care will be a burden."

She narrowed her gaze. "That's why you were asking about the mill earlier."

"It's a valid concern," he defended. "You've managed to operate a successful business venture—make that *two* businesses—while providing for your and your sisters' needs. No one wants to see that compromised."

She clutched at the jacket that held the remnants of his body heat and his woodsy scent. He had to be freezing in his suit vest and shirt.

"We're fine. Not wealthy, of course, but comfortable. Having Eli in our home doesn't jeopardize anything."

"Good. I'm glad. I would've shared that information had I known." He cocked his head to one side. "Claude's not the only one who consulted me. Reverend Monroe and some other prominent citizens have marched through my office this week demanding to know why I haven't relieved you of this responsibility."

"I don't want to be relieved of it!"

"You didn't say anything," he said somberly. "I knew you were growing fond of him, but I wasn't aware you had an eye on the future."

"And if I had, would you have supported my decision? Pleaded my case to the doubters?"

"Yes."

There wasn't a moment's hesitation. At his utter conviction, some of the starch went out of her. Now Isabel didn't know what to say or how to feel.

Ben lifted his hand as if to caress her cheek. She held her breath, her heart battling in her chest, at once craving and dreading his touch. At the last second, he curled his fingers into a fist and lowered his arm.

"I have no doubt you'll make a wonderful mother. If adopting Eli is what you've set your heart on, then I'll do everything in my power to make it happen."

To her horror, tears threatened. Her emotions swung from one extreme to another. This man had the power to infuriate her one minute and reach the most protected, private part of her the next. Who would've thought that the Debonair Deputy would be the one man to make her doubt her choices? It was dangerous to allow him to remain in her life, but she needed him. He'd be a powerful ally against anyone who would oppose her goal of becoming Eli's guardian.

He chafed his arms. "Come, let's return to the house. The temperature must've dropped at least ten degrees in the past hour."

She attempted to give him back his jacket, but he told her to keep it until they were inside. Once they returned, the warmth in the entrance hallway washed over Isabel, and she hurried to the fireplace just inside the parlor. The carpet where the children had been seated was empty. Cheerful voices carried in from a room farther down the central corridor.

Ben made quick work of his jacket buttons. "Would you like something to drink? I saw an urn of hot cocoa earlier."

Isabel nodded, eager to check on Eli. At the end of the papered hallway, double doors on their right opened into the biggest dining room Isabel had ever seen. A formal space with polished mahogany furniture and printed draperies, it could easily hold fifty people. Children sat around the massive table while their parents milled about the room. Her gaze found Eli seated beside Lillian, who held Artie in her lap. Wearing an intent expression, Eli was consuming a gingerbread cookie as large as his plate.

Bowls piled with jewel-toned fruits occupied the table's center space. Silver platters were laden with an assortment of cookies to choose from, thin ones sprinkled with cinnamon and various spices, round ones dipped in icing, and thick, doughy ones studded with cranberries. A three-tiered cake perched on a glass pedestal was slathered in white frosting and covered in candied cherries. It was almost too pretty to eat.

Ben bent his head toward her. "Looks to me like he's a bit too preoccupied to miss us."

"It's a lot to take in."

His hand skimmed her lower back as he leaned past her to get Merilee's attention. "May we have a moment?"

The smartly dressed woman left her granddaughters to join them in the entrance. Her gaze was curious as it landed on Isabel. "Are you all right, dear?"

"I apologize for the way I left things."

"I didn't intend to upset you."

"That's my fault," Ben said gruffly. "I will speak to Claude tomorrow, but I wonder if you'd mind giving him a message for me?"

Her brows drew together. "Of course."

"Tell him that Eli will remain with Isabel for the fore-seeable future."

"But the Watsons—"

"Weren't supposed to be consulted until I had spoken with Isabel." A muscle ticked in his jaw. "I have now, and she's informed me that she wants him to stay with her. He's thriving in her care. I have no objections, and neither should anyone else."

The firmness of his words bolstered Isabel. When she looked over and saw that Eli was beckoning her to his side, she excused herself and crouched beside his chair.

"Did you enjoy the story?" she asked warmly.

He nodded and smiled, crumbs clinging to his mouth. Some had found their way to his lap. Going on his knees, he chose another gingerbread cookie and handed it to her. She deliberately bit off the entire head, evoking a giggle.

The absolute trust in his eyes made her heart melt. He'd had a rough start in life, a history she knew little about, and she was determined to see he received the nurturing, love and guidance that every child deserved. God had brought Eli into her life for a reason, she truly believed that. She had the means and the desire to care for him, to step into a role she hadn't envisioned until now...motherhood.

After a few minutes, Ben joined them, gratefully ac-cepting the cookie Eli handed him. Isabel rose and placed her hand over his sleeve. His eyes were cautious and still carried remnants of his earlier apology.

"Thank you, Ben."

"No need to thank me." Then he said something that made her want to weep. "I believe in you, Isabel."

Chapter Thirteen

He was too old to sleep on cold, hard floors.

Admit it, you'd do it indefinitely if it meant you could be near Isabel.

After he'd stretched the kinks from his back, Ben tugged on his boots and rolled his pallet into a neat bundle. He considered keeping the nature of last evening's errand to himself. Mr. Warring, the livery owner, had found him at the Beaumonts' and informed him that one of his horses had been stolen. Ben had waited until the festivities were over before escorting Isabel and Eli home, then rode out straight away to Main Street to investigate the theft. A serious crime worthy of hanging, horse theft was rare in their town. He was inclined to believe it was the work of the blackguard who'd threatened Isabel's life. Or could it be Eli's guardian?

As he used the water basin Isabel had provided to wash his face and brush his teeth, he thought about the fallout of keeping Claude's visit a secret. The devastation he'd wrought, the damage to the trust he'd built with her, made his decision easy. Hiding information from Isabel would be foolhardy, especially if he wanted to remain in her life.

While he knew sticking around carried risks, he couldn't bring himself to walk away.

Ben opened the hut door and discovered a winter wonderland. During the night, what looked to be between six and eight inches of snow had fallen, blanketing the woods and structures in pure white powder. Icicles as long as his arm dangled from the hut's overhang. Standing there soaking in the hushed silence, he noted the absence of a familiar sound—there was no trickling water, no whir of the mill wheel.

Snow crunched beneath his boots as he ventured onto the stoop. Crisp air made his exposed skin prickle, particularly his ears. He quickly wound the scarf around his neck and closed the door behind him. Needing to inspect the livery in the light of day, he planned to skip breakfast and grab something later in town. Movement on the narrow footbridge suspended between the bank and the mill caught his attention.

Isabel. Her cloak swirled about her like a gray cloud. She hammered a piece of paper to the mill's door and crossed the bridge.

"Good morning," he called, tendrils of wispy fog curling about his mouth. "I take it the wheel is iced over?" His progress was hampered by knee-deep drifts.

"I've posted a notice letting folks know I'll open Monday to make up for it, weather permitting." As she neared, he noticed the rosiness of her cheeks. "The accumulation would've likely kept away a bulk of customers anyway."

"Has Eli seen this?"

Her mouth curved into a smile, and her eyes brightened. "He's begging to be permitted to play in it, so be warned. I've no doubt he'll bombard you the moment you step through the door."

"Are you going to indulge him?"

They fell into step together, picking their way past the hut, bits of snow dislodged by their progress. The serene beauty of snowcapped mountains soaring to the cotton sky belonged on one of those fancy Louis Prang holiday greeting cards he'd seen in the mercantile. Christmas was fifteen days away, so there was little chance the snow would stick around that long. A shame, considering they rarely got to celebrate a white Christmas.

"I don't see any harm in it as long as he's bundled up," she said.

"He'll have a fantastic time," he concurred, turning to gaze at the smoke spiraling from the cabin's chimney.

"Aren't you going to join us? He's planning a snow fort and an army of snowmen. I have a feeling you'd be more skilled in that task than me or my sisters."

The earnest query surprised him. After last night and their conversation in the garden, he wasn't sure exactly where he stood with her. It appeared she'd forgiven him. *Thank You for small mercies, Lord.*

"Isabel, I hadn't planned on staying for breakfast." His eyes locked with hers. "You recall Mr. Warring seeking me out last night."

She nodded, her fat braid slipping free of her cloak collar and swinging between her shoulder blades. How his fingers itched to explore her raven mane, to unravel the interwoven locks and watch them ripple down her back.

"Did something happen at the livery?"

He struggled to direct his thoughts along more appropriate avenues. "Someone stole one of Warring's horses. I searched the stalls and tack room, as well as the outdoor perimeter, and came up empty. I was hoping to conduct a more thorough search in the daylight. The snow will hinder my efforts, but it's worth a try."

She looked pensive. "I know what you're not saying."

"I don't have any other suspects at the moment. I've been here four years, and in all that time, there's only been one horse stolen. In that case, the animal was a Thoroughbred belonging to Albert Turner."

"Wasn't that connected to the trouble surrounding Caroline Turner McKenna and that unhinged maid working for them?"

"Yes. Quite a different scenario than swiping an aged working horse."

"The lack of answers is frustrating." Her pace slowed as they neared the front steps. "I know you're ready to sleep in your own bed and be among your own things."

"And I know you're impatient to see me gone." He offered a rueful smile. "But your safety is important to me."

Her curved black lashes swept down to hide her eyes. "I feel safe when you're around."

His initial instinct was to make light of the admission. It was a habit he'd honed over the years, a way of deflecting a young lady's praise and guiding the conversation into less serious waters. However, this time, Ben chose to revel in the pleasure pulsing through him.

"I'm glad I can be of some comfort," he said seriously. "Although you've proven you're handy with a blade."

That earned him a smile that made him feel like he was standing on a hot, sandy beach. He couldn't be certain exactly what she glimpsed in his eyes. Whatever it was, she averted her face and bounded up the steps. Ben scolded himself. Her confession that she'd begun to consider him a friend meant a lot. He didn't want to do anything to make her regret lowering her guard.

Once inside, Isabel called for her sisters. They replied from behind their closed door that they were helping Eli dress and would be out momentarily. Toasty waves of heat from the crackling hearth enveloped him. The spicy aroma of sausage made his mouth water. His stomach rumbled.

At Isabel's pointed smile, he said, "What's so funny?"

She unwound her scarf and looped it over the coatrack. "I'm surprised you're hungry, considering the number of cookies you consumed at the party."

He shrugged out of his coat, glad he'd taken the time to drop by his place last night and change into more comfortable clothes before returning. "I didn't have more than four."

Propping her hands on her hips, she raised her brows. "Four? You're in a state of denial, *mi amigo*. You sampled every kind of cookie on that table, some more than once. And have you forgotten the giant slice of cake you practically inhaled?"

Ben followed her past the table crowded with plates, utensils and dishes of sumptuous-looking food and into the kitchen. "I didn't realize you were observing me so closely." A tray lined with what looked to be miniature pockets of fried dough distracted him. "What are these?"

"Pumpkin empanadas." He reached for one only to have her smack his hand. "No sneaking."

Ben clasped his hands together and assumed his most hangdog expression. "Take pity on me, sugarplum, I beg you. Just let me have *one*. Consider it payment for assuming guard duty."

To punctuate his request, his ravenous stomach protested again. Isabel's laughter rolled over him, warming him to his toes. Her sparkling eyes invited him in, a silent communication that he was, at long last, included in her inner circle.

"Fine. *One*."

He chose the largest one and sank his teeth into the flaky golden crust. Pumpkin flavor exploded on his tongue. Hints of cloves, cinnamon and other mysterious spices had him groaning in appreciation. When he opened his eyes, he discovered her regarding him with an indulgent grin.

Arms folded across her chest, her braid trailing along her arm, she rested against the work counter. Ben acknowledged that returning to his cabin, his silent and empty kitchen and table set for one, would not be pleasant.

"You really enjoy food, don't you?"

"When it's prepared by a skilled cook such as yourself," he said between bites, "then yes, I most definitely do."

"And you enjoy your job, despite its many challenges."

"Yes."

"Why did you choose it?" she asked curiously. "Was your father in law enforcement?"

Polishing off the empanada, he rested his hip against the counter. "Both my father and my uncle started out in this line of work, but my father suffered a leg injury early on. He was chasing a suspect through the countryside and his horse went down, landing on his leg. He lay there for hours before someone finally found him." Taking note of her shocked expression, he went on. "At that time, I was their only child. My mother was scared out of her wits. She worried that the job would end my father's life before he'd had a chance to raise his only son." He shrugged. "Her fears, coupled with the fact the accident had left him with a bad limp, prompted him to switch careers."

"What did he wind up doing?"

"He's the county clerk."

"And your uncle? Is he a deputy like you?"

"Uncle Dwight is our town's sheriff." The affection he felt for his father's brother colored his tone. They exchanged frequent letters, keeping each other updated on work cases and life in general. "I had the great honor of working with him before I decided to move."

"You miss him."

"He's one of the best. Fair in his dealings. Intent on justice, but compassionate, too. He's the reason I got into law enforcement. Ma balked, of course, having never forgotten Pa's accident and his long recuperation."

She studied him. "He convinced her of the wisdom of letting you make your own choices?"

He smiled, remembering the heated discussions around their dinner table. "It took time—months, actually—but he finally wore her down."

"You clearly loved working alongside your uncle. Why leave?"

His smiled faded. "In the face of an untenable situation, I did what I thought was best."

Her brow creased in contemplation. Then a burst of insight. "The scandal you spoke of had something to do with it, doesn't it? But why would your flirting affect his career?"

Frustration welled in his chest. Would she ever see him as a man of depth and substance? Or would her poor view of men continue to color her opinion?

Pushing off the counter, he paced to the opposite side of the room. "My so-called flirting had no bearing on my resignation. None."

The abrupt end of his engagement had been the impetus for his ultimate departure. The only daughter of Mayor Augustus Ogden, Marianne had her pa wrapped around her finger. Mrs. Ogden had died when Marianne was an infant, so for years it had been Augustus and his daughter against the world. Because she'd promised not to breathe a word of Ben's condition, she'd led the mayor to believe his heart was fickle. Augustus had been outraged on her behalf. No one cast aside his precious Marianne and got away with it.

He'd launched a subtle but dangerous campaign against Ben, turning prominent town leaders against him. His family had suffered the sting of judgment. When his uncle's reputation began to suffer, Ben made the difficult decision to seek work elsewhere.

"So what happened?"

"Let's just say I angered the wrong people. The mayor, to be exact. My uncle got caught up in the scandal, unfortunately. I couldn't be responsible for his career imploding, so I left."

She clearly wasn't satisfied by his vague explanation but didn't fish for details. "And you started working here, with Shane."

"Not at first. I accepted a position in the northern part of Georgia, working with Sheriff Isaiah Moser. I was there for eighteen months. Then Uncle Dwight wrote to me about an open position here. He'd struck up a friendship with Shane before he became sheriff of Gatlinburg. I came to meet Shane and the rest is, as they say, history."

"You were forced to leave your home because someone decided to make trouble. How is it that you're not battling bitterness on a daily basis?"

"Oh, I wrestled with it for a long time. I was angry at the situation. Angry at God for allowing it. I felt cheated."

She slid her hand over her hair and along her braid, toying with the ends. "I'm acquainted with the feeling."

"But then I woke up one day tired of being angry. I began to focus on my blessings. Was this my desired future? Absolutely not. Not at first, anyway. But I had a boss whom I respected and enjoyed working for. I had a new community that embraced me. A fresh start, if you will." He flicked his fingers toward the window and the picturesque mountains. "And of course, living here isn't exactly a burden, is it?"

Lost in thought, Isabel picked up the empanada dish and carried it into the main room. Laughter could be heard in the girls' bedroom.

Ben stood behind his usual chair. "I don't blame you for being angry at your father. Because of him, you were cheated out of an ordinary childhood."

Her dark eyes flashed defiance. "I'm still paying for his mistakes."

"Being gossiped about isn't pleasant, but you're a strong woman. You've proved you can withstand the whispers and narrow-minded prejudices. You've flourished despite rough beginnings."

"You sound like Honor." Isabel's knuckles went white where she gripped the dish. "You're suggesting I forgive and forget."

"What has holding on to the past gotten you, Isa?"

Emotions marched across her face. Her throat worked. "I—"

A crash in the bedroom made the floorboards quiver. There was span of stunned quiet, followed by a panicked wail.

Isabel blanched. "Eli!"

Heart thundering, Ben rushed into the bedroom a step behind Isabel.

"What happened?" she demanded, falling to her knees on the rug. "Where does it hurt?"

His face leached of color, Eli pointed to his ankle. Fat tears rolled down his cheeks. His breathing came in spurts.

Carmen wrung her hands. "He was standing on the bed and waving a pretend sword around, talking about gumdrops or something. I didn't know he was going to jump."

Honor consoled her with a sisterly pat. "It's my fault, too. We shouldn't have allowed him to stand on the bed."

Ben crouched beside Isabel. "Can you show us exactly where it hurts, little man?"

His crying hitched. He pointed to the spot. The misery in his baby blues tugged at Ben's heartstrings. In his profession, he regularly encountered various mishaps and calamities. It was bad enough when adults got hurt, but defenseless children were a whole other level of nightmare. And sweet, bashful Eli... Ben had a personal investment in the kid.

Isabel shifted his riotous curls out of his eyes. "I'm going to roll your stocking off, okay?"

His reaction was one of immediate worry.

"I promise I'll be gentle."

Ben lifted his gaze to Carmen, who was shifting her weight from one foot to another and looking as if she might be ill. "We may need some damp cloths. Would you mind?"

Her eyes big in her face, she nodded. "Of course."

She swept out of the room. Honor joined her.

Ben held his breath as Isabel removed the stocking. When Eli whimpered, Ben cupped his shoulder. "Did you know Miss Isabel has patched me up before?"

The boy shook his head. His crying had all but ceased, leaving his face wet with tears. Ben fished his handkerchief from his pocket and dabbed the moisture away.

"I injured my arm," he told him. "And she took excellent care of me. I promise she'll make you feel better, too."

"How did you get hurt?" Eli ventured.

Still cradling Eli's foot, Isabel shot Ben a look that said he shouldn't have brought up this particular subject.

"Well, I was working. You know my job is to protect people." He searched for an appropriate response. "I was helping keep someone safe."

He sensed Isabel's regard and was stunned to see something akin to admiration there.

"Ben was very brave, Eli," she said, her gaze unwavering. "I'm convinced you can be just as brave."

"Like the gingerbread soldiers?"

A bubble of laughter burst out of her, and she returned her attention to her patient. "Yes, like them." She indicated his ankle. "Ben, what do you think?"

He bent close. "Looks a bit swollen to me."

"And I detect the beginnings of a bruise. It's going to be a day of rest for you, sweetie. If it swells any more, we'll fetch the doctor."

His mouth hung open in horror. "But the snow! We were going to play. Even Mr. Ben!" Eli's small hand clasped Ben's. "Don't you wanna build snow soldiers with me?"

Ben could well understand the boy's disappointment. The promise of a grand snow adventure had been snatched from him.

"I do, Eli. Very much. But Isabel's right. You shouldn't put weight on that ankle. It'd be painful, and you could aggravate the injury."

Isabel's brows tugged together. "How about I fix you some hot cocoa to accompany breakfast?"

Eli shrugged, his gaze downcast. She cast a helpless look at Ben.

"I have an idea," he blurted, pushing to his feet. "You can't go outside to play in the snow, but no one said the snow couldn't come to you." Reaching down, he swung Eli into his arms and carried him to the sofa. Honor and Carmen emerged from the kitchen.

To Isabel, he said, "Where's that copper basin?"

"The one we use for bathing?"

"That's the one."

She propped a pillow beneath Eli's injured foot. "In the shed."

Honor moved to stand behind the sofa. "We have a smaller one that will work to soak his foot."

"I don't need it for that." Going to the coat stand, he donned his outer gear. "I'll be back in a jiffy."

Quickly locating the basin, he carried it close to the cabin and, using a bucket, scooped mounds of snow inside. When Ben maneuvered the heavy basin into the cabin and situated it in front of the sofa, Eli's jaw hit his chest. His delight brightened his entire being, making Ben glad he'd had the idea.

"Now we can still make those soldiers, but on a smaller scale. We'll have to be careful not to make wet tracks all over the floor, though."

Eli's grin stretched from ear to ear. "Okay."

Ben caught Isabel's gaze. "I promise to clean up the mess."

"Thank you, Ben. I never would've thought to do something like this. You're great with children."

Long-suppressed yearning for a wife and kids broke forth, stunning in its intensity. He struggled to contain it.

Carmen nodded vigorously. "I agree. You should think of settling down and starting a family."

Honor didn't reprimand her this time. "You've made it plain you're as committed to bachelorhood as Isa is to remaining a spinster. Don't you want children?"

"Cozy family life isn't for me." He kept his gaze trained on his boots. If he looked at Isabel, she'd know his words didn't ring true. "I'm better off alone."

"Mr. Ben, let's play." Eli reached out and tested the wet powder.

"Good idea." He crouched before the basin. "The heat from the fire will soon melt it."

Grateful the girls let the subject drop, he focused on sculpting his snow figures.

Ben hadn't been forthcoming. Later that evening, as she hefted a pot of fragrant beef stew to the table, Isabel continued to ponder the puzzle he presented. He clearly enjoyed spending time with Eli. He'd gone out of his way to cheer him, going so far as to refill the basin with fresh snow twice so they could continue their play. The busy lawman surely had work to do—he'd spent scant time in his office these past few days. But he hadn't uttered one word of complaint, hadn't acted like being with them was a burden.

So why claim he wasn't fit for family life? The more she got to know the man behind the facade, the more Isabel was convinced he was deliberately being evasive regarding his reasons for being single. He'd admitted his parents shared a strong bond, and he spoke of his sisters with fondness. What was he hiding, then?

Honor started to place a fifth bowl on the table. Isabel put out a hand. "Ben's not joining us, remember?"

"Oh, I forgot." She wore an unhappy frown. "He's dining with Veronica Patton this evening."

The sharp stab of jealousy was unexpected. The thought of the beautiful, poised blonde with Ben evoked deep-seated denial. Why would the notion of them together trouble her to this extent? She didn't want him for herself.

Are you sure about that?

Of course she didn't. But she also knew that Veronica wasn't a good fit for him.

"He should be here with us." Carmen bustled in bearing utensils and cloth napkins.

Honor nodded. "I've gotten used to having him around."

Isabel grappled to regain her scattered common sense.

"We all have to keep in mind that Ben's time with us is temporary." She cast a glance at Eli, who was propped up by pillows and engrossed with his toy horse. "He's got a busy social calendar that I'm sure he's anxious to get back to."

Chapter Fourteen

Ben accepted the pie his hostess pressed upon him and ate without tasting. He shouldn't be here. He should be in the cabin across town, sitting down to good food and conversation at the Flores sisters' table.

"Thank you for the meal, Patricia." He'd dined with the Pattons enough times that Veronica's mother had insisted on dispensing with the formalities.

"You know you're always welcome, Ben." Pausing in her clearing of the table, she fiddled with the pearls around her neck. "We were wondering if you'd made any Christmas plans."

Across from Ben, Veronica picked at her dessert without eating. She'd acted annoyed the entire evening. When she didn't add to the conversation, her mother gave him a strained smile.

"Veronica and I were discussing the sheriff's trip to Norfolk, and we realized you might not have a place to go. We wouldn't want you to be alone."

"Oh, he hasn't been alone, have you?" Veronica's blue gaze speared him.

"You haven't been at the jail much this past week."

Seated at the head of the table, Silas Patton took a long draw on his pipe and eyed Ben over the rims of his spectacles.

"Even when Shane's in town, I tend to avoid long stretches at the jail. I prefer to make regular passes through town, stay informed on recent developments."

"But you haven't been making rounds," Veronica challenged, her chin at a militant angle. "You've been preoccupied with that orphan boy and spending an awful lot of time at the Flores farm."

Patricia resumed her seat and, smoothing her napkin in her lap, reached for her coffee. "I heard Isabel is thinking of adopting him."

Veronica scowled. "Bad idea, if you ask me."

Ben lowered his fork to his plate. "Why would you say that?"

"Must I list the reasons?"

Silas exhaled a line of piquant smoke. "No need, dear daughter. They're quite obvious. I'm sure the girl's aware of the difficulties, but she has no marriage prospects on the horizon. Thus, no children. She's desperate."

Ben tamped down his flare of temper. "Isabel is aware of the challenges. She cares about Eli, however, and is willing and able to overcome any obstacle that may arise."

Mother and daughter shared a significant glance, but then Veronica banished the annoyance from her face. "Let's not waste our evening talking of Isabel Flores and plans that don't concern us. I thought you'd like to know I've purchased a dress for the McKennas' Christmas party. It's a shade somewhere between periwinkle and blueberry."

"It certainly brings out your eyes, dear," Patricia inserted. "Just wait until you see her in it, Ben. You'll be scraping your jaw off the floor."

Veronica preened. "If you don't already have a shirt and vest to match, I'm sure Quinn can locate them for you."

"I don't follow."

"You're not the only one." Silas chuckled. "These females and their fashion. I'm happy if I walk out the door in matching socks."

"We'll want our outfits to coordinate, of course," Veronica told him impatiently. "Don't you remember we talked about this?"

"I don't recall discussing attending together, much less wearing matching clothing."

Hot color bloomed in her cheeks. "It seems your memory has been faulty of late, Deputy."

"I apologize. I have had a lot on my mind."

Veronica tossed her napkin atop her plate and abruptly stood. "Well, it's clear your thoughts didn't include me."

Her rush from the room was punctuated by the slamming door. Silas took another thoughtful puff on his pipe. Patricia's hand trembled as she lowered her cup.

"You'll have to excuse her, Ben. She hasn't been herself today."

He scraped his chair back. "I'll go talk to her." Grabbing his hat from the hutch, he inclined his head. "Thanks again for the meal."

Emerging onto the dark porch, he spotted the overwrought young woman's shadowed form near the lane and the break in the fence line. His long strides ate up the distance.

"Veronica—"

"I shouldn't have been rude."

She enfolded his hand in both of hers. With a start, Ben realized he felt nothing. Absolutely nothing. That wasn't the case with Isabel. The barest brush of her skin had him warm and tingly all over.

"I admit it," she rushed ahead, "I've been jealous. Ridiculous, I know." Her laugh had a desperate quality. "I mean, what could you possibly see in *her*?"

He tugged free. "Veronica, I have no intention of marrying. Ever."

"That's because you refuse to see what's right in front of you." She gripped his suit lapels. "I'm different than the others, Ben. I'm confident I can make you happy."

Shame pounded at his temples. He'd provoked this scene. He'd hurt her and others—the fact that it had been unintentional didn't matter.

"I'm truly sorry. I shouldn't have initiated a friendship with you."

"Friendship?" Her voice was shrill. She thumped his chest. "This was a *courtship*. How can you deny we have something special?"

"I was wrong." He whipped off his hat and, pacing a few steps away, thrust his fingers through his hair. "I've been wrong for a long time. It's time I stopped running from the truth."

"What truth?"

"I hope one day you'll be able to forgive me." Going to her, he cupped her shoulder. "You'll make some fortunate man very happy. It just won't be me."

Ben left her, more certain of his course than ever before. He'd walk this path alone and conduct himself with honor. No more disappointed hearts. He was done dragging others into his misfortune.

Now if he could manage to control his growing attraction to Isabel, he'd have no cause to worry.

Isabel had the distinct feeling she was being followed. Whether it was her imagination playing tricks or her instincts identifying an actual threat, she couldn't be sure. The gloomy afternoon, complete with thick fog hugging the mountains, evoked a menacing atmosphere. She increased her pace along the deserted lane, her gaze darting to first one side, then the next, searching the woods for signs of life.

Should've brought the horse. But she'd been restless and keen to stretch her legs. Walking to the mercantile alone would give her a chance to sort through the thoughts plaguing her. Ben had been busy this week. During his infrequent visits, he hadn't been inclined to relate how his dinner with Veronica had gone. And she hadn't asked.

A squirrel darted out of the underbrush and into her path. Gasping, Isabel came up short.

Her heartrate hiked. "It's an innocent squirrel, Isa," she muttered.

Clutching her empty basket, she plunged on ahead, skirts swishing. This was Ben's fault, she thought irritably. He'd convinced her the bank robber would want to silence her. Well, there'd been no indications he'd stuck around. They hadn't connected the attempted robbery of Quinn's store or the missing horse to the man who'd threatened her life. Those could be random, isolated events.

If she said that aloud to Ben, he would focus on two words—*could be*. Being prepared for the worst was a code he seemed to live by.

The crack of a limb startled her. She whirled to her right. There…a streak of movement through the trees. A man in dark colors, his face hidden by a low-slung hat.

Her feet felt weighted with bricks. *Dagger. Get your dagger.*

But he wasn't running toward her. He was running away, bent on escape.

Could this be the mysterious Happy?

Isabel didn't think. She bolted into the trees. "Wait!"

The man ran faster, weaving around bushes and tree trunks, dead leaves crunching beneath his boots.

"I only want to talk!" she called after him. Trying to track his progress while also trying to avoid obstacles slowed her down. Not to mention the fact she was wearing far more restrictive layers than him.

A stitch in her side that sharpened with each jolt of her shoes against the hard, uneven ground convinced her to give up the chase. Bracing her hand against a tree, she sucked in great gulps of cold air and battled crushing disappointment. This stranger had been following her for a singular purpose, and it wasn't to harm her. He had to be Eli's guardian. She felt it in her bones.

Returning to the spot where she'd dropped her basket, Isabel found the lane still empty. She hurried to town and bypassed the mercantile for the jail.

Claude Jenkins intercepted her outside the entrance. Tugging his sagging waistband farther up his girth, he said, "If you're looking for Ben, he's out on official business. Just left five minutes ago."

"Did he mention how long he'd be gone?"

"Not to me. If you don't mind my saying so, you look upset. Has something happened?"

Isabel debated what to do. "I encountered a man in the forest just now. He took off the moment I spotted him. I think it might be Eli's guardian."

He looked understandably concerned. "It's a possibility. Or it could turn out to be a traveler passing through who isn't keen on being social. Whatever the case, I'll round up some fellows to investigate. Maybe we'll locate his tent site, if not the man himself."

Claude glanced about as if ensuring no one could hear them. "How is young Eli?"

She bristled, well aware where this conversation was headed. "He's well, thank you."

"I have to tell you, I wasn't expecting to hear you wanted to raise him by yourself. The Watsons were crushed when they learned the news."

"How could they be? They haven't even met him."

"To them, Eli was their last opportunity to have a son."

"Eli was brought to my home, not theirs. They don't know that he can't sleep without his rocking horse. They don't know that he's suspicious of men or that he's got a tender scalp and you have to be extra gentle when combing out his curls. Mr. Jenkins, they don't know him like I do." Her voice shaking, she pressed her hand to her chest. "My sisters and I have become that boy's family."

His gaze reflected sympathy. "Taking him in is an admirable act of Christian charity. It's understandable you'd feel protective. Unfortunately, the Flores name has been sullied over the years. Are you certain you wish to expose him to the same derision you and your sisters have suffered?"

Isabel felt as if the banker had dealt her a cruel blow. Doubts rushed in, resurrecting shame and the impossible wish for a different legacy. But then, like a lifeboat come to save her, Ben's encouragement, his repeated assertions that her father's sins weren't hers to bear, bolstered her confidence.

She straightened to her full height. "Our father was a scoundrel, it's true, but those were his mistakes, not ours. I'm striving to regain honor and respect, a family legacy we can be proud of. If some people don't recognize the difference between the way Manuel conducted himself and our current lives, that's their problem. Not mine. And if Eli does experience a taste of the same small-mindedness, we'll be there to guide him through it. We'll teach him that

God loves each of us, no matter our heritage, no matter our personal failures. We'll teach him that God's opinion far outweighs anyone else's."

Feeling as if the pronouncement had freed her from a lifelong burden, Isabel actually smiled. "Now, if you'll excuse me, I have some shopping to do."

The banker's eyes were wide with what appeared to be reluctant admiration. It hit her then that her own actions had influenced, at least to some degree, how others treated her. Her father's shame ever present, she'd lived as if she were to blame. Well, no more.

And to think, Ben had inspired her transformed attitude. Ben, the notorious flirt she'd evaded for years. Ben, who'd turned out to be so much more than she'd ever given him credit for.

What does this mean, Lord? Was this the reason You placed Ben in the alley that night? Or do You have something more in mind?

Chapter Fifteen

The moment Isabel heard the approaching rider, she draped her cloak over her shoulders, seized the lamp from the table and left the cabin's warmth. She didn't care that it was past midnight or that her sisters and Eli were fast asleep. Worry fueled her quick jaunt to the hut. Ben had been gone the entire day, and she hadn't been able to shake the feeling something was amiss. She'd never heard from Claude, so she didn't know if they'd found the man in the woods or not.

Rounding the corner, she noticed Ben's horse wasn't hitched to the post out front. A large form came around the other side, and her heart lurched into her throat. She raised the lamp high.

"Ben?"

His pace slowed. "Isabel. Is something wrong?" He met her at the stoop. "I thought you'd be in bed."

"I couldn't sleep."

He opened the hut door, his teeth gleaming white. "Worried about me?"

She followed without waiting for an invitation and suspended the lamp from a peg. "As a matter of fact, I—" She gasped. "You're hurt!"

Grimacing, he gingerly passed his fingertips over the gash above his eye. "I tangled with an irate bull."

Pulling the lone chair to the middle of the floor, she pressed him into it. "That's what you've been doing all day?"

He grinned. "Not all day. I was trying to sort out a neighborly squabble after lunch. Seems Mr. Fairchild's sons have been trespassing on the widow French's property and fishing out of her pond without her permission. As I was leaving, I was compelled to investigate claims of a moonshine still. And finally, Ed Nettles begged me to help corral his rogue bull."

Isabel bent close to inspect the wound. "It needs stitches. I'll get my supplies."

His gloved hand closed over wrist as she made to leave. The buckskin was soft and warm and his grip firm. "No stitches, Nurse Flores."

"You might scar if you don't."

"Scars add character, don't you know?" His voice deepened to lush velvet.

The tranquil night, the realization that they were the only ones awake for miles, turned her blood to slow-moving honey. The indescribable yearning she'd fought to imprison broke free, like a mighty wall of water breaking through a dam, enveloping her and drowning out the many, many reasons why she should return to her cabin *right this second*.

Her gaze landed on the washbasin. "At least let me clean it. Do you have a fresh handkerchief?"

In answer, he released her wrist, removed his gloves and dug in his coat pocket. He said nothing as he held out the snowy-white cloth, but his eyes—oh, his eyes, they spoke volumes. Mouth dry, Isabel forced her shaky legs to the basin and dampened the material. When she returned to his side, she stumbled over his saddlebag.

Ben caught her around the waist. "Steady, sugarplum," he murmured.

Isabel settled one hand on his shoulder for balance before turning her attention to the gash. "D-does that hurt?"

His face was tilted up, and the faint light flicked over his features, creating a play of angles and shadows. "Stings a little. Nothing I can't handle."

"And your arm?"

"Is fine. I'm fine."

She dabbed the wound, aware of his large hands spanning her sides. "Your job is dangerous."

"It has some inherent risks."

She ceased her ministrations to gaze deeply into his eyes, which were a pulsing, vibrant sea green at the moment. "You regularly set aside your own comfort—indeed, you risk your safety in order to keep us safe. I admire you, Ben." His eyes flared in surprise. "Thank you for saving my life in the alley. And for everything you've done to help me since."

Before she could stop herself, she bent and pressed a kiss on his cheek. When she lifted her head, Ben cupped her cheek with a trembling hand.

"Isabel."

His expression was nothing like she'd seen before... earnest and vulnerable and laid bare. He guided her face down, and she willingly went along. Their mouths met and parted on twin sighs, as if they'd both been waiting a lifetime for this moment and couldn't quite believe it was real. The damp cloth slipped from her fingers to the floor. His lips sought hers again, tender and reverent, slow and sweet. This kiss was a poignant window into his soul, and she felt closer to him than anyone else in the world. Dizzy delight swirled through Isabel. She gripped his shoulder to keep from falling over.

* * *

Ben knew he was leading them both down a treacherous path that held no promise of rainbows and happy-ever-after at the end. He knew it, yet he couldn't let Isabel go. She was too precious, this moment too fleeting. Framing her face, he slowly rose to his feet. Her lids fluttered open, her eyes big and soft with wonder, her lips parted in protest. Her words from minutes ago—*I admire you, Ben*—scrolled through his mind again, shocking and powerful. Those words, coming from this beautiful, amazing woman, made him feel as if he could overcome any obstacle. He wrapped his arms around her and tugged her snug against his chest. Gazing up at him, she encircled his neck and tentatively stroked his hair.

"What are we doing?" she whispered, awe evident in her voice.

Ben brushed her lips with his own and smiled. "Something unwise."

"That's what I thought." Her hold tightened. "Kiss me, then, before we come to our senses and you banish me to my cabin."

He happily complied, the loneliness he hid from the world shrinking a little as he held her tight and kissed her. Isabel was everything he'd ever dreamed about in a woman. If he wasn't careful, he'd start dreaming about forever with her and Eli, the family he'd been denied.

Start dreaming about? Too late.

Isabel eased out of his arms, regret brimming in her eyes. "We should probably stop."

Ben came close to reaching for her again, but the futility of such an action prevented him from doing so.

He caressed the curve of her jaw. "We shouldn't have started, but I can't bring myself to wish it undone." He'd treasure these moments for the rest of his days.

She swallowed hard and nodded. Wrapped her arms around her middle.

Not fully trusting his self-control, he went to the wood-stove and began tossing kindling inside. Without Isabel's nearness to distract him, the dull ache behind his eyes registered again.

"Did you see Claude at all today?" she asked.

"No, why?"

"Earlier, when I was on my way to the mercantile, a man was following me."

"*What?*" He twisted around and stood up so fast the room momentarily tilted. He gripped the window ledge. "Why didn't you tell me?"

"Why do you think I came here at this hour?"

The dull ache became a fierce pounding. The gash's lingering sting was nothing compared to his sudden, intense headache. "Did he threaten you? How did you get away?"

"He's the one who escaped." Isabel came closer. "Ben, you've gone pale. Did the bull kick you in the head?"

He pinched the bridge of his nose. "No, I had my eyes on him instead of where I was going. Collided with the fence post. And what do you mean he escaped? Please don't tell me you tried to confront a stranger."

Her expression was equal parts worry and defiance. "Come to the cabin, and I'll fill you in on the details. Did you eat supper?"

"There wasn't time."

"I'll fix you a snack and an herbal infusion that should help you with that headache."

Here was an offer she wouldn't have made mere weeks ago. Ben was tempted. Not only would he appreciate something to relieve the pain, but he wasn't ready for their time together to end. "It's late. I wouldn't want to disturb the others."

"I know how to be quiet." She arched a single raven brow. "Do you?"

"I think I can manage it."

"Good."

In the cabin, he peeked in on Eli while Isabel put the kettle on. The boy looked more adorable than usual curled up on his side, his wooden horse clutched to his chest. Ben straightened the covers and tucked them more closely about his small form. Then he moved out of the room before he could succumb to foolish thoughts he had no business entertaining. It hadn't been easy, especially in the beginning, but he'd accepted that fatherhood wasn't part of God's plan.

He couldn't start daydreaming about Isabel as his wife. Nor could he envision fishing outings with Eli like the ones Ben had enjoyed with his own father. They weren't permanent fixtures in his life. Even if Isabel could overlook his condition—assuming she'd relinquish her prized spinsterhood—she didn't see him as husband material. His chest squeezed with longing for what could never be.

"How's he sleeping?" She placed a sachet of herbs in an enamel mug and poured steaming water over it. "Sometimes he gets restless."

"He didn't so much as twitch that I saw. Must be having dreams about candy castles and gingerbread men."

After divesting himself of his outer gear, he sank onto the sofa and stared at the smoldering logs. He was getting far too comfortable here. The longer the case of the missing guardian and would-be bank robber dragged on, the harder it was going to be to resume normal life.

After Isabel had provided him with food and drink, he listened as she recounted her encounter in the woods.

"I wish you hadn't chased him."

"Our thief wouldn't have run away. It was Eli's guardian, I'm sure of it." Seated opposite, she leaned forward, her eyes intense. "Happy watched us for who knows how long before deciding to leave Eli here. Stands to reason he'd stick around and make sure Eli was being treated right."

"But you couldn't have known that when you started after him. What if he'd been someone else with sinister things to hide? What if he'd produced a gun and got a shot off as he fled?"

The thought of her, wounded and alone with no one the wiser, turned his insides cold.

She blanched. "I didn't stop to consider the danger. I simply reacted."

"Like the night you faced off against a bank robber." He set his coffee on the low table between them. "Isabel, I commend your bravery. I do. But you have people depending on you. If anything happened…" He cleared his throat. "Please promise me you'll be more careful."

She slowly nodded. "I will."

"Say you promise."

"I promise."

"Good."

Her pledge didn't fully dispel his worries. That he'd kissed her proved he was starting to care far too much. He was breaking rules he'd established years ago, rules meant to prevent anyone from getting hurt. That kiss could not be repeated. If he hurt Isabel, he'd never be able to forgive himself.

"Got any plans for Christmas?"

Ben tilted his hat farther up his forehead and leveled an even stare at his friend riding alongside. Their progress through the woods was painstakingly slow. Around them, volunteers fanned out searching for signs of the stranger Isabel had encountered yesterday.

"Not yet." He didn't trust the gleam in the former marshal's eyes. "Why do you ask?"

"Just wondering." Grant's shrug was unconvincing. "It's ten days away. I figured with you spending so much time with Isabel and her sisters that you'd have received an invitation by now."

"I have." Isabel had yet to reiterate Carmen's spontaneous invite, and he wouldn't intrude on their private celebration without her wholehearted consent. "Haven't made up my mind what I'll do."

"Well, if you find yourself without somewhere to go, you're welcome at the O'Malleys'. It's what I like to call organized chaos." A grin eased the ruggedness of his features. Grant was doing a lot of that lately, his excitement over the baby obvious to anyone who talked to him.

Sunlight shafted through the trees to form pale patterns on the faded leaf cover. The occasional bird of prey flew overhead, their flapping wings and piercing cries interrupting the hush blanketing the winter landscape. Conversations he couldn't make out carried across the expanse as men rode in pairs or trios.

Ben shifted in the saddle and inhaled the crisp air. He was fighting drowsiness today, thanks to his late-night visit with Isabel. At least her concoction had worked. His headache was gone, and all he had was lingering soreness beneath the bandage she'd insisted he wear.

"Have you gotten Jessica's gift squared away?"

Grant flipped up the collar of his caramel-colored coat. "I ordered her a housekeeping book she's been wanting, but I'd like to get her something a little more sentimental."

"You're a blessed man, you know that? A nice home, a beautiful wife and a baby on the way. Don't ever take that for granted."

"I won't." His gaze grew serious. "I came close to losing

her once upon a time. That small taste of life without her was enough for me."

When Grant Parker first arrived in Gatlinburg, injured and disoriented, he'd been suffering from amnesia. Jessica gave him shelter and helped him try to solve the puzzle of his identity. Once they learned he was a US marshal, Grant returned to Arlington with his brother, Aaron. It hadn't taken him long, though, to figure out Tennessee was where he wanted to be, with Jessica as his wife.

"What are you getting Isabel?"

The question didn't register for a long minute. "Why would you assume I'm giving her something?"

Grant feigned innocence. "Oh, I don't know. Maybe because you've been practically inseparable the past two weeks?"

Ben glanced around to be sure no one was close enough to overhear. So far, his sleeping arrangements—and Isabel's part in the robbery—had remained a secret. She wouldn't thank him if that news hit the local grapevine.

"In a professional capacity, might I remind you. We aren't courting." His hand closed over the saddle horn as their embrace taunted him. He couldn't stop thinking about those fleeting moments when she was in his arms, yielding to whatever was pulling them together instead of fighting it. "Eli, on the other hand, could use shoes that fit him better. And some more clothes. Maybe a picture book, too. He loves it when Isa reads to him."

"Isa, huh?"

Scowling, Ben guided his horse around a wide fissure in the ground. "Drop it, Parker." A sudden flurry of activity to their right snagged his attention. "Looks like they found something. Let's go check it out."

When they arrived at the spot, farmer Lester Thomas broke apart from the group to address Ben. "It's a squatter's campsite, all right." He spat a long stream of tobacco juice into the leaves and pointed to a crude fire pit. "Ashes are still warm."

"There are signs of a lone horse," Lester's son called. He used his boot to dislodge debris from the hoofprints.

Ben and Grant dismounted and took their time inventorying the scene. As he riffled through the ashes with a stick, Grant's features went taut. "How far are we from Isabel's?" He kept his voice low.

These men were under the impression they were searching for a man who might have stolen Warring's horse and been involved in the attempt on the bank. No one besides Grant knew about the connection to Isabel.

Ben spun in a slow circle and took note of the land features. "About half a mile. Maybe less."

"Not a coincidence, I'd surmise."

"No." He struggled to keep his apprehension from showing. Crouching on the opposite side of the extinguished fire, he said, "So who is this guy? The thief who threatened Isabel's life, biding his time until he can try to silence her? Eli's mysterious caretaker? Or someone else with an entirely different motive we can only guess at?"

"Take your pick."

"I'm tired of waiting around to find out." He stood and, instructing those volunteers who could continue searching to do so, strode for his horse.

Grant followed. "What are you going to do?"

"What I should've done from the beginning," he said. "I'm going to patrol the streets and lanes of this town until I catch him."

"Oh, yeah? When do you plan to eat? Sleep?" Grant mounted his horse.

Back in the saddle, Ben resettled his hat on his head. "I'll figure it out as I go."

"I'll help you."

"I won't be the reason you're not at home with Jess. I enjoy her cooking too much to risk making her mad."

"You're only one man. With Shane in Norfolk, this town's troubles have been falling to you. Let me help." Grant's gaze and voice were in one accord—he was intent on having his way, left over from his life as a marshal used to throwing his weight around. "I'm positive some of Jess's cousins will pitch in, as well."

"If you're sure I won't have a bevy of irate wives after me, I won't turn away the assistance. Isabel and Eli deserve a hassle-free Christmas."

Grant's regard turned thoughtful. "What happens once you get the answers you seek? Will you bow out of their lives?"

The thought of living like the reserved strangers they used to be cut deep. "It's what Isabel will want."

That kiss was an aberration, a momentary lapse in judgment, a desperate attempt to assuage both their lonely hearts.

"What about you?"

"I've learned what I want doesn't matter."

Chapter Sixteen

Sometimes Isabel had full confidence in her ability to meet Eli's needs. Other times, like this one, doubts poked that confidence full of pomander-sized holes. He'd woken from a brief nap in a terrible mood that lingered, no matter what she tried. She prayed for guidance and insight, keeping in mind that he was adrift in a new world. He was missing his mother. Confused by his guardian's actions.

"I want Mama!" Thin arms folded tightly across his chest, his wooden horse trapped in the crook of his elbow, he refused to budge from the sofa.

The mantel clock struck six. Carmen was visiting a friend, and Honor was with John. It was going to be a long evening.

Isabel set the book she'd hoped to entice him with on the cushion beside her. "I miss my mama, too."

His dark brows furrowed. "You do?"

"Mmm-hmm." She brought their one and only family photograph over and lightly tapped her mother's image. "That's her. Her name is Alma, and she lives in another town now. I don't get to see her as often as I'd like."

He scrutinized the photo with curious eyes. "Who's that?"

Isabel frowned. "My papa, Manuel."

"Where's he?"

"He passed away." She returned the frame to its usual spot.

"Like my mama."

"Yes."

"Are you sad?"

Isabel searched for the appropriate response. "I have been." Sad that Manuel couldn't hurt their family anymore? No. Sad that she'd missed out on a typical father-daughter relationship? Absolutely.

Eli tucked his chin under and pulled his horse up to hide his face. Her heart broke for him. Scooting closer, she rubbed his back.

"Eli, I know you're missing your mother and the home you shared with her. That's okay. That's to be expected. You can talk about her as much or as little as you want." He shifted his head so that his right cheek rested on the horse's head, but he didn't meet her gaze. "I want you to know that you don't have to worry about the future. You have a home here with me."

He sat up, the wariness in his eyes out of place in such a young child. "I can stay here forever?"

She smiled. "Would you like that?"

"Can I sleep in the hut with Mr. Ben sometimes?"

Isabel couldn't keep her surprise from showing. "Ben won't be camping out there for long. He has his own cabin closer to town."

"Oh."

Grateful he didn't ask why Ben was staying on their property, she reached for the book. "Living here means you'll get to go to school eventually and learn to read. You won't have to wait for one of us to read you stories—you'll be able to do it yourself."

He didn't look cheered by the notion. "My mama used to sing a lot."

"She did?"

"She sang to me and the baby in her tummy."

Shock reverberated through her. Surely she'd heard wrong. "Eli, are you saying you have a sibling?"

He scrunched his nose. "What's that?"

"A sibling is a brother or sister."

He shrugged and plucked at the horse's yarn hair.

At the heavy tread on the porch, Isabel left Eli to peer through the window. The sight of Ben's profile caused her heart to leap with equal parts anticipation and relief. This latest revelation added a layer of troubling intrigue to Eli's past, and she was eager to hear Ben's take on it. He might possibly summon conclusions beyond her realm of experience.

When she swung the door open to grant him entrance, he was scanning the property as if his sight enabled him to see through night's cloak of darkness. His black coat molded to his broad shoulders and muscular arms, and he looked every inch the strong, commanding lawman. He turned his head, and that intense gaze punched into her. Secrets shared between them swirled in the vivid depths. Was it possible he'd grown more handsome? Before their paths collided this Christmas season, she'd never given much thought to what she found attractive in a man. Certainly she hadn't thought about hair color. Now she was convinced red was the way to go, rich, vibrant and gleaming where it caressed his pale skin. She'd run her fingers through those silken strands and would dearly like to do it again.

His mouth was pensive tonight, unlike when he'd dared kiss her. Then, those sculpted lips had been soft and molding, exquisitely tender, evoking dreams of romantic fairy tales.

"Evenin', Isabel." He raised his brows. "May I come in?"

Startled out of her reverie, she flushed. Had he guessed the direction of her thoughts?

"Of course." Shutting out the cold, she pointed to the square piece of white gauze above his eyebrow. "How's your wound?"

"I'd forgotten it was there." He lifted his hat and, setting it on the table, scraped his hand over his bristled jaw.

"You look exhausted."

One corner of his mouth lifted. "That bad, huh? I've been in the saddle much of the day."

"You do smell like horse and leather. And spruce trees."

"Anything else?"

"Maybe a little like a campfire."

"Maybe I should come back in the morning." He slapped his gloves against his pant legs, his exaggerated frown at odds with the twinkle in his eyes.

Isabel cast a quick glance at Eli, who was watching them over the top of the sofa. She leaned close. "I'm actually glad you're here."

He repeated her action, bringing his lips perilously close to her ear. "And why is that, sugarplum?"

His peppermint-scented breath stirred her hair. Tingles of awareness sizzled across her nape. "Someone's having a rough evening."

His attention swerved to Eli, which made it easier for her to breathe. No more teasing. No more thoughts about ill-advised midnight kisses, either.

"How's my favorite little man?"

Ben's query was met with a shrug.

"Would you like a glass of milk, Eli?" she interjected.

"Okay."

"Stay here while I go in the kitchen with Ben."

Ben followed her to the kitchen and took up a post in the doorway so he could watch Eli. "He's not acting like himself," he said quietly. "He's not getting ill, is he?"

"He woke up from his nap crying. I think he had another bad dream."

The doorjamb supporting his weight, he angled his head toward her. The intermittent light around the cabin glinted off his badge. He was wearing a white shirt with thin caramel stripes underneath his tan vest. A sage-colored cotton scarf kept his neck warm.

"About his ma?"

"I'm not sure." She removed a glass from the hutch and placed it on the counter. "Ben, he said something tonight that troubles me."

The shadows beneath his eyes seemed to deepen.

"He said his mother was pregnant. When I asked if he had a brother or sister, he wouldn't say."

His jaw went slack. With a quick glance toward the living room, he crossed to where she was standing near the stove. "Do you believe he's talking about something that really happened, or is it the product of an active imagination?"

"He was serious." Somehow her hand came to rest on his chest. "Ben, what if Eli's mother died in childbirth?"

His chest rose and fell in a ragged breath. He pinched his nose between his thumb and forefinger. "If Shane was here, he'd have found this guy already. He would've gotten the answers you seek."

"I understand you're frustrated. So am I. But you've done the best you could with what little you have to go on. It's not like you can interrogate a small child, especially one who's suffered a trauma."

He sighed and shook his head.

"What more could the sheriff have done that you haven't?" Beneath her splayed fingers, his muscles bunched. His solid warmth flowed into her palm and traveled a languorous path up her arm. She surreptitiously lowered her arm to her side.

His gaze became hooded. "I don't like feeling as if I've failed you. Or that boy in there."

"Trust me, you haven't. You've watched over us. Made us feel safe. You've championed my cause. That's not what I consider failure."

Ben reached up and smoothed a stray tendril behind her ear. "I want you to get your heart's desire, Isa. Raising Eli on your own, independent of any man."

What had once been her ideal now struck her as hollow. Because of Ben.

Isabel would take that secret to the grave. He was a committed bachelor and she an avowed spinster.

"In order to accomplish that, I need to find the person who dropped him here. Any lawyer worth his salt will want to know we've exhausted all resources in our search for extended family members. Constantly worrying about someone coming to claim him will wear away at your peace."

Ben's focus wasn't on his task, and his finger came in contact with the hot pan. He tried to hide his wince, but as he lifted his sore finger to his mouth, Isabel shot him a knowing look.

"I had no idea you were so prone to accidents, Deputy."

"It's your fault," he quipped. "Being around you distracts me."

Beneath her plain white apron, she wore his favorite plum-colored blouse and matching dangly earrings. The outfit, combined with her intricate and severe French braid, hinted at a dour librarian persona. Ben knew better. The woman he'd held in his arms was vibrant and giving.

And beyond reach. Or did you conveniently push that tidbit to the recesses of your mind?

She watched over Eli as he transferred the cookies to a plate. "I wasn't there when you tested your hard head against a fence post."

"True. Turns out your presence isn't necessary. Thoughts of you are enough to pose a danger."

She frowned, and her dark eyes grew troubled.

"Done!" Eli set the spatula down with a clatter. "Can I eat one now?"

"Yes, you may." Isabel handed him a warm cookie. "You and Ben worked hard on these."

Eli's smile smacked of contentment. They'd managed to cajole him out of his cranky mood by making plans for a Christmas tree and myriad decorations. Then Isabel had suggested making cookies, and the boy had leaped at the chance, as any child would've done.

The three of them alone in the cabin, doing domestic things, was wreaking havoc on his heavily fortified defenses. Maybe it was the atmosphere of hope this season imparted. Carolers in the streets, happy shoppers and satisfied shopkeepers, extra time set aside for family and friends, the planning of gifts. Or maybe it was the change in his and Isabel's relationship and the fact that her home felt like a haven.

Movement at the front door sent the deep thoughts scattering. Isabel went to investigate, her surprised greeting bringing both Ben and Eli into the dining area. As soon as his gaze came to rest on John and Honor, he knew the Flores sisters' lives would soon undergo changes.

Ben was certain the others didn't see what he saw— Isabel visibly setting her mind to dwell only on her sister's happiness, just as he had done when Grant and Jess conveyed their good news. He went to stand beside her and, without thinking, settled a hand against the middle of her back.

The couple remained on the threshold, John's arm snug around Honor's shoulders.

"Is Carmen here?" she said, her sparkling gaze darting to the bedroom.

Isabel clasped her hands at her waist. "No, she's with Rosa. How was your evening? You're home earlier than usual."

The pair looked at each other and shared bright smiles. Honor snuggled closer to his side. "John proposed tonight."

John looked as if he'd lassoed the moon. "She said yes."

Isabel was silent long enough for the couple to notice. Then she rushed over and enveloped Honor in a hug. "Congratulations, sis. I'm thrilled for you both."

Ben took the opportunity to shake John's hand and offer his own well wishes. "When's the big day?"

John looked at his fiancée with raised brows. "Our cabin's ready, save for a thorough cleaning."

A becoming blush bloomed in the pretty girl's cheeks. "We discussed holding the ceremony in February." She took hold of Isabel's hands. "What do you think, Isa? Would that be too soon?"

Isabel's eyes shone with affection and pride. If there was the tiniest hint of sadness, Ben was convinced the couple didn't notice. They were too wrapped up in each other.

"I think any day you choose will be perfect."

"Then I vote for Christmas Day," John teased, chuckling.

Honor's blush deepened. "I have to have time to ready a dress, my love."

"I don't care what you wear, you know that."

Beaming with happiness, Honor suggested they visit

Rosa's house to tell Carmen. John readily agreed—he was so smitten, Ben was fairly sure he'd have agreed to ride to Canada if she'd asked—and they left as quickly as they'd arrived. The silence in their wake was rife with unspoken emotion.

"Isabel—"

"I don't know about you, but I'm ready to try one of those cookies." She scooped Eli into her arms. "What do you say, Eli? Want another cookie?"

At his nod, she carried him to the kitchen. Ben played along, ignoring the obvious, biding his time. Isabel avoided his gaze, and he debated whether or not to leave. The wobble in her voice as she uttered a bedtime prayer with Eli made up his mind. As she exited the bedroom and eased the door shut, he caught her wrist.

Her lips parted, and her gaze slid away. "It's late, Ben. You should probably go."

Threading his fingers through hers, he urged her closer to the fireplace. "I will soon. I won't be sleeping in the hut tonight, so I'll need you to be extra vigilant. You have your dagger with you, right?"

Her sleek brows knitted together. "That and a hunting rifle. Where will you be?"

His thumb traced across her knuckles in a back-and-forth motion. "Patrolling the streets. There's a greater chance of encountering strangers under cover of darkness."

She flicked a glance at his bandage. "You'll be careful?"

"I'll do my best." Releasing her hand so he could think, he said, "Isabel, I want you to know—" He couldn't reveal his secret, but he could offer a shoulder to cry on. "I understand how certain changes in our lives can bring unexpected challenges. It's natural to have mixed feelings about Honor's engagement."

"I'm happy for her," she stated, her expression earnest.

"I know, but—"

"Surely you don't think I'm jealous?"

"Of course not. I think you're a good sister who wants the best for her siblings, even if that means their fulfilled dreams affect you in unforeseen ways. You're going to miss her."

"She's not moving out of state."

"But she won't be here with you and Carmen. She'll have a new family, new responsibilities."

"Are you trying to upset me?"

"I'm trying to be a good friend."

I want you to trust me enough to share your hurts, to let me in when you keep the whole world at bay.

She inhaled sharply. "So be a good friend and cease this talk."

Confused by this need to push his way past her defenses, he did as she suggested. "Fine."

He was at the door when she called for him to wait and didn't at first recognize the battle light in her eyes.

"We haven't discussed what happened in the hut."

"What is there to say besides I would dearly love to do it again?" She gasped. "But I won't."

"Because kissing is for serious romance," she retorted. "Isn't that what you said? What happened, Ben? Did you forget your own rule? I told myself I wouldn't pry into your relationship with Veronica. You haven't breathed a word about your dinner with her, however. You've acted as if she doesn't exist."

"I haven't spoken of what transpired, because it's nothing to be proud of. I reiterated my stance. She didn't take it well. We will no longer be spending time together. Does that satisfy your curiosity?"

She crossed her arms over her chest. "Not fully, no.

Considering what happened between us, I want to know— did you kiss her, too?"

"Besides you, the only other woman I've kissed is Marianne Ogden, my former fiancée."

Isabel narrowed her eyes. "Your former *what*?"

"You heard me."

"You were engaged to be married?" She gaped at him. "I don't believe it."

"Want her address?" *On second thought...*

"You said you hadn't been burned by love."

"I never said that. You assumed." He shoved his hand through his hair. Talking about this was a bad idea. "We were young. Things didn't work out. It wasn't a tragedy."

At least, the part about not marrying Marianne. In hindsight, he'd been spared a lifelong union with a woman whose loyalty wavered depending on the circumstances, a woman who'd used his reticence to her advantage, repainting their breakup in order to portray herself as a victim. The other part had cut at the root of his masculinity. His inability to sire children had made him feel abnormal. He wasn't about to share any of that with Isabel.

"Tell me what happened, then. If it wasn't serious."

"Why should I when you aren't willing to open up to me?" He pivoted toward the door.

"You were right," she rushed out.

He didn't turn his head; instead kept his gaze on the wooden slats inches from his face. "About?"

"Honor and John." She edged closer. "I do have mixed feelings. Not having her around is going to take some getting used to." She sighed. "I've had to act strong for my sisters ever since I can remember. I worked hard to shield them from my parents' unhappy marriage, to take the brunt of the town's ridicule. As the oldest, I was the most logical target." Her voice dropped an octave, and there was no denying her pain and disillusionment. "Sometimes, though, I wonder what it would be like not to have to be the strong one. To have someone I could lean on."

Ben squeezed his eyes shut. With everything in him, he wanted to hold her in his arms. Comfort her the only way he knew how. Promise he'd be there for her when she was feeling sad or lonely or overwhelmed.

But he couldn't do that, could he? He wouldn't be around. Not forever. Because he was broken. Less than whole.

"The first step to dealing with problems is admitting them," he said woodenly, lifting the latch. "Good night."

She didn't react until he was on the porch. "I opened up to you like you asked." Confusion colored her voice. "And your response is to offer empty platitudes? You're honestly going to walk away right now?"

"I'm sorry."

More sorry than you'll ever know.

Chapter Seventeen

She was a bigger fool than Sally Hatcher, Veronica Patton and the Smith sisters combined. Isabel pounded at the red-hot metal with all her might. She'd bared her soul, fully expecting Ben to repay the favor, and for what? He'd expected her to trust him but he wasn't prepared to reciprocate?

Isabel had ignored her instincts and allowed him into her life. She'd stupidly forgotten the potency of his practiced charm. Ben was a master at making a woman feel like she mattered to him when, in reality, none of them did. Marianne Ogden must've ripped his heart into shreds and neglected to instruct him how to put it back together again. As a result, he was exacting his revenge on every susceptible heart unfortunate enough to cross his path. He could, too. Because he was extraordinarily handsome. He possessed a certain boyish charm that made it difficult to be mad at him. Most importantly, he was a devoted lawman bent on protecting others…true hero material.

She'd known what he was and had still succumbed, making her worse than the others he'd duped. She pounded the metal too thin and it cracked.

With a frustrated growl, she set the tongs aside and

tossed her gloves to the ground, belatedly registering the shiny black boots in the patchy grass. Her gaze racing up the tall, formally dressed masculine form, it took a moment to reconcile his identity with his presence on her farm. Why would the mercantile owner pay her a visit?

"Mr. Darling. To what do I owe the pleasure?"

His keen gaze roved over her work area before returning to her. "Please, call me Quinn. I beg pardon for interrupting your work."

His smile was kind, his accent reminiscent of his Boston roots. The heir to a clothing empire, he'd left the family business to strike out on his own. He'd wound up marrying his shop assistant, Nicole O'Malley. Theirs was one of the families Isabel had admired from afar, a model of devoted commitment and proof that some people did find the real thing.

"Do you have a moment to discuss a business proposal?"

His words sparked suspicion. "Does your visit have anything to do with Ben MacGregor?"

In the shade of his black bowler hat, twin raven brows lifted a notch. "In fact, the deputy is the reason I'm here. Is that a problem?"

Removing her apron, she projected a calm she didn't feel. Ben hadn't just walked away. He'd added insult to injury by sharing her secret without permission. "He told you about my knives."

He inclined his head. "He was in the store this morning at the same time I was lamenting my dissatisfaction with my current supplier. I've had several customer complaints. Ben took me aside and suggested I come and see you."

"I don't sell to locals."

"Your identity could remain anonymous." He grew thoughtful. "Sometimes that increases customer interest. The mystery, you know."

"You haven't even seen my product."

"I have faith in Ben's judgment." He smiled. "I'm also a businessman. I would of course like to see samples before making a formal offer."

Isabel pondered his request. Selling her wares in town would add to her earnings. Circling her portable forge, she said, "I have several I can show you."

They strolled to the cabin in silence. Quinn gestured to the handful of wagons outside the mill. "I thought you usually filled the miller position."

"Carmen volunteered so that I could work on an order."

Volunteered might not be the best description. Still humming with frustration and hurt, Isabel had craved privacy today. Alone in her makeshift forge, she was able to make use of a physical outlet for her heightened emotions. Because she had so rarely asked for a break from the mill, her sisters had instantly agreed to help. Carmen was better with the customers, and Honor had been happy to spend the morning with Eli.

Considering Honor was still in a state of euphoria, she likely would've been content no matter what task was set before her.

When they stepped inside, Honor and Eli emerged from the kitchen, where they were heating water to wash dirty laundry. Quinn greeted them warmly, his gaze growing puzzled as he contemplated Eli.

Isabel put it down to curiosity. He was a topic of interest. It wasn't every day a boy was found wandering the woods alone.

Going to the hutch, she removed the walnut box where she stored her finished products. She placed it on the table and lifted the lid. "As you can see, I have these smaller ones, what Ben refers to as gambler's daggers, as well as larger ones."

Quinn studied them one by one, taking them out and testing their weight and strength, admiring the various handles. He seemed partial to those blades paired with antler and bone. When he was done, he folded his hands behind his back.

"I have to agree with the deputy. You're a skilled craftsman, Miss Flores. If you're amenable, I'd like to stock your knives in my store." He named a price and a percentage he'd take in commission that struck Isabel as fair.

She glanced at the weapons. "I accept your offer, Mr. Darling."

His handsome face brightened. "It's Quinn, remember? And I'm very happy to hear that. I look forward to establishing our working relationship. My next question is this—what will you choose to do about your identity?"

Isabel didn't give herself a chance to think. "Display my name. It's time I stop worrying about my father's reputation and start building my own."

He smiled. "You're making the right choice."

They decided he'd select five from her collection to start with, since Isabel was reluctant to part with them all. After he'd made his choices, he cast a furtive glance at the kitchen.

"Would you mind if we spoke on the porch for a moment?"

More intrigued than concerned, she led him outside and waited for him to speak.

"I have a strong sense of having seen Eli before."

Her heart leaped into her throat. "Where? When?"

"In the store." His eyes were intense. "Earlier in the fall, I had a young female customer come in and order a particular fabric for some baby clothes she wished to sew. She made an impression because she was a new face. Not only that, she was pregnant and far too thin for her condition. I was so concerned that I concocted a fake contest in which the customer who ordered that particular item received complimentary sacks of flour, sugar and salted beef."

She reached out and wrapped her fingers around the wooden post. "Did she have blond hair?"

"Yes. Did you know about her?"

"Eli has spoken of her. We haven't gotten much information and didn't want to press him. Thinking about her makes him sad. H-he said she died."

Sympathy swirled in his eyes. "He was with her that day. I gave him a bundle of licorice." He frowned. "I kept thinking they'd return, but they never did."

"He mentioned a sibling, but we didn't know whether or not to believe him." She gazed at the window, but the curtains blocked her view. "He's so young."

"Would you like me to go over my ledgers from that time? I may be able to discover her name."

"Yes, please." Isabel sighed. "I have to tell Ben."

"Stop by the store when you're ready."

"Thank you, Quinn."

After relating the nature of her errand to her sisters, Isabel saddled Honey and headed to Ben's place. Like it or not, she and the deputy were a team. Her connection to him was no longer merely professional. And while her feelings for him simultaneously confused and terrified her, she was certainly capable of focusing on their mission— finding answers for Eli.

Chapter Eighteen

"Annie Howell." Quinn ran a finger over the ledger entry. "That's her right there."

They were crammed into the mercantile's windowless, narrow office, Quinn scated at the desk and a welcome buffer between Ben and Isabel. Standing on either side of the businessman, their gazes clashed. The worry glimmering in her eyes amplified the feeling of helplessness that had taken up residence in his gut. There were too many unanswered questions. This was the part of his job that made him crazy. He knew from experience he wouldn't know a moment's peace until he solved the mystery.

Isabel had awakened him from a fitful slumber. Her presence in his home had been jarring, bringing him to full alertness in half the time it would've taken a cup of coffee. Still upset over their heated exchange, she'd reverted to her old manner of addressing him—as if he was unworthy of her valuable time.

He never should've breathed Marianne's name.

Isabel bent over the desk and squinted at the page. "Does it indicate where she was staying?"

"Afraid not." Quinn sank against the chair. "I recorded the item she traded in and the amount of credit she had left over." He looked at Isabel. "In fact, this credit should go to Eli."

She straightened, her expression somber. "He could use clothing items. I'll compile a list."

"I'm sorry I couldn't be of more help."

Quinn's assistant appeared in the hallway outside the office. "Sir, the postmaster sent over a telegram for the deputy. It just came in."

"Thank you, Henry."

Ben accepted the message and, unfolding it, quickly scanned the contents. "I have to go to Pigeon Forge." He couldn't avoid telling Isabel. "There was a robbery last night. The sheriff has a witness whose description fits our man."

"I want to come with you."

His shock was tempered by the knowledge that Isabel's quest for answers trumped her discontent with him. Ben cast a sideways glance at the shopkeeper, who'd twisted in his seat and was observing them both. "We've taken up enough of your time, Quinn. You've been a huge help."

"I wish I could've done more."

"You gave us a name. That's a key piece of information."

They filed out of the office and into the crowded mercantile, garnering many curious glances. Once outside, Ben navigated the busy street, his mind racing ahead. Isabel kept pace beside him. "This involves me, Ben. I want answers as much as you do."

He unlocked the jail and proceeded to gather extra weapons from the safe. "Our bank robber has nothing to do with Eli."

"You can't know that for sure. The timing is suspicious. What if the bad man Annie spoke about was the same person who held a gun on me?"

He swiped one of the Winchesters from the rack above

his desk. "What will people say if they find out you spent the day with me? No one knows you're involved in this."

"It's a risk I'm willing to take."

He stopped what he was doing. She'd remained by the door, an immovable sentry. "Our thief isn't the real reason you wish to go, is it? You think you might learn something about Annie and her baby."

"Pigeon Forge isn't that far from here. It wouldn't be a stretch to think she'd visit Gatlinburg, especially if she had relatives living in the area. This Happy person could be a resident of one of the outlying coves."

Without a description or actual name for Eli's caretaker, Ben hadn't been able to adequately canvass those residents who shied away from town.

He closed the distance between them and settled his hands on her shoulders. "What purpose will it serve to learn Annie and her child died in childbirth?"

She lifted her chin. "Eli won't be left wondering what happened to his loved ones. He's young now, but he'll ask questions as he grows older. He deserves to know the truth."

"What if we locate Annie's parents or grandparents or cousins? Decent people who might want to raise Eli?" He tightened his hold. "If that's the case, you need to prepare yourself for what might happen."

Her eyes clouded over. "I'd have no choice but to give him up."

That would devastate her. Him, too, if he were honest. He'd grown fond of Eli. Like any natural father, Ben was driven to protect the boy.

"And I'd have no choice but to uphold the law."

Her palpable sorrow kicked him in the sternum. "Eli deserves to have a family. He should be raised in a loving, nurturing environment, whether that's provided by me or blood relatives. I only want what's best for him."

Like she wanted for her sisters. Why did others' happiness have to cost Isabel hers? She'd shouldered the burden of her father's sins so that her sisters could have a better life. They'd been affected, too, but not nearly to the extent she had. They'd retained their faith in love and marriage. Isabel couldn't even bring herself to consider opening herself up to it. Eli had been like a gift, an amazing opportunity for Isabel to be a mother to a needy boy. That there was even the slightest chance it could be ripped from her made him feel ill.

Ben dropped his arms and turned away before he could do something stupid. "I can't promise this trip won't turn out to be a waste of time."

"I know."

With the desk safely between them, he leveled her a warning look. "I also can't promise to keep your name out of it."

That no one had discovered he'd spent numerous nights on her property was surprising.

"I know that, too."

"Fine." He consulted the clock on Shane's desk. "I've got to let Grant know where I'm headed and ask him to cover for me until we return late tonight."

"And I need to inform my sisters."

"I'll meet you at the edge of town in an hour. Beside the abandoned well."

Once she'd gone, he sank onto the desk and glanced at the ceiling. "Whatever we're headed into, God, I ask You to give us the strength to handle it."

Isabel's pulse raced later that afternoon as Pigeon Forge's sheriff lifted a wanted poster from the stack and placed it on the desk.

"Isabel?" Ben bent slightly to peruse the image. "Is that him?"

The scene in the alley rushed at her, the cold dread of her brush with death easily conjured. "Y-yes. That's the man who threatened my life."

Sheriff Langston's astute gaze shifted between them. "My witness didn't interact with him. He hid in the shadows while Theron Franklin filled his pockets with my citizens' hard-earned cash." He scowled. "Can't expect a young man to face off against a criminal, but I wish he'd been quicker to come and fetch me."

Theron Franklin. According to the poster, he was wanted for the murder of a young man from the middle of the state and other, less serious crimes. She couldn't suppress a shiver. Ben shifted closer but didn't touch her. He'd spoken very little during the long ride here. Not that she'd been in the mood to chat, either, not with anticipation warring with dread. She had to remember that God had a plan. Until today, she'd been confident that plan was for her to become Eli's permanent guardian. The possibility of relatives who might want him had put a dent in her confidence. Perhaps Eli's presence was always meant to be temporary.

Lord in heaven, Your Word promises to give me strength when I need it. Please lead us to the answers we seek. Please help me to accept Your will, no matter what it may be.

She glanced at Ben's profile. His jaw was locked tight, his mouth hard.

Help Ben accept it, too.

She wasn't the only one whose life had been affected by Eli's arrival. Watching them together as they made cookies yesterday, it had been impossible not to notice their deepening connection. Ben was the epitome of patience. Unlike Isabel, he was okay with messes. He'd let Eli measure the ingredients, mix the dough and roll it into balls.

And Eli's initial reticence around the lawman was a thing of the past. Absolute trust had blazed from his big blue eyes. How easy it was to imagine the three of them as a real family. Ben would make a good father. No, a *great* father. He'd never do anything to hurt his children. He'd guard and protect them, nurture and guide them.

If she wasn't an avowed spinster and he a confirmed bachelor, they might've raised Eli together. Given him lots of brothers and sisters…

"Isabel?" Ben's fleeting touch on her elbow halted the disconcerting train of thought.

"Yes?" Both men were watching her. "Sorry, I didn't hear what you said."

Ben's brows tugged together. "The sheriff hasn't heard of Annie, but there was a lady by the name of Ethel Howell who lived on the outskirts of town."

"Was?"

The sheriff laced his fingers over his chest. "She passed several months ago. Late July. No surviving kin that I'm aware of."

"Would you mind if we went out to her place and took a look around?" Ben asked.

"Be my guest. I can't say what the status of the place is. Could've been ransacked by looters by now. Or four-legged critters may have moved in."

"We'll proceed with caution. Thank you, Sheriff."

"I'll contact you if I get more information about Theron."

"Let's hope next time he strikes, you'll be there to capture him." Ben pointed to the wanted poster. "He's proved he's willing to do whatever is necessary to get what he wants."

Isabel took one last look at Theron's likeness and prayed she'd never meet him face-to-face again. There'd been times she'd wished Ben hadn't happened upon that deserted alley. Now she thanked God for sending him when He did.

Outside the jail, people bustled about the streets with packages in their arms, their friendly faces and good cheer a sign of the season. Christmas was approaching, and instead of making preparations, she was playing detective with Ben.

He must've noticed her distress, for as he unhitched their horses, he said, "You've been distracted ever since we got here. What's the matter?"

She gestured to their festive surroundings. "We don't have a tree. Eight days until Christmas, and I haven't started a single pie or cake. The gifts aren't ready." She walked to the boardwalk's edge. "I know those things pale in comparison to the reasons we're here."

His eyes softened with understanding. "It's hard to enjoy the preparations when you're worried about your future."

"I wanted to make this Christmas special for Eli. And now that I know this year will be Honor's last under our roof…"

"You still can, you know." He tilted his chin to the festooned storefronts and wagons creaking past. "I don't have anyone depending on me. I have time to devote to this case. There's no reason for you to be dragged into this."

There wasn't an ounce of self-pity in his voice. Still, something about his stance struck her as off. And his expression told of dreams relinquished. Did Ben truly wish to be alone? Or did his past entanglement with this Marianne woman strike fear in his heart to ever try again?

"I'm already square in the middle of it. I insisted on coming along, remember?"

He cast her a wry glance. "I remember."

He handed her Honey's reins, and they led their animals along the street. Isabel noticed that, for most women they passed, one look at Ben wasn't enough. They smiled and batted their eyes. Some even said hello. In the past, he would've poured on the charm. Not today. He didn't even seem to notice they existed. If she were honest, she'd admit he hadn't lived up to the Debonair Deputy's reputation in weeks.

Ben stopped before a steaming cart. "Do you like roasted chestnuts?"

As it was midafternoon, and they'd eaten a hasty packed lunch on the way, the treat would be a perfect snack. "Very much."

When she fumbled for her reticule beneath her cloak's folds, he forestalled her. After paying the man for two full sacks, Ben handed her one and they continued on their way. The sound of musical instruments drew her attention. In an empty lot beside a leather goods store, a crowd had gathered to listen to carolers.

Noticing her interest, Ben nodded toward them. "We've got time to listen to one or two songs."

"Are you sure?"

He gave her a half smile. "Let's pretend for a few minutes that we're not on a serious mission but out on a holiday shopping excursion."

Despite the strain that had characterized their interactions of late, he was trying to give her a bit of cheer. His thoughtfulness touched her. "I like that idea."

They spent a good half hour listening to the carols. Isabel couldn't help humming along with the familiar songs. It was a moment to reflect on the reasons for Christmas and God's unconditional love. He wasn't like her earthly father. God saw her faults and loved her anyway.

Too soon, it was time to go. They mounted their horses

and rode in silence to the homestead that once belonged to Ethel Howell. The isolated property had an abandoned, unkempt look. There were no animals stirring about. One of the windows had broken panes.

After securing their horses, Ben told her to wait while he walked the perimeter and peered into the windows. Satisfied there weren't any unwelcome human guests inside, he stepped onto the low porch. "Ready?"

Nodding slowly, she stared at the house and wondered if what was behind the door would grant them the answers they sought.

Chapter Nineteen

The interior of Ethel's farmhouse was dark and dusty. While Isabel tugged aside curtains to admit more light, Ben picked up a dining chair off the floor and righted it.

He checked the kitchen cabinets and drawers. "Doesn't look like anyone's bothered the place. There's silverware and a silver tea service in plain view."

"I feel strange doing this. Like I'm invading someone's privacy."

Isabel hovered in the doorway, too beautiful for his peace of mind. Being alone with her on the open road or a busy street was one thing. Here, in this house, he was attuned to the oddest things. Her soft, rhythmic breathing. The sigh of her full skirts against her leather boots. The tiniest hint of her orange-laced scent teasing his nose.

"We're searching for information, nothing more."

Her lips turned down at the corners. "I didn't see any personal effects in the living room."

"Let's check the bedrooms." He walked behind her to the rear section, his gaze drawn to her exposed nape above her cloak and the stray tendrils caressing her smooth golden skin. He paused in the hallway outside the first one. "You want this room while I take the next?"

She took a deep breath. "Sure."

Ben was accustomed to this type of work. Isabel wasn't. "If you come across anything you'd rather not examine, holler for me."

He proceeded to the second room, his gaze alert to clues but his ears straining for Isabel's movements. *Focus, Mac-Gregor.* This must've been reserved for guests, because there was nothing of interest. He was heading to the last room when she called for him, a curious note in her voice.

"What have you found?"

"Look at this." She handed him a photograph of a family. Mother, father and two older adolescents…a boy and a girl. "Turn it over."

He read the neat script aloud. "'Jim, Abigail, Annie and Harry.'"

Isabel came closer, her brown eyes alight with excitement. "Annie must've been Ethel's granddaughter. Look at her. It's obvious she had lighter hair than the others. And Eli has her chin." She tapped the young man's image. "And her brother, Harry? Don't you agree the name could be mispronounced by a small child?"

He raised his head. "You think Happy is actually Harry?"

"Maybe Eli's initial attempts to say his name sounded like the word *happy* and it stuck."

"Makes sense." He motioned to the open box on the bed. "Are there any other photos?"

She shrugged. "I haven't had a chance to go through that stuff. This was on top."

"Looks like important papers. Some letters. We should take them with us to sort through later. I'd like to talk to Ethel's neighbors." Ben glanced out the window. Because they had opted to listen to the carolers, they'd lost some daylight. "I didn't pack supper and had planned on eating at one of the establishments in town before heading back."

Isabel's forehead bunched. "I thought we weren't going to remove anything."

"If we stay here any longer, we'll be forced to rent rooms for the night."

"My sisters would be worried."

"As soon as we're finished with Ethel's belongings, I'll mail them to the sheriff and he can bring them back out here."

She agreed to his plan. Ben did a final check of the house before carrying the box outside and putting it into his saddlebag. They rode to the farm they'd passed earlier and spoke with the owners. The couple confirmed that Ethel had grandchildren but said they hadn't seen Annie or Harry in a while. Apparently Ethel had become a recluse in recent years. She'd paid a young man to fetch her items from town and assist around the farm, but he turned out to be a swindler.

Ben and Isabel thanked them for their time. What was supposed to be a quick meal in town turned out to be an ordeal that lasted an hour and a half. The harried waitress failed to place their order and then served chicken that was too tough to eat. The proprietor had apologized and set things right, but it had cost them traveling time. The sun had long since dipped below the mountain ridges when they started the trek back to Gatlinburg. As darkness blanketed the countryside and stars began blinking in the expanse above, cold seeped into his bones. He glanced at Isabel riding alongside. She was an indistinct form on horseback, her cloak's hood covering her head and her scarf pulled up over her chin.

"You okay?"

"Thinking about Annie, is all. How did she wind up

in Quinn's store? Was she married to Eli's father? How is Harry involved?"

"The neighbors might've been more informative if Ethel hadn't avoided contact."

Conversation dropped away as they rode in companionable silence for a few minutes. "I don't know how you do it," she finally said.

He turned his head to meet her gleaming gaze. "Do what?"

"Your job. I'm discovering it's harder than it looks."

He smiled for the first time since embarking on this trip. "You thought all I did was amble through the streets with my weapon on display, didn't you?"

"I don't know what I thought," she said seriously, "but this isn't it."

The terrain steepened, and he focused on guiding Blaze up the bumpy lane. "I can't promise you the perfect outcome, Isabel. I wish I could, but I've learned that these matters often can't be wrapped up in a tidy bow. Life is messy and unpredictable. Some puzzles are never solved."

"Thank you for caring about Eli. You didn't have to go to all this trouble, especially with Shane out of town."

"He's a special little boy." He shrugged, striving for nonchalance. "Be tough *not* to care." *About him or you.*

By the time the gristmill came into view, Ben was exhausted. Isabel advised him to go home, and he was debating the wisdom of that. If anything happened to her or the others because he'd chosen the comfort of his own bed, he'd never forgive himself. This many weeks after their run-in with Theron, it wasn't likely he'd come after her. Not likely, but still possible.

"Whose horses are those?" Isabel's strained question shattered the silence.

Beyond the darkened hut, lights blazed from the cabin windows, and a pair of horses waited out front.

"This isn't the typical hour to host visitors," he said, apprehension building.

"I hope it's nothing serious."

While she was worried about Eli, Ben was coming to a different conclusion. It was possible someone had need of his services and, considering he'd been seen with Isabel and Eli about town recently, had thought to search for him here. Whoever was inside that cabin would wonder what he and Isabel were doing coming home in the wee hours of the morning.

Leaving their horses with the others, he followed her inside, his gut clenching at the sight of Myron Gallatin and his pa, Sal. Their shared smirks weren't lost on Ben. They wouldn't let this opportunity to stir up trouble pass them by.

"Evenin', Deputy." Myron made a point to check his pocket watch. "Or should I say good morning?"

Isabel's anxiety gave way to white-hot outrage. How dare these men intrude upon her home and compel her sisters to entertain them until Ben's return? Honor's features were pinched, her eyes bloodshot. At Isabel's entrance, they'd both sprung up from the sofa, shoulders sagging with relief.

Honor noticed her glance at her bedroom door. "Eli's sleeping."

Rounding the side table, she halted in between the fireplace, where Myron lounged with his arm across the mantel, and the rocking chair occupied by his father. "Why are you here?"

Sal's mouth flattened with displeasure at her abrupt manner. Pushing upright, he ignored her, his granite gaze zeroing in on Ben. "I've got a problem out at my lumber-yard, Deputy. Someone broke into my office. I searched for you in town and came up empty." He smirked. "Then my boy here reminded me how much time you'd been spending with the Flores family of late, so we decided to pay them a visit."

Myron let his arm slip off the mantel. His gaze, sliding between her and Ben, held a mean streak. "Thought it was my imagination playing tricks on me when I saw MacGregor leaving your property the other morning. Then Carmen here told us he's been staying here since early December. Not a smart move for someone who'd prefer to stay out of the gossip mill."

"My presence here has been strictly in a professional capacity." Positioned near the door, he stood with his hands on his hips, weapon in clear view. He looked mad enough to spit nails. "It's long past a decent hour to keep these ladies from their sleep. Let's discuss the particulars of your dilemma outside." He opened the door and waited, silently daring them to defy him.

Sal jerked his head in Ben's direction. "Let's go."

Before they could exit, Ben blocked their way. "Aren't you forgetting something?"

Myron rolled his eyes before dipping at the waist. "Thank you kindly for your hospitality, ladies."

Isabel didn't move as father and son trudged onto the porch. Ben's gaze sought her out, and he mouthed, *I'm sorry.* Tugging on his hat's brim, he murmured a good-night and closed the door. Honor hurried over to lower the latch.

"Please forgive me, Isa." Carmen flopped onto the cushions and shoved her unruly hair out of her eyes. "I didn't mean to let it slip, but they were here for so long and you know how the silence makes me nervous—"

Fatigue washing over her, Isabel sat beside her. "It's not your fault."

Honor peeked through the curtains. "Hateful men. I was near the end of my rope, I tell you. I was almost to the point of getting *Abuelita*'s broom and shooing them out of here."

"How long were they here?"

Carmen shuddered. "About an hour and a half. That Myron makes my skin crawl."

Honor let the curtain fall into place. Joining them, she perched on the sofa's edge. "Isa, I think they'll take pleasure in spreading this news."

"I agree. But we have nothing to be ashamed of."

"What will everyone say?" Carmen leaned forward. "No one knows of the danger you've been in. They'll draw conclusions."

"Wrong ones," Honor added darkly.

The same smothering feeling that any threat of scandal kindled came over her. Reminding herself she had to be strong for her sisters, she projected a false calm. "I'm sure a solution will present itself. Right now, I'm too tired to think. Let's get a good night's sleep and discuss this in the morning."

They both agreed and trudged off to their room. Isabel checked the yard and was relieved to find it empty. Although she had plenty to occupy her thoughts, she fell asleep almost instantly.

The late night caused them to oversleep Sunday morning, and they bustled about trying to complete chores, eat breakfast and dress for services.

On the way out the door, she tapped Eli's shoulder. "You need a haircut, young man."

"I don't like haircuts." His bright demeanor fading, he hung on the post beside the steps. "Mama said I didn't have to if I didn't want to."

Isabel pictured the photograph of a young Annie and Harry. *What happened to you and your baby, Annie?*

Honor stopped beside him. "You don't see Ben going around with unruly hair, do you?"

Eli shook his head.

"I'd say he'd even be willing to accompany you to the barber if you ask."

His blue gaze swung to Isabel. "Can we ask him today?"

Surrounded by churchgoers who'd soon hear how Ben had brought her home at an indecent hour? No, thanks.

"If not today, then we'll see about paying him a visit tomorrow."

Eli seemed to accept that answer, for he hopped down the steps and across the yard to the wagon. Carmen closed the door and, coming alongside Isabel, gave her a reassuring squeeze.

"It's going to be okay. Even if tales do get around, you're strong enough to handle it with grace. It's what you've been doing for as long as I can remember. I haven't ever told you, Isa…" Her eyes glistened, and she blinked. "Thank you. For everything. You're my hero."

Emotion clogged her throat. She hugged her back. "I love you, *hermana*."

"I love you, too. And I don't want you to worry about Honor's leaving. I don't plan on getting hitched for many years to come."

Their conversation was cut short by their sister's impatient bid for them to hurry. Carmen rolled her eyes. "She can't bear to be apart from her precious John for more than a few hours at a time."

"That's not it." Honor's eyes narrowed. "I don't like walking in late, and you know it."

During the brief trip to church, Isabel warded off further arguments by peppering Honor with questions about her upcoming nuptials. All three fell silent, however, when they rode into the yard. Thankfully, no one sent them scandalized glances or stared in stark disapproval. But it was early yet. Myron and his pa hadn't had time to spread their venom.

Lord Jesus, help me please. I'm not as strong as Carmen thinks. I need You.

They chose their usual seats in the last pew on the right side of the aisle. As in the yard, they weren't met with undue curiosity. It appeared she'd been granted a reprieve. One that was short-lived, unfortunately. As soon as the hymns had been sung, the reverend made an announcement that made her head begin to pound.

"Before we begin, Deputy MacGregor has an announcement to make."

Eli was perched in Isabel's lap. Her arms went stiff where she held him, and he angled his face up to hers in silent question. She gave him a reassuring smile and ordered her body to relax. Maybe this had nothing to do with her. Maybe—

"Good morning, folks."

Handsome in his black suit, his copper hair damp and slicked off his forehead, Ben faced the crowd with his natural confidence. His vivid gaze touched on each pew, jarring to a halt when it landed on her. He gave a slight nod. Isabel's mouth went dry. Had anyone noticed?

"I have a confession," he said. "One that will hopefully clear up a recent misunderstanding."

His attention on her didn't waver. Her first impulse was to shout at him to stop. Her second was to gather Eli in her arms and rush from the building. She did neither. Like everyone else in attendance, she sat in rapt silence waiting for him to continue.

Chapter Twenty

A hush descended on the crowd. Some exchanged curious glances. Other scooted to the edge of their seats, intent on capturing every word. Isabel remained as still as
a statue, a misleading facade considering her heart thun-
dered against her ribs and she felt woozy.

"First of all, I'd like to thank everyone for the patience
and support you've extended in light of Shane's absence."

"You're doing great, Deputy," someone called out.

"We love you, Ben!" A female admirer, of course.

Ben flashed a smile, the affable, charming one she
hadn't seen for quite some time. But there was no accompanying twinkle in his eyes this time.

"You are aware of the attempted bank robbery that occurred at the beginning of the month. At the time, I made
a decision to leave out a pertinent piece of the puzzle."

Murmurs and whispers shredded the silence. A couple
of rows in front of Isabel, Grant Parker shifted in his seat
and cast her a quick glance over his shoulder. The brush
of his blue gaze spoke of understanding and empathy. *He
knew.* Not surprising, she supposed, considering he was
Ben's closest friend. Apart from the fact Grant was a devoted husband, they had a lot in common.

"I've come to realize that might not have been the best decision." His expression grave, he slipped his hands in his pockets. "The fact is, I wasn't alone in that alleyway. There was the thief, me and someone else." Honor laid her hand on Isabel's shoulder. Ben's focus swerved to her. His eyes begged her to understand. "Someone whose bravery astounds me, in both this life-threatening situation and in ordinary, everyday life. That person is Isabel Flores."

Audible gasps bounced against the walls. Pews creaked as every single person there turned to stare at her. Feeling as if she were in a dream—or nightmare, depending on how one looked at it—Isabel couldn't bring herself to meet those stares. She fixed her gaze on Ben like a drowning person clinging to a rope.

"Isabel is the one who foiled the robbery. Isabel confronted the criminal, who we now know is Theron Franklin. I happened upon the scene, and Theron would've dragged her off if not for her quick thinking."

Undoubtedly confused by all the attention, Eli twisted and buried his face in her shoulder. She rubbed soothing circles on his back.

"She didn't ask me to omit her role. I did it without consulting her. I was trying to protect her privacy, but in doing so, I accomplished the opposite of what I intended. You see, because of the danger Theron posed—she's the only one who saw him without a mask—I decided to remain on the Flores farm. I've spent many nights over the last weeks in their warming hut." Most of the crowd resumed their front-facing positions so they could watch Ben. "Yesterday, Isabel and I made a quick trip to Pigeon Forge. Turns out Theron is continuing his crime spree."

Conversations broke out across the high-ceilinged room. Ben held up his hand in a bid for silence. When that didn't work, he lifted his fingers to his mouth and let loose a piercing whistle. "Ladies and gentlemen, let me assure you, I will do everything humanly possible to protect our town."

"When you're not protecting the miller, you mean." The snide remark came from none other than Sal Gallatin. Isabel's cheeks burned.

Ben ignored him. "In order for me to do this, I'll need everyone's cooperation. I've got Theron's likeness on this wanted poster. I'd like you all to familiarize yourselves and be on the lookout." He withdrew a paper from his suit pocket, unfolded it and held it aloft. "On a different matter, if anyone here has any information regarding a man named Harry Howell, please see me after the service. Thank you for your time."

Ben shot Isabel one final look before taking a seat on the first row. Carmen leaned close to whisper in her ear. "See? That wasn't so bad."

The reverend's words washed over Isabel in an unintelligible hum. Her body thrummed with the urge to flee. She couldn't foster anger toward Ben. He'd evaluated their options and decided this was the best course of action. By making his announcement, he'd lessened any damage Sal and Myron's tales would've wrought. It was the calculated move of an experienced lawman, yet the picture he'd painted cast her in the best possible light.

If she hadn't been lost in thought, she would've noticed the reverend was wrapping up his sermon. She would've slipped out the door during the final prayer. Too late, the rustle of skirts and thud of boots on weathered wood signaled the service's end, and Isabel found herself surrounded by people eager to praise her courageous act.

Not everyone paused to chat, though. The Smith sisters flounced by without acknowledging her presence. The Pattons stuck to the far wall, bypassing the gathered throng around her pew. At the glint of pale blond hair, Isabel caught sight of Veronica following in her parents' wake. She glanced toward the front, to where Ben stood in conversation with the reverend and his wife, and an expression of intense longing tightened her features.

Isabel felt sorry for the other woman. Before spending time with Ben, she wouldn't have understood. Now she could commiserate. Ben wasn't the type of man to inspire gentle, staid feelings. He was the flesh-and-blood representation of every girl's hero. But did Veronica and the others realize he wasn't invincible? Had they discovered, like she had, that his hadn't been a charmed life? That he'd suffered hurts and disappointments? That he was lonely?

She'd stood in that barren, pitiful cabin he called home and ached for him. He might claim to prefer solitude, but he didn't actually seek it, did he? He made a point to avoid eating at that table set for one. When he wasn't dining amid the Plum's customers, he joined various families across town. He'd eagerly accepted any and all invitations to dine with her and her sisters. He thrived on the company of others. His claims of embracing bachelorhood were a front. Isabel wondered if the opposite was true…did he in fact long to be a husband and father? And if so, why would he go to such great lengths to pretend otherwise?

She was still wrestling with the troubling thoughts when Ben sauntered over and greeted her and Eli, who'd moved to the seat beside her. He'd gotten sleepy during the service and, to combat that, had begun to play with his toy horse.

Most everyone had left the building, including Honor and Carmen.

"Are you upset with me?" His gaze was intent.

"No, but you could've warned me."

"There wasn't time." His eyes darkened, braced as if for battle. "Was anyone rude or condescending?"

"Quite the opposite, thanks to you."

He relaxed. "I told the truth, nothing more."

He'd held her up as an exceptional example of bravery, when she'd actually been reacting out of desperation.

"Did anyone talk to you about Harry?"

"Unfortunately, no. That doesn't mean no one will approach me in a less public place. There's still a chance." He shifted his stance. "Listen, you may not like this, but I've shared what we learned yesterday with Grant. His work as a marshal gives him valuable insight into cases like these. They've invited us to eat with them, and I think we should go."

"I know you're close friends with them, but why me?"

"We can talk to Grant together. Get his advice." He noticed her sideways glance. "Eli's invited, too, Isabel. You're a pair. A package."

Because she was hungry for answers, she found herself in the Parkers' home a half an hour later. Jessica made Isabel and Eli feel welcome, treating them as if they were frequent guests. While the men situated the horses in the barn, Jessica enlisted Eli's help in preparing the table. Isabel set to work, as well, slicing up the roast while her hostess transferred vegetables and rolls to serving dishes.

When they were in place around the table and enjoying the delicious meal, Grant proved a competent host, keeping the conversation light and interesting. He was a considerate man, as astute as he was handsome. That he included Eli when many adults would've ignored him sealed Isabel's high opinion of Ben's closest friend. His obvious devotion to his wife filled Isabel with a curious yearning for something she'd long spurned…a loving husband of her own.

She'd known that not every family was as miserable as hers had been. She'd seen evidence that some marriages thrived. Being in Grant and Jessica's home, talking with them, witnessing their happiness up close, pierced her already thin armor.

Ben caught her staring at the couple—how could she not, when their love and devotion practically permeated the air around them—and lifted his brows in question.

Isabel dropped her gaze to her plate. How embarrassing if he guessed the truth. She struggled to combat the intimacy of the situation, the false sense of connectedness she felt with him. They weren't here together because they were courting. They were here on official business. She'd do well to remember that.

He'd never held a sleeping child.

Ben shifted to a more comfortable position on the cushions, one arm anchored around Eli. The ladies had insisted on clearing off the table and suggested they retire to the living room to wait for dessert and coffee. Almost as soon as Ben had claimed a spot on one end of the delicate new settee, the boy had climbed onto his lap and laid his head on his chest. For a split second, Ben had gone still, his breath frozen in his lungs. Eli's initial reticence had waned, but he hadn't exhibited this level of trust before. It hadn't taken him long to doze off. The simple act had humbled Ben, and his protective instincts had intensified.

"You're a natural with him, you know."

Seated on one of two matching chairs angled toward the settee, Grant crossed his arms over his chest, stretched out his legs and hooked one ankle over the other.

Ben leveled him a warning glare, but he wasn't deterred.

"It's the truth," he said innocently. "Anyone can see that a bond has formed between you."

"I have a responsibility to see that he's taken care of."

Grant narrowed his gaze. "You're forgetting who you're talking to."

Eli's soft curls tickled the underside of Ben's chin, and he released a heavy sigh. "You're right, he's more than that."

The ladies' muted chatter filtered in from the kitchen. Satisfied he wouldn't be overheard, he said, "I care about what happens to him."

"You care about him," Grant countered. "And he's not the only one you care about."

Ben had no way of escape, not without disturbing Eli. "You can stop now."

"Ben, listen to me—"

"This subject isn't up for discussion. Nothing has changed."

Ben studied their decorated tree in the corner. The edges of the gold foil ornaments faded, the colors blurring together. He *had* developed feelings for Isabel. But he wasn't so far gone that he couldn't recover what ground he'd lost. Someday he'd settle Eli's guardianship and he'd walk away. He'd adjust to seeing Isabel and the boy on Sundays and occasionally in town. He'd watch over them from afar. And if Shane came back before this case was solved, then Ben would hand it over to him.

"You're the most hardheaded person I know," Grant said, his frustration unmistakable.

Footsteps announced the ladies' approach. Jessica bore a tray with a tea service and cups. Behind her, Isabel balanced a stack of plates and handful of forks. Her dark eyes soaked in the sight of Eli asleep on his lap and softened with unnamable emotion.

"Who's hardheaded?" Jessica inquired as Grant leaped up to assist her. "Surely you weren't talking about Ben. That would've been like the pot calling the kettle black."

Chuckling, Grant centered the tray on the low table. Jessica retrieved the dessert.

Catching Ben's wide-eyed gaze, Isabel said, "Looks like a work of art, doesn't it? Jessica called it a coconut flummery."

Jessica's smile was modest. "It's an old recipe that dates to the War Between the States. Sponge cake on the bottom, topped with custard and then meringue mixed with coconut shreds. Time-consuming, but not difficult."

Ben shook his head. "You spoil him, you know that?"

Instead of refuting it, the couple grinned at each other.

"Would you like me to take him so you can eat?" Isabel said, gesturing to Eli.

"I don't mind waiting. Besides, he's comfortable where he is."

"Yes, he certainly seems so." She looked thoughtful.

Jessica doled out the pieces, setting aside one for Ben. They discussed the upcoming Christmas play and the celebrations the O'Malleys had planned. Halfway through her dessert, Jessica got a strange look and covered her mouth.

Grant shifted forward to place his cup on the table. "What's the matter?"

"I—" She abruptly shot to her feet. "Excuse me."

She rushed to the kitchen and out the back door. Grant cast them a worried look. "I'll go check on her."

"Yes, of course, go."

Seated on the sofa with at least a foot of space between them, Isabel radiated confusion. "I wonder what's wrong. She seemed fine. In good spirits, even."

Ben knew the reason for Jessica's hasty dash outdoors… plenty of expectant women suffered from queasy constitutions. He looked over at Isabel, the urge to smooth the pleat marring her brow difficult to resist. She was wearing another somber blouse with matching drop earrings. She looked crisp, neat and schoolmarm prim. That was a veneer she wore to deter men's attentions. Ben had experienced firsthand the warm, ardent, at times spirited woman she truly was.

"I'm sure it's nothing serious."

She angled toward him. "Do you think it was something we ate?" Her raven brows dipped low. "I feel fine. Do you feel all right?"

He nodded. "There was nothing wrong with the food, Isa."

Grant reentered the house and poked his head into the living room. "She wanted me to tell you she got a bit overheated. I'm going to take her a damp cloth."

He bustled about the kitchen. When the door closed again, Isabel didn't attempt to hide her bafflement. "Overheated? It's forty degrees outside."

"Maybe she's hot natured?" He winced at the rise in his voice.

Isabel cocked her head to one side, her heavy black braid sliding across the cotton material. "You know something, don't you?"

He swallowed hard and smoothed a gentle hand over Eli's curls.

She rested her hand over her heart. "Please tell me there's nothing seriously wrong with her."

"Isabel—"

"Jessica's young and healthy. And Grant *adores* her. If anything were to happen to her—"

"She's pregnant."

The words spilled out of his mouth in a bald statement.

"Oh." Her eyes went wide.

Ben watched the news sink in. Wonder and surprise shifted to wistfulness. His throat constricted. She shared the same aspirations as almost every other woman on the planet.

* * *

"Tell me something. If you were to find a man who was able to meet your lofty standards, how many would you want?"

Something painful shadowed her face. "I'm not getting married, remember?"

"Humor me."

"Three," she said shyly, her focus on Eli. "Maybe four."

Ben nodded as if her admission hadn't gutted him. "What about you?"

Me? Oh, I can't have children. I'm sterile.

"I'm in the same boat at you. I'm a bachelor for life."

"But if you were to meet a woman worth giving up your freedom for?"

I already have. She deserves a whole man, one who can give her what I can't.

Since his reality was zero, he threw out an unlikely answer. "Six. Eight. Ten. The more the merrier."

Isabel went still. "You're serious?"

The problem was he could picture a life with her. Him, Isabel and Eli. A houseful of fat babies, chubby-cheeked toddlers and attention-hungry kids. Ben's arm tightened around Eli. Or not. For a man who couldn't have *any* children, one would be a precious gift.

"You want the honest truth? I'd be grateful for any God chose to give me."

Chapter Twenty-One

"This is interesting." Carmen waved the letter to get their attention. "Ethel's sister, Hazel, is questioning her about the lad she hired to help around the farm. Seems Ethel doesn't trust him and is worried about his blossoming interest in her granddaughter."

Isabel's gaze clashed with Ben's. He and Honor were seated on the opposite side of the table from her and Carmen. While the adults pored through Ethel's belongings—mostly letters from relatives and official documents—Eli drew pictures of stick figures and hummed the carols they'd sung in church that morning. He seemed to like music. If he expressed interest in learning to play an instrument, who would she get to teach him? Would she have enough money to purchase said instrument and pay for lessons? Questions like these were popping into her mind with increasing frequency. She tried to combat the doubts. While she might not be able to provide him with every opportunity, she would love and guide him to the best of her ability.

"We've established that his name is Wesley, right?" Honor paused in the reading of a different letter. "But we don't have a last name."

Ben drummed his fingers on the smooth wood. "The neighbors we spoke with indicated he turned out to be less than honorable."

"What confuses me is the sheriff indicated Ethel didn't have family in the area," Isabel said. "When and how did Annie and Harry come to be in Pigeon Forge? Were their parents with them?"

Honor sighed and refolded the paper. "This one doesn't have any pertinent information."

"On to the next." Ben handed her another from the pile, an air of determination shimmering about him. He'd shed his suit coat and tie, leaving his pin-striped shirt open at the throat. He'd rolled his sleeves up almost to his elbow. Isabel's gaze kept returning to his exposed neck, smooth and sun kissed. Below the open collar, in the V of his shirt, his skin was paler. Like flawless, sculpted marble, except his flesh wasn't cold and unforgiving. He was incandescent heat and suppressed strength. Sunlight slanting through the window picked up the mahogany tint of his forearm hairs. Isabel's fingers itched to touch the corded muscle, test the width of his wrists, trace the outline of his square hands. He was mere inches away in physical terms, but there was a chasm she couldn't cross.

Talking to Ben about fictional children hadn't been wise. He'd meant to shock her with his outrageous answer. Instead, he'd blasted open a cavern of curiosity and deep-seated longing. Why would he feel the need to do such a thing? More than ever before, she was certain she'd misjudged him and was only now unveiling layers of the Debonair Deputy he'd prefer to keep hidden. They weren't so very different, after all. They both projected personas that didn't reflect their true hearts. She knew her reasons. What were his? He'd rejected the suggestion it had anything to do with his former fiancée. Maybe he wasn't being forthcoming. Perhaps he'd been hurt so badly he couldn't bring himself to speak of it. Because what else could it be?

He noticed her staring and frowned, twin lines carved on either side of his mouth. The gathering at the Parkers' had put a strain on him as well, it appeared. When they'd left Grant and Jessica's two hours ago, she'd craved a break from the confusing emotions Ben evoked. And he'd been quieter than usual. Instead of retreating to his cabin, however, he'd suggested they search for answers. Having her sisters assisting them made the work go faster. More importantly, they weren't alone.

Seated beside her at the table's end, Eli stopped coloring. "When do I get to read?"

Isabel smiled. "After Christmas, I'd be happy to teach you letters and numbers. Would you like that?"

He nodded and went back to drawing. Although she sensed Ben's perusal, she didn't meet his gaze. Silence descended as they resumed reading. The occasional crumbling of a log in the fireplace mingled with the clock ticking and the scrape of Eli's pencils across the tabletop.

A low whistle escaped Ben's lips. "Ethel had a propensity to vent her frustrations with friends and family across the south. Listen to this from Corrinne Johnson in Georgia. 'I'm as appalled as you are by young people's easy dismissal of moral codes, not to mention the Lord's commandments. To think your own granddaughter was duped by a charming liar is unbearable. Whatever will you do?'"

Carmen snatched the letter from his hand and skimmed the contents. "Wesley was successful in pursuing Annie." Her brown eyes danced with the thrill of discovery. "He's got to be you-know-who's father."

"Certainly sounds plausible." Honor glanced at Eli. "A last name would be useful."

Ben agreed. "First thing tomorrow, I'll send a telegram

to the sheriff and ask him to do some further digging for us. There are neighbors we didn't talk to."

"It's a starting point."

Isabel had received a reply yesterday from the lawyer Lucian had recommended. As expected, he'd advised her to gather as much information on Eli's parentage and his guardian as possible before pursuing legal guardianship.

They pored through the rest of Ethel's things but found no further clues. There was no way to know if Wesley married Annie or whether or not he was the father of her second child. Ben was disappointed but undeterred. He planned to ride into the more isolated coves the next day. To Isabel's annoyance, he refused to allow her to accompany him.

On the matter of his staying the night, he heeded her wishes and went home. Theron was miles away. Weeks had passed since their run-in, and he hadn't sought her out as they'd both feared. She was safe. Ben's guard services were no longer necessary.

The moment he'd gone, Isabel sagged against the door, a combination of relief and melancholy washing over her. He wasn't supposed to have this effect on her. He wasn't supposed to have single-handedly dismantled her solid stance against marriage, replacing cynicism and bitterness with brilliant, tantalizing hope.

Her sisters left Eli playing on the rug to interrogate her.

"What's going on between you two?" Honor looked concerned.

"I don't know." The state of her heart was a mystery. Her life's course, which had been pretty much set since her father's scandalous death, had veered into dangerous territory.

"You both need to cease being stubborn and confess your love. Then you can marry him, move into his cabin and leave the family farm to me." Wearing a triumphant grin, Carmen fluttered her hands to encompass their surroundings.

Isabel's jaw sagged. "You're *eighteen*. What makes you think you can run this farm and gristmill by yourself?"

Honor gave a disbelieving laugh. "That's the part you're protesting, Isa?"

Carmen's expression turned smug. "Good point. Why *aren't* you denying you love the deputy?"

Panic seized her. She couldn't have been so imprudent as to have developed feelings for Ben. Pushing past them, she said, "This is a ridiculous conversation."

"She's retreating," Carmen said in a dramatic whisper, "which means we've hit the nail on the head."

"Isa, wait. Hear me out." Honor caught her elbow. "There's no shame in admitting you were mistaken."

"Mistaken about what?" she huffed.

"Many things. Life. Marriage. What it means to care about someone, to be committed to that person's happiness."

"What exactly are you saying?"

"That you've fallen for Ben and the prospect of being his wife both thrills and frightens you."

"His wife?" Pulse racing, her heart rejecting Honor's claims, she shook her head. "You're wrong, *hermana*. The happiness you've found with John is coloring your thinking. I'm not dreaming about wedded bliss with the Debonair Deputy!"

"Perhaps not with the Debonair Deputy," she agreed. "But what about Ben MacGregor?"

Carmen's nose scrunched up. "You're not making any sense."

Honor made a dismissive gesture. "Isa understands what I'm saying, don't you?"

She sagged against the sofa, unable to meet her sisters' gazes. Honor was right. She might not have been in danger of falling for the suave charmer, but the thoughtful, caring, valiant white knight who epitomized service to others? That man, the one behind the badge, was impossible to disregard.

"He's not interested in marriage or family," she said quietly.

Honor rubbed Isabel's arm. "Take heart, dear sister. You're proof that stubbornness doesn't have to be a lifelong ailment."

He'd never taken a child to get a haircut before.

Eli was introducing him to a whole new world of firsts.

Ben crouched before the terrified boy and attempted to assuage his fears. "You see these men? They're here to get their hair trimmed like you."

Every seat in the barbershop was occupied, and every customer was riveted to the scene playing out before them. He could've done without the audience.

Eli's eyebrows crumpled above worried blue eyes. To a four-year-old, the array of shaving razor blades and pointy scissors would be intimidating, especially if he hadn't had a professional cut.

"I wanna go home."

Ben dismissed the weight of the others' curiosity. Losing his patience wouldn't benefit anyone. "I have an idea. How about I sit in the chair and you sit on my lap while the kind barber here fixes you up right?"

Eli tilted his head back and contemplated the amused white-haired man waiting by the chair.

"I've got steady hands," he said. "See?" He held out his age-spotted hands for Eli to inspect.

Ben squeezed his shoulder. "You're safe with me, Eli. I won't let anyone hurt you."

He transferred those big blue eyes to Ben. "Okay."

Feeling as if he'd won a major skirmish, Ben grinned and sat down. When he patted his thigh, Eli scrambled onto his lap. One of the men winked at Ben and the rest beamed in approval, as if he was part of that exclusive group called fatherhood. The barber draped a towel over each of them and started chatting about boyhood adventures on his family farm. To Ben's surprise, Eli didn't squirm or try to evade the scissors. When his curls were gone, he stared for long minutes into the mirror.

"What do you think, little man?" Ben prompted.

The barber smoothed a nice-smelling pomade on his brown hair. "I, for one, think you look fine and dandy."

A slow smile appeared on Eli's face. Ben winked at the barber. "Looks like we have our answer."

They hadn't taken more than a couple of steps from the shop before encountering Isabel. She exclaimed over Eli's spiffy new look.

"Here to check up on us?" Ben said.

She straightened and motioned over her shoulder. "I had to mail a package. My last order of knives before Christmas. Now that I'm here, you can go about your business."

He pointed to the Plum Café on the opposite side of the street. "First I have to fulfill my promise. I told Eli I'd treat him to a slice of pie."

Her raven brows hit her hairline. "Before the noon meal?"

"It won't hurt this once. A big glass of milk will balance it out."

Eli slipped his hand in Isabel's. "Can we go, Isa?"

"I'm not sure…"

Eli bounced on his tiptoes. "Please?"

"Fine. You win." She tapped his nose. "Dessert before lunch it is."

As they crossed the street, folks greeted them with frank curiosity. Ben knew they looked like a normal family. Mother, father and child out running errands. If only he could offer Isabel a shot at a normal life. The regret he'd wrestled with for six years threatened to smother him.

I thought I'd laid these dreams to rest years ago, Lord.

The last few weeks in Isabel and Eli's company had taught him his error.

I thought I had finally accepted my solitary path. Like the apostle Paul wrote in Philippians, I've learned to be content no matter the circumstances. But Isabel has caused me to feel things I've never felt. She's special, Lord. But then, I don't have to tell You that.

The Plum Café was a cheerful space. The sunlight-yellow curtains and tablecloths, anchored by green glass lamps, lent the dining room a springlike air. The new look was Ellie Copeland's doing. The pregnant widow, hired to fill the cook's position, had altered more than just the café. She'd transformed the reclusive owner, too. Now she and Alexander were ensconced in wedded bliss and hopefully enjoying their visit to his family's Texas ranch.

Ben looked forward to their safe return. Ellie's baby was due in March, and he worried about how such a daunting journey might affect her. Of course, Alexander was devoted to his wife's well-being and couldn't wait to be a father. He'd indicated they would make multiple stops along the way to give her a chance to rest.

"Good morning, Ben." Sally Hatcher, the waitress he'd had a not-quite relationship with, greeted him with a breezy smile. A new beau had erased any lingering pique she might feel. "Your usual table is occupied."

His old habit of flattery and teasing didn't come as naturally as it used to. Maybe because he was wrapped up in hopeless longing for the woman at his side?

"That's all right, Sally. How about that table beside the fireplace?" He nodded to the far corner.

"It's all yours."

About half the tables were occupied by folks lingering over a late breakfast. They watched Ben, Isabel and Eli with the same interest Sally displayed. He supposed the sight of Gatlinburg's most determined bachelor and headstrong spinster would arouse questions. Seemed to him it'd be obvious that Eli was the reason for their continued association.

Blond braids swaying, Sally brought the adults coffee and a glass of milk for Eli. Soon, hefty slices of Christmas cake were set before them. Studded with almonds and dried fruit, the cake was as colorful as an ornamented tree.

Ben lifted his fork. "With Ellie out of town, who's doing the baking?"

"Jane and Jessica."

"And how's Flo doing with the rest of the meals?"

"Not so bad. Alexander hired someone to help out." She blew her bangs out of her eyes. "So far, no one's complaining." Sally shifted her attention to Isabel. "How's your cake? Need more cream for that coffee?"

Isabel had been pensive since their arrival. She smiled and shook her head. "No cream, thank you. And the cake's delicious."

"Mine's delishush, too," Eli announced, some of it smeared atop his upper lip.

Isabel's tension melted as they shared a laugh. The door opened, letting in a waft of frigid air, and Sally went to greet the customers. Feminine voices drifted ever closer. When Isabel frowned, Ben twisted in his seat and saw Lynette and Laila Smith bearing down on them.

The sisters stationed themselves at his elbow. They wore matching black coats with fluffy ermine collars and bonnets boasting white and black feathers tucked beneath a wide swath of red ribbon. Their almond-shaped eyes blasted him with reproach.

Laila swatted his arm. "Ben MacGregor, you've been a naughty man."

Lynette bobbed her head with such force her feathers flapped like wings in the breeze. "It isn't like you to neglect your obligations." Her hazel gaze slid to Isabel and Eli, cool disdain gracing her features.

Isabel's expression was devoid of emotion. In the chair beside her, Eli chewed more slowly, his eyes big in his face.

Ben wiped his mouth with his napkin. "You'll have to remind me what it is I've done."

"It's what you *haven't* done." Laila's chin jutted. "It wounds me that you've forgotten our Sunday evening ritual."

"It wounds me, too, dear sister." Lynette placed her gloved hand atop Laila's. "I'm certain the good deputy has a perfectly good excuse."

They looked at him in expectation. He realized they were waiting for him to charm his way into their good graces. They'd be waiting a long time.

"I admit our traditional game night escaped my attention. As you're no doubt aware, the past few weeks have kept me busy. I hope you'll accept my deepest apology."

They exchanged perplexed glances. "Of course we understand the burden that's been placed upon you," Laila rushed out. "We will be patient until you can resume your social activities."

"Ladies, I'm afraid our weekly visits must come to an end."

The color drained from Laila's cheeks. "Surely not!"

"We didn't intend to back you into a corner." Lynette sputtered. "Is this your doing, Miss Flores?"

"Absolutely not—"

"Oh, but it is," Ben smoothly inserted, folding his arms over his chest. "I have you to thank for my new approach to bachelorhood, remember?"

Isabel gasped. "Me? What have I to do with your marital status?"

His gaze bounced between the sisters. "Isabel opened my eyes to the fact that, despite my stated intentions, I've given Gatlinburg's eligible ladies the wrong impression." Sensing their disbelief, he hung his head. "I may as well make an announcement." Pushing his chair back, he stood and addressed the room's occupants. "Ladies and gentlemen, let it be known that the Debonair Deputy is no more. I'm a committed bachelor. It's time I started living like one."

The occupants' reactions ranged from humorous incredulity to approval. What he hadn't expected was for his announcement to cause anyone to swoon. Laila's eyes rolled back in her head and, if it weren't for Lynette's quick thinking, she would've hit the floor in a dead faint.

Chapter Twenty-Two

"I can't believe you caused a girl to swoon." Grant's eyes danced with laughter. "I mean, I knew girls were apt to act a tad daft around you, but this takes the cake."

"I'm not to blame here. I can hardly be expected to control a lady's constitution."

He scraped his hand along his jaw. "Noted. But I can't imagine this went over well with Isabel."

Blaze shifted beneath Ben, and he smoothed his hand along his neck. They'd been waiting in this copse near the abandoned hunter's shack for ten minutes, and both he and his horse were raring to get moving. Ben was determined to search out every cove, every mountainside homestead in his quest for answers. Someone had to have seen Harry Howell, maybe even befriended him. The number of locals who eschewed town life was adequate enough to prove daunting. It was a challenge not to let this task, akin to searching for a needle in a haystack, overwhelm him.

"Isabel didn't stick around long enough for me ascertain her state of mind."

Ben had leaped into action the moment Laila went down, calling for damp cloths and removing his jacket to form a pillow for her head. By the time he'd gotten her settled in a chair with a bracing cup of tea, Isabel and Eli were gone.

Grant guided his horse closer. "You're aware of what your announcement will lead people to believe, I presume."

"That I'm sticking with my convictions?"

"Nope. That you're besotted with Isabel and playing pa with Eli has finally won over the resolute deputy."

A bright red cardinal and his mate alighted on a branch near Ben's head. He shifted his gaze from the birds to the surrounding forest when the sound of hooves striking the hard earth registered through the trees. It gave Ben an excuse to ignore his friend's theory, which struck far too close to his heart's secret desire.

"Who exactly have we been waiting on, Parker?"

"See for yourself."

As the riders neared, he recognized them as members of the O'Malley clan, both born and married in. Brothers Josh, Nathan and Caleb. Their father, Sam. Lucian Beaumont, Megan's husband. Evan Harrison, husband of Juliana. Originally from the neighboring community of Cades Cove, Evan had moved his wife and kids to Gatlinburg last year so they could be close to her family. Former barbershop owner Tom Leighton, who was married to Jessica's twin sister, Jane. The only one missing was Nicole's husband, Quinn.

When they'd all exchanged greetings, Ben lifted his hand. "Thank you for coming." He spoke around a knot of gratitude. There was no question that the law-abiding citizens of Gatlinburg loved and supported their sheriff, Shane Timmons. To have that same level of support directed at him was humbling.

His mount positioned near the front of the group, Evan tugged his black Stetson lower over his eyes. "Grant told us about your case. We're happy to help."

"He threatened us with bodily harm if we didn't keep our traps shut." Nathan grinned, his teeth flashing white.

Caleb spoke up. "To be more precise, brother, he threated to sic our wives on us."

Josh shrugged. "Same thing."

The men shared a few chuckles. Grant snagged Ben's gaze. "Hope you don't mind their involvement. We needed more men, and you can count on them to be discreet."

"I'm grateful." He swept his arm in a wide arc. "We've got a lot of ground to cover. Your assistance is going to make my job easier."

He removed the photograph from his satchel and passed it around. "Harry was maybe fifteen or sixteen at the time this was taken. He will have matured, but the identifying scar above his right eyebrow should be visible."

When they'd all had a chance to view it, Lucian whirled his horse around. "Let's go knock on some doors, gentlemen."

They split up into pairs, leaving an odd man. Sam O'Malley chose to ride along with Josh and Caleb. After agreeing to a meeting time and location, they spread out in different directions. Ben and Grant took the southeast trail leading away from town. They visited numerous households. Some folks were helpful, others openly hostile. No one admitted knowing Harry.

It was nearing one o'clock when he and Grant ate their packed lunch on the lane's edge. The sun's warmth helped dispel some of early winter's grip.

Grant tossed his apple core to the ground. "I didn't get the sense that anyone was lying, did you?"

"No."

"Maybe the others are having better results."

Ben chewed the fresh-baked bread and ham Jessica had provided but didn't register the taste. Isabel was counting on him to find Harry so she could proceed with the guardianship. He wanted answers for her and Eli. That way they could celebrate Christmas free of worry.

Grant took a long draw on his canteen. Finished with his meal, Ben refolded the handkerchief and handed it to Grant.

"Thank your wife for the food."

"Will do."

They continued on their journey, traveling deeper into the mountains. By late afternoon, the cold stiffening his joints was matched by his disappointment.

"Let's call it a day," he told Grant.

A half mile from their meeting place, Evan and Caleb intercepted them.

"There's something you'll want to see, Deputy." A reserved man, Evan kept his opinions close to his vest. Today was no exception. Ben couldn't decipher if their discovery was good or bad. Caleb had already redirected his horse, so he was no help.

Grant shrugged and uttered a succinct command to his horse. They followed Evan and Caleb onto a rutted track that in summer would be overgrown with brush and weeds. Up ahead, Lucian and Nathan appeared to be standing guard over something while Sam and Josh remained astride their horses. Tom scouted out the area beyond them.

It soon became clear the men were guarding someone, not something. And that someone was sprawled on canvas-type bedding, weaving between sleep and wakefulness. Even without the empty whiskey bottle lying a few feet away, it wouldn't have taken great detective work to figure out the man was skunked. He reeked of alcohol.

Ben crouched on one side, Grant on the other.

"Looks like our man," he said.

"A dirtier, scruffier version," Ben agreed, eyeing the

hatless drunkard's unkempt hair and beard. There, clear as day, was the distinctive scar. They'd found Eli's guardian.

Reaching over, he jostled the man's shoulder. "Hello, Harry."

Christmas was in five days, and Isabel and her sisters, along with an ebullient Eli, were finally getting around to decorating a tree. As when they'd hung the evergreens, they were doing it without Ben, even though Eli asked about him every ten minutes and his absence depleted some of the joy from the experience. With each passing day, another piece of her heart was claimed by the lawman. She thought about him every moment he wasn't with her. And when he *was* around, she could hardly concentrate on anything besides him.

She thrust the needle through another piece of popcorn and poked her finger. Wincing, she sucked on the sore spot. *Is this what falling in love feels like?*

The renegade thought slammed into her. "Surely not."

"Surely not what?" On the opposite end of the sofa, Honor was assisting Eli with the cranberries.

"Never mind."

Carmen was returning with more popcorn when she veered toward one of the windows. "Someone's coming."

Isabel glanced at the mantel clock. "Are you expecting a visit from John this morning?"

Honor shook her head. "He didn't mention anything. Can you make out who it is?"

Clapping her hands together, Carmen whirled and grinned at Isabel. "It's the deputy."

"Ben's here?" Eli popped up and ran to the window, going on his tiptoes to try to see out.

Despite her racing heart, Isabel restrained herself from doing the same. Yesterday's scene at the café ran through her mind again. He hadn't needed to make a public announcement. He'd done it for her sake. To convince her he'd reformed? Or to remind her his commitment to bachelorhood was as strong as ever?

His familiar stride resounded on the porch, followed by a succinct rap. Isabel let Carmen and Eli greet him like lovesick puppies. She pretended to be preoccupied with her task.

"Ben!" From the corner of her eye, she saw Eli hold his arms aloft. "Are you here to help?"

Ben boosted him into his arms and followed the direction of Eli's pointing finger. "That's a mighty fine tree, little man. I'd love to help you, but I have important business to tend to."

Eli's lips pursed. "Deputy business?"

"That's right."

Ben's gaze settled on her, glowing with appreciation as he assessed her appearance. Isabel touched a finger to the paste jewel pin above her ear. She'd skipped the usual woven braid and opted to leave her long tresses free, held back on either side with matching hairpins. While her navy vest and accompanying white blouse weren't new, they fit her like a glove, and the pearl buttons added a feminine flair.

"Isabel." He cleared his throat and shifted Eli to his opposite side. "I need you to come with me."

His somber manner registered. Her stomach fell to her toes.

Eli placed his flattened palm on Ben's cheek. His easy way with the lawman tugged on her heartstrings. Isabel wouldn't be the only one who'd miss Ben once he withdrew from their life. And he would.

"Can I go, too?" Eli said.

Ben's smile was strained. "I wish you could, but Isabel and I have some adult matters to tend to."

Carmen held out her hands. "And Honor and I can't finish this tree without you."

He willingly went to her, his arms fastening around her neck.

Isabel set her things aside and, joining Ben at the door, put on her gloves and cloak. She bade her sisters goodbye and dropped a swift kiss on Eli's cheek, then accompanied Ben out into the bright day.

Blaze turned his head as if to appraise them, golden tail twitching.

"Where are we going?"

He lifted his hat off his head and ran his fingers through his short fiery locks. "We located Harry yesterday. He's currently cooling his heels in my jail."

"What? Where? Why am I just now finding out about it?"

He grimaced. "He wasn't in a state to be interviewed yesterday."

"What's that supposed to mean?"

"He was foxed, Isa. After leaving the Plum, Grant and I, with help from the O'Malley clan, searched the mountains. We'd just about given up when we stumbled across his campsite. He was sprawled on the ground, oblivious to the world."

Isabel covered her mouth. What kind of man had been taking care of Eli?

He gripped her shoulders. "Let's not jump to conclusions, all right? I haven't pressed him for details. I wanted to wait so we could question him together."

Touched by his thoughtfulness, she leaned in and hugged him. Beneath her cheek, his breathing hitched.

He hesitated a mere second before looping one arm low on her back.

"You okay?" he murmured.

She felt his fingers tangling in her hair. When he brushed his cheek against the side of her head and his lips stirred the loose strands, longing zipped through her like a bolt of lightning. Instead of burrowing closer, Isabel forced herself to step away.

"Isa?"

"I'm a little overwhelmed," she admitted, eyeing the ground. "I've prayed for a chance to confront Harry, and now that I have it..."

"It's normal to be nervous." He ran his knuckles gently along her cheek, the supple buckskin of his gloves a caress against her chilled skin. "I'll be with you the whole time."

"What's he like?"

He stepped back. "Quiet. Scared. Isabel, we found him with Warring's missing horse."

"Oh, no."

"He claims he was desperate and chose the oldest one to borrow. He insists he was planning on returning it."

"What's going to happen?"

"I've spoken with Warring. As long as Harry agrees to pay the rental rate, Warring won't press charges."

"That's generous of him," she said. "What about the mercantile? Was he the intruder Quinn found?"

"He denies it. And since Quinn didn't get a good look at the man, there's no way to know for sure."

"You've got good instincts. What do you think?"

He exhaled roughly. "I think he's a frightened young man who's found himself in desperate circumstances."

"Has he spoken of Eli or his sister?"

"Not yet. I'm hoping seeing you will persuade him. He chose you, after all, to care for his nephew."

Isabel hoped he was right.

At the jail, Harry was sprawled on a cot, one arm thrown over his face, when she and Ben entered.

"I've brought you a visitor." Ben removed the key ring from his belt and unlocked the cell door, throwing it wide.

Harry planted his boots on the floor and sat up, his confused gaze sliding from Ben to Isabel. His tousled hair was a light brown hue. His scraggly beard couldn't detract from his pleasant features. He was younger than she'd thought, about her age.

"What's she doing here?"

She clasped her hands at her waist. "Hello, Harry. Or should I call you Happy?"

Grief flashed in his blue eyes—the same as Eli's—before he covered it with false apathy. "How'd you figure it out? Did the boy tell you my real name?"

"How about we not discuss this through the bars? Have a seat out here." Ben dragged a chair near the cell.

Isabel chose one beside Shane's desk. Ben propped his weight on his desk, long legs stretched out in front of him.

Harry obeyed, smoothing his hair with a trembling hand. His expression was wary as he shifted on the hard wood.

"How about you start at the beginning?" Ben prompted.

When Harry pursed his lips and stared at anything but them, Isabel spoke softly. "I know you care about your nephew."

Scruffy eyebrows tugged close, he rubbed a jagged gouge in the chair arm with his thumb.

She leaned forward. "What happened to Annie? Did she pass away during the birth?"

Harry's harsh inhale was loud in the room. Eyes awash in sorrow, his throat convulsed. "How do you know about that? I shielded Eli from what was happening. I didn't want him to see his ma…" Bowing his head, he gripped the bridge of his nose.

Ben shot Isabel a quick glance. "The boy mentioned that he had a sibling. He hasn't shared any other details, however."

The room was quiet save for the wood crackling in the stove and the occasional loud conversations of people passing the jail. Harry finally lifted his head to look at her.

"How is he?"

"He's as good as an abandoned child could hope to be." Anger warred with sympathy. "I understand you're in mourning, but I'd like an explanation. I've been caring for Eli as if he were my own. I believe I deserve to know why you chose to leave him on my doorstep, don't you?"

Harry sighed. "It's not a nice tale. A fine lady like you wouldn't understand."

"I assure you, I'm acquainted with the unsavory side of life."

Ben removed his gloves and tossed them on the desk. "Isabel can handle whatever you have to say."

"We paid a visit to your grandmother's home," she added. If they couldn't convince him to confide in them, he'd leave this jail and possibly skip town for good. "We know about Wesley."

Harry bolted out of his seat. Ben had his weapon drawn in the blink of an eye.

"*Sit down*, Howell."

Fury blazing, Harry dropped into the chair and gripped the arms until his knuckles went white. Through clenched teeth, he rattled off a few unsavory words.

Ben glowered at him. "I'd thank you to watch your language."

"My apologies, ma'am. I can't think about that man without wantin' to strangle the life out of him. He's a lyin', thievin' scoundrel. He took advantage of my sister. Duped her into believing he cared. But then he—" He clamped his lips together.

Sheathing his weapon, Ben paced to the window and leaned his weight against the wall. "This would be easier if you'd tell us the entire account, start to back."

"And what then? You gonna stick me in that cell again?"

"After you've satisfied our questions, you're free to go."

"Our parents died several years ago. Cholera. We went to live with Grandma Ethel. I dealt with the change all right, but Annie missed our home. She'd left friends behind. She was lonely. Prime pickings for a blackguard like Wesley Norton. I didn't trust him from the moment I laid eyes on him. Grandma wouldn't listen. She and my sister believed his pitiful story."

"Did they marry?" Isabel said.

"Nope, not even after it got out that she was expecting."

"The sheriff there didn't act like he knew you existed. Did you not go into town?"

"Rarely. My grandma was what you'd call a recluse. And after Annie got pregnant, there was no question of us mingling with polite folk." Old memories reflected in his eyes. Pain was there. And guilt. "Once Eli came, Wes started taking off for weeks at a time. Annie was devastated, but she'd always forgive him. He had no interest in being a father. I'm more a pa to that boy than Wes ever was."

"Where is he now?"

Harry frowned. "I don't know."

Ben shifted his stance. "Is he aware that Annie's gone, along with his second child, too?"

Harry's lips parted and, for a split second, denial was stamped over his features. Then his gaze slid to the floor.

Isabel's heart thudded. "Her baby didn't die," she murmured, willing it to be true.

Ben came to stand beside her chair, his hand resting on her shoulder. "Harry, what happened to the baby?"

The young man before them seemed to age before their eyes. He bore the weight of the world on his shoulders.

"Wes was livid when he learned she was expecting again. He started throwing stuff. Yelling. Scared my grandma out of her wits. I got my rifle and ran him off the property. The next day, I packed up our meager belongings and moved Annie and Eli to the outskirts of Gatlinburg. We lived in anticipation of his retaliation. They weren't married. And Wes didn't care to be a father, but he considered Annie and Eli his possessions. We were well aware that he wouldn't take kindly to us up and disappearing like that."

"What about Ethel?" Ben probed. "She wasn't scared?"

"She was, sure, but she was also a stubborn old coot. We tried to convince her to come with us. She refused. We didn't tell her where we were going in case Wesley tried to coerce her to spill the beans." Harry stroked his beard. "The three of us found an abandoned hunter's shack. We struggled to put enough food on the table. I hunted and fished, but there weren't a lot of vegetables to be had, and I made infrequent trips to town. I sometimes wonder if I made the right decision, moving Annie in her condition. Toward the end, she was weak. Maybe if she'd had more to eat, more milk and fresh eggs..." He broke off, unable to continue, sorrow a visible cloud around him.

Ben's fingers flexed. Isabel lifted her hand and covered his, the feel of skin upon skin a welcome distraction from the powerful grief they were witnessing.

"The baby came early," he rasped. "I tried to help Annie. By the time I realized she was in trouble, it was too late to fetch anyone. She lingered long enough to tell me what to do for the baby. And to name her. Fran Ruby Norton."

Unable to remain detached, Isabel stood and crossed to the broken man. Kneeling before him, she placed her hand on his arm. "I'm so sorry for your loss."

His mouth pursed. "You've a kind heart, ma'am. And brave. That's why I picked you. The way you handled Wes in that bank alley, I knew you were the right person to take in my nephew."

Isabel stared at him in confusion. "What are you saying, Harry? The man in that alley was Theron Franklin."

"Theron doesn't exist. At least, not anymore. Wes killed him and assumed his name."

Isabel twisted to meet Ben's arrested gaze. "You know what this means?"

"Our thief is Eli's father."

Chapter Twenty-Three

"You were there that night and didn't try to intervene?" Ben demanded, feeling his blood pressure rise. "What if I hadn't come along? Would you have left her to Wes's mercy?"

Harry held up his hands. "I had Eli with me. Keeping him safe was my first priority. I made a promise to my sister."

Not pacified, Ben pressed on. "How did you even know he was in town?"

"Eli and I came to the mercantile for supplies. We didn't come often, and when we did, I made sure we didn't draw attention to ourselves. I caught sight of Wes as we were leaving. We ducked into the alleyway and stayed there until sundown."

"I can't believe he is Eli's father." Isabel kneaded her forehead. "That man is dangerous. He would've killed me had he gotten the chance. The wanted poster said he murdered an innocent man. It's a good thing you got your sister and Eli away from him."

"What happened to the baby?" Ben asked. "How did you care for her?"

"I was scared out of my mind," Harry said. "I had no

idea what to do. Even if my grandma had been alive, I wouldn't have taken Fran back there. Too risky. I packed our meager belongings and headed for Cades Cove. Grandma used to tell us about some friends she had there. A pastor and his wife. Thought I'd look them up and appeal for help."

"And did they help you?"

His features softened with remembered relief. "They agreed to care for her until they could find a permanent home."

"How long ago was this?" Isabel glanced at Ben, and he could read her intent.

"Mid-October. Fran was born on the fifth, and we went to Cades Cove about a week later."

"She's two and a half months old," Isabel murmured. "Lots of couples would want to adopt her, I'm certain."

"I haven't received word. We agreed it would be best not to correspond for a while." Guilt and regret was stamped upon Harry's features. "They offered to take Eli, too. I thought I could keep him with me. However, the more time that passed, I realized how much I wasn't able to do for him. I was too ashamed to admit I'd failed, so I picked you to be Eli's caretaker."

The young man cared about his niece and nephew in his own way. He'd been put in a tough position and hadn't had anyone to guide him. No one to turn to for advice. Still, he'd made poor choices.

"What's your plan, Howell? Were you going to leave town and never look back?"

He flinched. "I know what you probably think of me. Those kids are my blood kin. Annie's offspring. She wouldn't be pleased at what I've done, but I can't take care of a newborn! Eli's old enough, I guess, but I don't have enough to put food in my own belly, let alone a kid's.

I couldn't provide for Annie. Look what happened to her." He shook his head, his eyes bleak. "No, they're both better off with folks who can provide a good, safe home." His gaze traveled to Isabel. "You are planning on keeping him, right?"

"You took a huge risk, you know," she chided. "Judging me based on a single encounter. I could've been a cruel person."

"But you're not."

"I choose to believe God had His hand on this situation. I care about Eli. To answer your question, I've contacted a lawyer. That's why I've been desperate to find you. He advised me to get as many answers about Eli's guardian or parentage as possible before starting legal proceedings."

Harry visibly relaxed.

"Are there any relatives who would fight Isabel's petition?" Ben said.

"No. There's no one."

"Harry, I'd like to meet Fran. Would you take me?"

He jammed a thumb against his chest. "Me? Now?"

Ben smothered a groan. "Isabel—"

"Yes. Will you?"

Harry didn't consider her request long before agreeing. "Sure. I'll take you. I'll need a horse, though."

"Isabel, I'd like a word with you in private." Ben pointed to the cell. "Howell, you wait in here."

Though he didn't look pleased about it, Harry did as Ben instructed, plopping on the cot and leveraging his boot against the bars.

Outside on the boardwalk, Isabel crossed her arms and jutted her chin. "Don't try to dissuade me, Ben. You won't succeed."

"I know what you're thinking. The chances that Eli's

sister hasn't yet found a family are low. You said it your-self. Who can resist a helpless infant?"

Her ire dissolved. Stepping close, she laid her hand on his arm. "At this point, I only wish to meet her. Fran is Eli's sister. He should be allowed to know her. If she has been taken in, I'd like to talk to her caretakers and learn if they'd be willing to foster a relationship between them."

"Sounds reasonable." He wasn't convinced there wasn't more to it, though. "I don't want you to be disappointed. Or hurt."

"You can't protect me from those things, Deputy, but you can be around to offer me a listening ear or a shoul-der to cry on if I need it."

His chest tightened. He wouldn't make promises he couldn't keep. This case was almost complete, ready to be tied up with a shiny ribbon like a Christmas present. Then he'd have to do what he'd been dreading…say good-bye to Isabel.

"I'm not letting you go to Cades Cove without me," he warned.

"I wouldn't dream of leaving you behind."

Isabel wasn't willing to examine too closely her con-suming determination to meet Eli's sister. Ben's frequent, contemplative glances as they made the brief journey to Cades Cove threatened to unravel her composure. He thought she was fooling herself. Perhaps she was.

Nerves assailed her when they crested the final ridge and the picturesque valley with a patchwork of winding streams, pastures and tidy farms greeted her. By unspo-ken agreement, they paused to take in the view. Ben and his steed stood between her and Harry. He wore resolve like a second skin, his hard-edged lawman persona firmly in place. Harry's freshly shaven face bore witness to his inner conflict. Ben had taken him to his place to wash up. He'd even lent him a fresh shirt. His kindness was one of the many things she loved about him.

Isabel closed her eyes tight. *Loved?* Truly?

Had she done the unthinkable?

She sensed movement beside her. "Isabel?"

Opening her eyes, she found Ben's gaze locked on her, his forehead furrowed in concern. "Are you all right?"

Floundering in the clear green depths, she acknowledged what her heart had been trying to tell her. She'd fallen for Ben MacGregor. She wasn't the first, and she wouldn't be the last. Pain shafted through her. This love had the power to wreck her.

Unable to speak past the terrible emotions ravaging her, she nodded and urged Honey into motion. As they made their way down the mountain, she begged God to take away the feelings. She'd lived twenty-two years without Ben. Isabel couldn't let one unusual Christmas—a few enchanted weeks spent with a man who'd awakened dreams long denied—destroy her future. God had not only blessed her with a home and loving sisters, He'd brought a special little boy into her life. Focusing on those things, instead of mourning what she'd never been promised, would surely carry her through this grief. It had to.

When they'd reached level terrain, Harry relayed the direction of the pastor's home. To distract her from her nervousness, she guided her mount even with his.

"What are your plans for the future? Will you return to Ethel's farm?"

His gaze soaked in their surroundings. "That place never really was my home. I was toying with the notion of returning to my parents' old place. Selling Grandma's farm would give me enough funds for a fresh start."

Her next question was hard to pose, but she had to be

sure. "And if you were to be successful, is there a possibility you'd change your mind about Eli?"

"You don't have to worry, Miss Flores. I love my nephew, but I ain't ready to be a pa. I'll attest to that before a judge."

"What if, in the future—"

"I wouldn't do that to him, not after he's settled in with you." The corners of his eyes crinkled. "I would appreciate it if you'd let me visit from time to time."

"As long as you're not in the state Ben and the other men found you in."

He blushed. "That's not typical for me, ma'am. I've been in low spirits and indulged in immature behavior."

Ben's beautiful mouth shifted into a smirk. She averted her gaze and concentrated on the path. When they arrived at the modest home a stone's throw from the church, a short, birdlike woman answered their summons. Her brunette hair was parted in the middle and scraped into a tight bun. Upon recognizing Harry, a quick smile softened her severe appearance.

"Harry, what a surprise!" Her gray eyes inventoried them. "Who have you brought with you?"

He swept his arm to encompass them. "This is Miss Isabel Flores and Deputy Ben MacGregor, both of Gatlinburg."

Once they'd exchanged polite greetings, Agatha invited them inside and, bidding them to make themselves comfortable, hurried to fetch coffee. Harry perched on the edge of a brown chair. Ben paced before the fireplace. Isabel sat on one end of the patterned sofa. The Browns kept a clean, comfortable, clutter-free home. A simple cross fashioned from unpolished wood hung above the door through which Agatha had vanished.

The utter silence blanketing the house dampened her spirits. Fran wasn't here.

Their hostess hurried back and doled out mugs of steaming coffee. "I apologize that my husband isn't here to visit with you. We had a death in our congregation this week, and he's comforting the family." When she'd gotten comfortable on the opposite end of the sofa, she glanced at Ben before addressing Harry. "What brings you here? Has something occurred that requires the law's intervention?"

"Our trip has nothing to do with the kids' father. His whereabouts are unknown." His knees bobbed up and down. "I, uh, was wondering about Fran. Miss Flores has taken Eli in and has plans to adopt."

"Is that so?" Agatha's keen gaze lit with curiosity. "I thought you'd planned to raise him yourself."

As he had with Ben and Isabel, Harry explained his change of heart. "Eli's flourishing. He not only has Miss Flores to look after him, but her sisters, as well."

Isabel felt compelled to add to the conversation. "I've been responsible for my younger sisters ever since my father's death two years ago. My mother moved away. My middle sister, Honor, will soon be wed. My youngest sister, Carmen, will continue to live with me and Eli until the day she marries."

"And what about you?" Agatha cocked her head. "Do you plan to marry, as well? Raising a child alone is a sober undertaking."

"I don't plan on marrying." *Because the man I love doesn't plan to, either.*

"Isabel's up to the task, Mrs. Brown." Ben cradled his mug in his hand. "She's got her sisters and friends. Most of the community supports her decision."

"I suppose there's always the chance you'll meet someone later on."

Isabel pressed her lips together to hold back a retort.

"Mrs. Brown, seeing as Miss Flores will be Eli's ma, she'd like to see Fran."

Agatha's expression sharpened. Isabel was certain she was leaping to the same conclusions Ben had. Folding her hands in her lap, she prayed for guidance. "I don't plan to challenge the couple's claim. And I understand they may wish to set a meeting time for another day. I simply feel the need to see her. Eli has become very important to me, and I'd like to tell him about her."

Agatha sucked in a bracing breath, sent a prayerful glance toward the ceiling and stood. "There is no other couple, Miss Flores."

Jaw sagging, Harry popped out of his chair. "You mean she's still here? In your care?"

"That's right. There've been several couples who've expressed interest, only to change their minds once we told them of her origins. They're frightened of future entanglements with a vengeful outlaw."

Ben looked as stunned as Isabel felt. "Is she sleeping? We don't wish to disturb her."

Checking the watch pinned to her bodice, Agatha said, "She's been asleep for more than two hours. It's about time for her to stir. Her baby bed is in our room." Motioning for them to follow, she led the way into a narrow hall and to the corner room. Isabel noticed Ben hung far behind, his steps reluctant.

Harry was the first to peer into the bed. A huge smile cracked his face. "She looks exactly like Eli did at that age," he whispered in an awe-filled voice.

Isabel's heart swelled when she saw the tiny infant cocooned in a pure white knitted blanket. Harry was right. Fran was a miniature version of her big brother. Downy, dark brown hair capped her head. Long black lashes rested in the crescents beneath her eyes. Her nose was as tiny as her pink mouth.

"She's beautiful," Isabel breathed.

Agatha stood by the single window, curtains drawn to block light. "She's a good baby."

Isabel noticed Ben remained in the doorway. When she waved him over, he shook his head, his eyes flat. Emotionless.

"Would you like to hold her?" Agatha said.

Isabel nodded to Harry. "Her uncle should go first."

"Very well."

Agatha moved in and, gently scooping up the baby, placed her in Harry's unpracticed arms. A wide range of emotions flitted across his face. His throat working, he gave her to Isabel. Snuggling the baby close to her chest, Isabel inhaled her sweet fragrance and marveled over her perfectly formed fingers and nails. A quick smile curved Fran's mouth, and both Isabel and Harry chuckled.

Isabel turned toward Ben. "Would you like to hold her?"

His jaw hardened. "I'm sorry, I can't."

Then he pivoted on his heel and stalked out.

Chapter Twenty-Four

❧

"He just walked out, Honor. Can you believe it?"

Isabel spoke in hushed tones so the others in attendance wouldn't overhear. Two days had passed since their trip to Cades Cove, forty-eight hours that had been both packed with activity in preparation for Sunday's celebration and also agonizingly long.

Elegant in her red dress, her long hair twisted into a loose knot, Honor kept her gaze trained on the children at the front of the church. Carmen had taken Eli up to meet some of the other kids his age. The annual children's play would begin in fifteen minutes. The room hummed with anticipation. Candles flickered on the greenery strung along the window ledges. Adults were dressed in their finest clothes. Children participating in the performance wore costumes. Megan and Lillian Beaumont were in charge of the event. As usual, they'd done an outstanding job on the backdrop. The church had been transformed into the village of Bethlehem.

"Maybe he was tired. Or wasn't feeling well." Honor shrugged. "He's been working long hours to compensate for Shane's absence. Sleeping on the hard hut floor hasn't allowed him to get much rest, I'm sure."

"You didn't see his face. He didn't only leave the room. He left the house altogether."

Twisting on the pew, she surveyed the crowd, anxious for a sign of Ben. After leaving the Browns', they'd returned to Gatlinburg in a cloud of introspective silence. Back at the jail, Ben had offered Harry a spot in his barn for a night or two. That was all the information she had. She hadn't seen either man since.

"Ben cares about Eli as much as I do," Isabel murmured. "Why wouldn't he at least want to get a closer look at Fran? He acted almost scared of her."

"Some men are intimidated by infants."

"Ben isn't intimidated by anything." She caught Honor's stare and lifted one shoulder. "What? It's true."

She blew out a frustrated breath. "If you two weren't so determined to cling to your shortsighted ideals, you could be having a wedding of your own." She tipped her head closer. "You love him, Isa. Admit it."

Isabel's skin prickled. She sensed him before she saw him. He stood, boots planted apart, his all-black ensemble making his hair gleam and his eyes glitter like fine jewels. The moment he spotted her, he strode in her direction.

"He doesn't look like a man in love," she said involuntarily.

"Perhaps he's as good at hiding his true feelings as you are."

Rising to her feet, she touched a self-conscious hand to her upswept hair. No braid for her tonight. "Ben. I was beginning to wonder if you were coming. Eli's been asking for you. Will you sit with us?"

"I'm not staying for the performance. I only stopped in for a moment. May I speak with you outside?"

She hoped her disappointment didn't show. With a nod, she left the pew and accompanied him out into the chilly evening. Multicolored light spilled through the stained-glass windows and formed patterns on the ground. Twin sconces on either side of the double doors helped dispel the darkness. He led her to the corner closest to the cemetery.

"I'm taking Harry to Pigeon Forge tonight. He doesn't have a horse and has no money to buy one. He's pretty sure the neighbor we spoke to took in Ethel's horses when she got too ill to care for them. The profits from the sale of one will go to Warring. He's going to put her house up for sale and hope for the best."

Isabel digested this information. "Christmas is in three days. Couldn't he wait until after? He could spend it with us. Eli would be tickled."

"He may not come out and say it, Isabel, but he's hurting. Seeing his niece again opened old wounds. It's my opinion that he's craving space and privacy to grieve."

Isabel dearly wanted to ask Ben about his own peculiar reaction to the baby, but his features were closed off in warning. She'd never thought she'd miss his playful teasing.

"How long will you be gone?"

He looked away. "I can't leave the town unattended for long."

"Will you spend Christmas Day with us?" When he remained frustratingly silent, she added, "I know Carmen invited you, but I failed to add my own sentiments."

"I can't."

"Oh." Her lungs deflated. "You have plans with Grant and Jessica?"

He waited until a couple ascended the steps and entered the building to meet her gaze head-on. "Our time together is over, Isabel. You have Harry's permission to adopt Eli. The case is closed."

She fell back a step, the wall behind her providing much

needed support. "I wouldn't call it closed. We haven't found Wesley. And Fran still doesn't have a home."

Caution pulsed in his eyes. "I'm going to fill in the sheriff about the developments and reiterate the importance of locating him. I'll also send a fresh batch of letters to the other local law offices. They'll be more alert once they learn two young children's welfare is an issue. I'll hire someone to guard your place."

"Absolutely not. I can protect my own."

Piano music filtered outside. "We'll discuss it once I get back. In the meantime, Clayton Chapman has agreed to stand guard."

Denial rose up so fast she couldn't contain it. "I don't want another man in my life. I want you. Only you."

The blurted confession hung there, suspended between them.

He looked floored. His eyes churned with suppressed emotion. At his sides, his gloved hands opened and closed.

Peeling back her protective layers and offering him a piece of her heart had taken guts. Isabel hadn't planned on revealing her true feelings, but now that she had, she felt lighter. Open to possibilities.

"Say something," she rasped.

With a quick glance at the entrance, he moved close and cupped her cheek. "I'm honored, Isa. Truly. Thanks to you, I'll always look back on this Christmas with fondness. It'll go down in history as the year Gatlinburg's deputy and courageous miller joined forces to help a vulnerable child." His words pricked the bubbly hope inside her. But he didn't stop there. "We always knew there'd be an end to this."

She curled her hands around his coat lapels, the wool scratchy against her skin. "It doesn't have to end." She forced the words out. She had to be brave with him or else regret it for the rest of her life. "We could be together. The three of us. A-and maybe Fran, too…"

"No." He was shaking his head, rejecting her outright. Tugging free, he backed away, hands up as if to ward her off. "That's a fanciful dream I won't have any part of."

"It doesn't have to be a dream." She tried one last time, feeling as if her heart was cracking wide open. "If you care about me—"

"I do. As a friend."

Clasping her hands together and pushing them hard against her sternum, she tried to assuage the pain there. "I—I see."

"I'm sorry, sugarplum." His voice was scratchy. "I can't be what you need me to be."

He left without another word, his broad form swallowed up by the night shadows.

Exhaustion dogged Ben late Christmas Eve night. He'd been in the saddle for hours and longed for a hot soak and a good night's sleep in his own bed. Instead of riding to his cabin, though, he went to the jail, where he wouldn't have to face his loneliness head-on. He wouldn't have to stare at his pitiful decorations and think about all the families across town preparing for tomorrow's festivities.

Lighting a match and putting it to the kindling in the woodstove, he sighed. How many times had he replayed Isabel's confession and wished he could've reacted differently? He'd come perilously close to sweeping her into his arms and begging her to be his bride. His determination not to be selfish had prevented him.

He was making himself some coffee when the door scraped open and in strolled Grant.

Ben aimed an exaggerated look at the clock. "Why aren't you at home with your wife?"

"Hello to you, too," he drawled, dropping his hat on Shane's desk. "I thought I'd check in and hear how things went in Pigeon Forge. I went to your place first. When I didn't see any lights on, I figured you were either asleep or still on the trail. Then I passed by and saw Blaze out front."

He gestured to his desk. "I had some paperwork to do."

Grant planted his hands on his hips. "You expect me to believe that?"

"With everything going on the past few weeks, I've gotten behind."

"It's Christmas Eve."

"Unlike you, I don't have anyone at home to fuss if I'm not there." He winced at the hint of self-pity in his voice.

"You have the power to change that."

"Forget I said it."

"Isabel—"

"Don't, Grant," he grumbled. "I'm saddle weary and hungry enough to eat my shoe. I can't listen to your well-intentioned lecture."

"The Plum's open for another hour. Let me buy you supper."

Ben sighed heavily. "I'll take you up on that offer if you promise not to talk about her."

"You have my word."

His friend honored his vow. While Ben gobbled up smoked ham, turnip greens, corn bread and mashed potatoes, Grant nursed coffee and spoke about every subject except the one that mattered. Once the bill was paid, they exited onto the deserted boardwalk.

"I'll see you at services in the morning, right?" Grant prompted.

"Wouldn't miss it."

"And then you're joining us for Christmas dinner at the O'Malleys'."

Ben had nowhere else to go, and spending the day alone in his cabin would drive him batty. "How could I turn down the opportunity to partake in one of their famous feasts?"

Grant opened his mouth to say something, then thought better of it. He clapped Ben on the back. "Good night."

Ben decided to ride to the Flores farm. He was careful to remain out of view of the cabin. The man he'd hired, Clayton Chapman, emerged from the shadows cast by the hut.

"Checking up on me, Deputy?" He grinned, revealing several missing teeth.

"I trust you to do your job." He stayed in the saddle. "Anything unusual to report?"

"It's been quiet. You going inside?" Clayton gestured to the cabin.

"It's late. I'm not going to disturb them."

While he watched, a light in the living room was snuffed out. Was that Isabel preparing to retire? Had she had a busy day of baking and putting finishing touches on the gifts? Were all the presents wrapped and stowed beneath the tree? He remembered his own childhood and the excitement he and his sisters had shared the night before Christmas. Eli would have difficulty falling asleep, which meant Isabel would, too.

If he'd made a confession of his own, he could be in there with her right now, telling Eli stories until he couldn't keep his eyes open. Afterward, he and Isabel could snuggle on the sofa while the flames danced in the hearth. He'd hold her close and steal a kiss or three.

If he hadn't fallen ill, if he could offer Isabel the same things every other groom had to offer, he'd have been down on his knee so fast her head would've spun.

The other man spoke into the silence. "Don't worry, Deputy. I'll make sure they're safe and sound."

Ben thanked Clayton and, battling his instincts, left the farm. He wasn't responsible for them anymore. His job was done.

"Wake up! It's Christmas!" The bed dipped, and hot breath fanned her cheek. Eli's fingers tangled in her unbound hair, twirling round and round, hopefully not making knots. He'd gotten into the habit, and she wondered if he'd done the same with Annie's. "Isabel?"

She stretched beneath the covers and fought to open her eyes. "Is it light outside?"

"Yes! That means it's Jesus's birthday!" Eli bounced on the mattress. "Time to open the stockings and presents!"

Scooting up to rest against the headboard, she pushed strands out of her eyes and smiled at this overt display of excitement. He'd had an awful time going to sleep last night. Who could blame him? This was his first year with a Christmas tree, at least one he could remember. Isabel was excited for him. She couldn't wait to see his face when he opened his gifts. Most were practical, of course. There were a few nonessential, just-for-fun items, too.

Eli cocked his head. His face screwed up the way it did when he was thinking hard. "Why don't we give Jesus presents?"

The question was insightful for one so young. "We don't give Him presents in the usual sense, but we can express our love through other means. Throughout the year, not only on December twenty-fifth. When we show kindness to others, when we help those in need, that pleases Jesus. He also knows that we love Him when we obey His commands."

Eli considered this for a minute. "I think He'd like the cross we made for the tree, don't you?"

She leaned forward and caressed his cheek. "I think so, yes."

He jumped off the bed. Isabel shivered when her stocking feet touched the cold floor. Hurriedly pulling on her dressing gown over her nightclothes, she ran a brush through her hair and tied it back with a ribbon.

Eli hopped from one foot to the other. "Is Ben coming today? Will he eat with us like he used to? I want to show him the stockings hanging from the mantel."

Needles of regret pricked her. Isabel prayed again for fortitude. She'd been honest with Ben about her feelings, and he'd returned the favor. He didn't want a future with her. Hiding her sorrow and humiliation from her family hadn't been easy. Every night since, she'd waited until everyone was asleep to curl up on the sofa and let the tears flow unchecked, pouring her heart out to God. He alone could heal her wounded heart.

It was Christmas Day, however, the day marking the birth of their Savior. She couldn't dampen everyone else's joy by giving in to the clouds of depression weighing on her. Tomorrow, she promised herself. Tomorrow, she could drop the pretense and mourn her loss. Today, she was going to be grateful for her blessings.

As she prepared breakfast with Eli's help, her mind drifted to Cades Cove and the precious baby girl there. She couldn't stop imagining Fran living here, brother and sister reunited. Isabel hadn't voiced the budding yearning in her heart. An unwed spinster adopting one child raised eyebrows. Add a second child—an infant, no less—and she'd likely face direct opposition. That didn't keep her from dreaming, however.

The Browns' children were adults. While Agatha and

the reverend didn't mind caring for Fran, they'd agreed on the condition the situation was temporary. Isabel understood their need to be honest about the baby's parentage. Would that honesty prevent Fran from finding a home?

"Good morning." Carmen bustled in, bright-eyed and perky even before her morning coffee. She scooped Eli up and twirled him in a circle, narrowly avoiding a collision with the hutch. "Merry Christmas!"

Eli's giggles tickled their ears. Honor joined them a quarter of an hour later, not in the mood to talk until after she'd consumed food and coffee. They were finishing their meal when someone rapped on the door. Isabel's heart climbed into her throat. Could it be…

But it was only Clayton Chapman, the man Ben had hired in his place. He turned down her offer of breakfast and placed an unwieldy burlap bag inside the door.

"What's this?"

"Christmas delivery." His eyes twinkled with mischief. "Ben stopped by about an hour ago and asked me to bring it over. Wouldn't explain why he couldn't do it himself."

Ben didn't want to see her, that's why.

"Thank you, Clayton." Her mouth felt full of rocks.

Tugging on his hat brim, he mounted his horse and left. Her sisters and Eli gathered around. Carmen shifted the material, peeked inside and removed a folded piece of paper. Since there was no specific name, she opened it and began reading.

"'To the Flores sisters, please accept these humble gifts as tokens of my appreciation. You have a knack for making a man feel welcome in your home. Forever your servant, Ben MacGregor.'"

Honor and Carmen looked at Isabel to gauge her reaction. "That was thoughtful of him," she said matter-offactly. "I suggest we put them with the others and open them after we've read the account of Christ's birth."

Eli trailed after Carmen, watching closely as she extracted each wrapped gift.

"Oh look, there's one with your name on it."

He clapped his hands together. "Ben got me something?"

Crouched on her knees at the tree's base, she encircled his waist with one arm. "He wouldn't leave you out."

Isabel lifted the heavy Bible from its usual place and waited for everyone to get settled before opening it to the book of Luke. Of course she was reminded of the morning Ben had read this same passage. So much had changed since then, it felt like a lifetime had passed.

When they'd taken turns sharing things they were thankful for, Honor assumed the task of passing out presents. Eager to watch the others' reactions, Isabel left her gifts untouched. Eli was a delight. He exclaimed over every item, no matter what it was. She could tell his favorite was the tin box of miniature metal soldiers Ben had picked out. He lined them up in a single row on the coffee table and studied each one up close.

Honor exclaimed over Ben's choice for her—a book of recipes. For Carmen, he'd chosen a crimson scarf with golden thread. She wound it around her neck and modeled it with flair. "How do I look?"

"Gorgeous, as ever," Isabel said. A crate with her name on it waited at her feet. She hesitated to uncover the contents.

"Stop stalling, Isa," Carmen cried. "I'm impatient to see what he got you."

Isabel slowly peeled the checked material back and gasped. Honor poked her head close.

"Deer antlers?" Honor looked intrigued.

Carmen gave an exaggerated frown. "What was he

thinking? That's the least romantic gift a man could give a woman!"

Isabel lifted one and tested the hard, bumpy surface. She disagreed. While this wasn't romantic in the usual sense, it proved he'd taken the time to decide on a gift suited to her exact needs. He would've had to get these from a hunter or scour the forest floor for them, a tedious and time-consuming task.

"I can use these for knife handles."

"Still not impressed," Carmen sniffed.

Honor smiled. "He knows what Isa likes, that's all."

Isabel lugged the crate to her room. Opening her bedside stand, she removed the fabric-covered box containing her gift for him and slid it into her reticule. She would give it to him at church. In such a public setting, she wouldn't be tempted to make a fool of herself. With the entire town watching, she'd act like a mature adult who could accept when the man she loved didn't love her in return.

Chapter Twenty-Five

He'd spent several Christmases apart from his family, but this was the first time he'd truly felt alone. As happy, chattering families filed past his spot on the stairs on their way inside the church, Ben told himself to get used to the feeling. His friends had found love and were navigating married life. The more years that passed, the more of an outsider he'd become.

He'd almost convinced himself to go in and find a seat when he recognized Isabel's wagon rolling into the yard. Sunlight bathed the day in cheery warmth. A white Christmas was rare here, and this year was no different. The cold was enough of a reminder that winter was settling in, however. Without Isabel and Eli, it would be interminable drudgery.

She and her sisters chatted as they hurried past conveyances and horses. Eli noticed him first and, grinning widely, broke into a run.

"Ben, look!" Little legs pumping, he raced up the stairs and produced a tiny soldier from his coat pocket. "I brought one with me."

Smiling, Ben crouched to his level and examined the

toy. "I'm glad you like it, little man." He gently ruffled his hair. "Merry Christmas, Eli."

Eli leaned close and hugged his neck. Ben's chest grew tight. He'd give anything to be this boy's father. The image of Isabel cradling a sleeping Fran rose up to torment him.

The girls arrived at the foot of the stairs. Ben stood up, his gaze riveted to Isabel's beloved face. He'd missed her. Missed sharing details of his life. Missed seeing her hard-earned smiles.

"Good morning, ladies."

Isabel's attention shifted elsewhere, away from him. He hated that he'd caused this rift between them. A clean break was best, he knew that. It would enable them both to heal and move on with their lives.

Except, when he looked at her, he couldn't see himself coming out on the other side of this ache. The woman he adored was in front of him, and he had to pretend everything was fine. That being near her wasn't destroying him from the inside out.

The girls thanked him for his gifts. As they passed him on the stairs, Isabel's brown-black eyes darted his way, and he glimpsed her misery. Straightening her shoulders, she fished something from her reticule and held it out to him.

"What's this?"

"A present for you."

He would've opened it, but she angled her face away. Holding out her hand, she summoned Eli. The group entered the church without him. Ben forced his feet to move. He found an empty spot at the back and turned the gift over and over in his hands. At the service's conclusion, he returned the others' well wishes with false enthusiasm. When he noticed Grant speaking to Isabel in the corner, dread filled him. Surely his friend wouldn't reveal his secret. But she didn't approach him afterward. She didn't even spare him a glance.

At Sam and Mary's, he summoned the strength of mind to act pleased to be there. He praised the food, thanked those who gave him gifts and accepted a second helping of pie. By midafternoon, he craved solitude.

Grant waylaid him in the barn. "Caleb told me you're leaving." He caught sight of the bowie knife and leather sheath and let loose a whistle. "That's a fine weapon. Where'd you get it?"

Ben let him inspect the handle and test the blade. "Isabel made it."

His gaze reflected wonder. "Did she carve the image of your badge into the wood, too?"

"She's a talented lady."

"This is a personal gift, my friend."

"If it was that important to her, she would've stuck around to watch me open it."

"What happened between you two?"

He sighed. "Nothing. I made sure of it."

Sympathy tightened his friend's face. "I'm sorry, Ben. Look, why don't you stick around? The day's only half-over. What are you going to do at home besides stare at the walls?"

"Who knows, I may go fishing. Haven't had much time for that lately."

He looked disbelieving. "It's too cold."

"It's never too cold to fish." He led Blaze into the sunlight.

Grant followed. "Did we do something to make you uncomfortable?"

"If there's anything the O'Malley clan knows how to do, it's making a guest feel like part of the family."

He wasn't about to confess that being the only single

person above twenty had amplified his despair. Shoving his boot in the stirrup, he grabbed the saddle horn and levered himself into the saddle.

"Enjoy the rest of your day," he said.

"I'll swing by later to check on you." Grant's blue eyes squinted in the light.

"Don't you dare," he grunted. "I'm a grown man. I don't require a caretaker. Spend the day pampering your wife."

"Tomorrow then."

Ben took his time getting home. Once there, he busied himself tidying up the place. Several weeks of neglect had resulted in a layer of dust. He chopped wood. Read magazine articles he'd read before. Completed a word puzzle. And, more out of boredom than hunger, indulged in the leftovers Mary had insisted on sending with him. Outside, dusk descended, followed by full evening darkness. He couldn't wait for bedtime. The sooner this day was over, the sooner he could focus on the future. A new year would be upon them, which meant a fresh start. Who knew? Maybe he'd take a holiday of his own once Shane returned. He'd certainly earned it.

He could travel down to Georgia. His parents and sisters would be overjoyed. Besides, it would do him good to put some distance between himself and Gatlinburg for a little while.

The knock, when it came, was barely audible. Ben lowered the magazine and cocked his head. Had to be his imagination. Unless an emergency had arisen, no one would venture out on Christmas night.

The sound of shuffling feet on the stoop convinced him there was an actual visitor. He pushed out of the chair and crossed to the door. He was without his boots, his gray wool socks visible, and he'd long since shucked his vest and suit jacket. Whoever was out there would have to understand he hadn't been expecting visitors.

"How can I help—"

"Hello, Ben."

"Isabel." Even the blast of cold air couldn't unmuddle his thoughts. "What are you doing here?"

She lowered her hood, allowing him a generous glimpse of her hair. The loose locks flowed like ebony ribbons over her cloak and past her shoulders. His mouth went dry.

Her eyes were huge in her face, dark and mysterious. "May I come in?"

He shuffled out of the way. "Of course."

Closing the door, he remained silent as she glanced around, removed her gloves and began unbuttoning the clasps. She must plan on staying a while.

He fisted his hands. "Why are you here?" When her elegant brows dipped and her mouth pursed, he returned to his seat and sank into it. "What did Grant say to you?"

"He didn't tell me your secret." Laying her cloak over one of the chair backs, she advanced, her expression a curious mix of vulnerability and soldier-like determination.

"But he told you I had one?"

"I already knew that." She didn't stop until she stood directly in front of him, her boots nudging his. His breathing grew shallow. "He said you were keeping something from me and, since we're both stubborn and hardheaded, I should try to get it out of you."

Ben found it difficult to think. She was wearing that plum blouse again. A calculated move? Normally its strict confines lent her a schoolmarm air. However, with that glorious hair streaming free, her plush lips begging to be kissed, the effect was obliterated.

He gripped the chair arms, the cushioning not giving him much to cling to.

"That's not the only reason I'm here," she said huskily. Inching even closer, she braced one hand on the chair edge by his left shoulder. With her other hand, she cupped his cheek. "I want to prove something."

Pulse racing, he stared helplessly up at her. "Prove what—"

Her mouth pressed against his, sweet and shy and shattering. Rational thought was impossible. Reaching up, he framed her face, glorying in the silken sweep of her hair against his hands. With Isabel in his arms, he was home. They could be on the beaches of California or the rivers of Louisiana and still they'd be home. She was his everything.

Caught up in the rapture of her petal-soft caresses, his soul soaring on the heights of the wind currents, he temporarily forgot why he'd ever driven her away.

Ben's touch was a healing balm to her bruised and battered heart. He clung to her like a drowning man to a line of rope tossed to him in a stormy sea. Moving her hand to his shoulder, she struggled to stay upright. His lips were sure and seeking. And then he was planting kisses on her jaw and temple, his fingers roaming through her hair in endless exploration.

Triumph singing through her veins, she eased away, testing the ability of her knees to hold her. Smiling, she gently smoothed the strands that had fallen into his eyes.

"We've established you want more than friendship."

The warmth cleared from his eyes. Slowly, his features shuttered, locking her out. Pressing the heels of his hands to his eyes, he muttered, "I like kissing you. That proves nothing."

Hurt sliced through her. Why did he insist on pushing her away? He returned her feelings. He *had* to.

"What did Marianne do to you?"

Ben shoved out of the chair and stalked to the bed. Pivoting, he crossed his arms and regarded her as if those tender moments hadn't happened. "Do? Marianne didn't do anything except speak the truth. That I'm half a man. Damaged goods." He pinched the bridge of his nose. "I got sick the summer of my nineteenth birthday, so sick I almost died. To my family and friends' amazement, I recovered. But the illness took its toll. Due to my age, the prolonged high fevers and way it affected my body, the doctor informed me that it's extremely unlikely I'll ever father a child."

Shock riveted her to the floor. This was the last thing she would've guessed he was hiding. His grief surrounded her, claiming her in its powerful grip. No children? No babies with dark red hair and sparkling green eyes? Flashes of Ben and Eli together rose up to taunt her. He was *good* with kids. He had much to offer. Knowledge to impart. Love to bestow. Because she loved him, she felt the loss as if it were her own. *Why, God?*

The question reverberated through her, a cry of anguish. The injustice hurt her heart. Isabel looked into his eyes. The weariness, the cost of bearing this burden, had scarred him. Ben had wrestled with this sentence for years. Everything made sense now.

"Oh, Ben, I'm so sorry. I can't imagine how difficult it must've been for you, receiving a diagnosis like that. That's a heavy burden for anyone to bear, but for a nineteen-year-old...and then your fiancée..." Anger at a young woman she'd never met filled her. "She was mistaken. She was young and naive and very, very wrong."

Aching to comfort him, Isabel started forward. His neck stiffened, so she stopped. Her heart broke for him. "Did she spread this? Is that why you left?"

"She didn't breathe a word. Too much of a lady to discuss such indelicate matters, I suppose. She did lead her devoted father to believe I'd simply changed my mind about marrying her, and he set about avenging her honor. He was the mayor. People believed him."

"And because you were in a position of authority, they wanted rid of you."

"Yes."

"I hate that you had to endure those trials." How badly she needed to hold him. "But you know something? I'm glad Marianne was a blind fool. I'm glad she didn't see your true worth, because if she had, I wouldn't have met you." Her throat closed up at the mere thought. Approaching him as one would a skittish deer, she moved closer. "You, Ben MacGregor, are the most generous, kindhearted, courageous man I've ever known. You'd give the shirt off your back to help someone. You'd give your life for the people of this town."

His brows drew together. "Why aren't you leaving?" His expression hinted at a world of sadness. "You were supposed to offer platitudes, make an excuse we both knew was false and bolt."

Isabel drew in a deep breath. This moment would define her life. She couldn't allow fear to cripple her.

"Because I love you. Not for what you can give me, but for who you are."

"Isabel," he breathed, a battle raging in his eyes. He mournfully shook his head. "But children—"

"Can be brought into our lives in various ways." She curled her fingers around his and held on tight. "God's shown us that, don't you agree?"

His gaze grew intense. "You'd truly give up the chance to bring a child of your own into this world?"

"If it meant being with you? Yes."

He cupped her cheek. "Isa, you have to be *sure*. One

hundred percent sure. No changing your mind a year or a decade from now. And no clinging to hope that the doctor was wrong." His throat worked. "Because I couldn't bear to disappoint you."

"My sweet man, even without a diagnosis like yours, there are no guarantees for any married couple. Think about it. We both know at least one couple who were unable to have children. They either come to terms with it, or they grow their families in unconventional ways."

"Like adoption."

"Like Eli." She smiled hopefully. "And maybe Fran."

A tremulous smile curved his lips. "You're amazing, you know that?"

He bent his head and placed a brief, tender kiss on her lips. Pulling back, he gazed deeply into her eyes. "I love you, sugarplum." His smile grew brighter, and the old, familiar twinkle returned. "I've loved you since the moment you got me shot."

The joy his declaration gave her couldn't be measured.

"Excuse me?" She swatted his chest. "It appears your memory of that night differs from mine."

"Fine. Since the moment you played nurse and stitched me up, then." He chuckled. "Despite your hearty dislike of me, you were gentle and thorough."

Amazed at how their relationship had altered, she lowered her gaze to his chest. "I didn't dislike you, you know."

"You disapproved of me."

"I misjudged you," she admitted. "You were right. I *had* allowed my lingering resentment toward my father to cloud my thinking. It was easier to condemn your behavior than actually get to know the man behind the badge."

Ben tipped her chin up. "And you were right about me. I used charm and flattery to avoid dealing with my diagnosis. I didn't take into account anyone else's feelings except my own."

"It took an outlaw and an abandoned little boy to force us to look beyond the surface and discover something precious." Awe filled her voice.

His smile bathed her in glorious love and affection. "Sometimes God has to do drastic things to get our attention."

"I'm grateful He cares enough to do that. I'll never forget this Christmas. He not only brought my dearest love into my life, but He gave me—rather, He gave *us*—the opportunity to be parents."

Happiness danced in his brilliant green gaze. "This is also the Christmas that we get engaged, is it not?"

Isabel gasped as he went down on one knee, clasped both her hands and peered up at her with such intensity she could hardly breathe. The spinster was about to be proposed to.

"I love you, Isabel. I can't promise you a life without hardship. And I can't promise I won't mess up sometimes and you'll get so angry you'll wish I was sleeping in the warming hut again."

She laughed through her glistening tears.

"But I can promise I'll spend every day by your side, giving my all to you and Eli." His smile grew lopsided. "And maybe, hopefully, Fran." He squeezed her fingers. "What do you say? Will you marry me?"

Framing his face with her hands, she bent and kissed him. "That was a fine proposal, Deputy MacGregor," she whispered against his lips. "One I wouldn't dream of passing up."

"Merry Christmas, sugarplum."

"Merry Christmas, my love."

Epilogue

Three months later

"Why am I not surprised to find you here?" Ben murmured, his arms sliding around her from behind.

A delicious shiver overtook her. Although they'd been married for six weeks, her husband's nearness never failed to fill her with contentment. Isabel settled against him, his chest a solid support, his body heat enveloping her.

She covered his hands with her own. "She's precious, isn't she? I could stand here for hours and watch her sleep."

Ben was silent for a moment. His breath stirred the tendrils at her nape. "Before Fran came into our lives, I never knew a smiling, toothless infant could capture your heart without saying a single word."

"We are blessed, aren't we?"

"More than I thought possible."

The dark-headed infant shifted beneath the pink-and-white knitted blanket, a gift from her aunt Honor. Her forehead wrinkled. Her mouth puckered, then relaxed. She was a happy baby as long as her tummy was full, and she already seemed to adore her big brother. Her blue eyes lit up whenever he paid her attention.

The past three months had passed in a blissful blur. The week after Christmas, Ben had gone before the church and announced their engagement. Other than Veronica bursting into tears and fleeing the building, and a few misty-eyed young women whose hopes were forever dashed, the news had been well received. Honor and John had decided to hold their ceremony in January so that Ben and Isabel could marry mid-February. Between preparations for both big events and packing and moving Honor's things to John's place, the days had been filled with a flurry of activity.

Ben had sold his cabin to a single farmer. In order to have more space and privacy, they'd decided to build on to Isabel's cabin. An opening had been cut in the wall opposite the other bedrooms and a room added on. Boasting one window and a woodstove, the room was large enough for their bed, dresser, washbasin stand and a handmade crib for Fran. Isabel and Ben had combined their personal things and made it into a cozy, relaxing space. Eli had a room to himself, but he typically sneaked into Carmen's halfway through the night.

Because Isabel now had two young children to tend to, Carmen had volunteered to take over the running of the gristmill. She'd proven to be a capable miller. And of course, their customers were drawn to her perky personality. Isabel wasn't the only one who'd noticed the increase of single men bringing their corn to be ground into meal. While Carmen was old enough to start thinking of marriage, Isabel had made sure her youngest sister felt welcome to stay as long as she wished. Ben treated her as another sister, one he could tease mercilessly since his own were so far away.

"I have news."

Hearing his serious tone, she turned in the circle of his

arms and entwined hers around his neck. His expression was peaceful, which put her worries to rest.

"Shane and I received a telegram from Knoxville. Wesley's been captured. He's currently cooling his heels in a jail cell and will no doubt remain there for the rest of his life. Since he's been charged with the more serious counts of murder, he may even face death."

"I'm so relieved that we don't have to worry about him showing up here."

"Even if he had dared to come sniffing around, I never would've let him within a foot of you or the kids."

"I know." Ben would take his last breath protecting those he loved. "I'm just glad he won't be able to hurt anyone else."

The lawyer she'd hired to handle Eli and Fran's adoption had paid them a visit a few days after their wedding. He'd conducted interviews with various townspeople and, satisfied Ben and Isabel were honest, decent people, had said he'd recommend the judge grant their petition. Last week, the official letter had arrived. In the eyes of the law, Eli and Fran were their children. Isabel had written Harry about the news and invited him to visit when he was ready. She hoped to receive a response soon.

"Papa!" The front door slammed. "Papa? Where are you?"

The commotion woke Fran, whose startled cries never failed to tug at Isabel's heart. Ben and Isabel shared a smile. The demands of parenthood were many, they'd discovered. But the rewards made every sleepless night, soiled diaper and grumpy outburst worth it. Dropping a brief kiss on her lips, he released her to tend the baby while he went out to see what Eli wanted.

Murmuring soothing words, Isabel scooped the infant into her arms and cuddled her close. In the living room,

Ben had crouched in front of Eli. The boy put both hands on Ben's shoulders. They looked like any typical father and son. They might not be related by blood, but the pair had forged a deep bond in a very short time, one that would strengthen and grow with each passing day. Her heart bursting with gratitude, she joined them.

"Mama, there are people coming to see you. Look!" He flung a hand toward the window.

She squinted through the glass. "Ben, did you know Shane was coming? He's got his whole family with him."

"I had no idea."

They stepped onto the porch to await their surprise guests.

The sheriff walked beside Allison, his arm looped about her shoulders. The vivacious blonde carried their infant son in her arms. Even from here, Isabel could see the glint of the light hair he'd inherited from his mother. Their other children, Matilda and twins Izzy and Charlie, tripped along behind them. Walking at a much slower pace, the café owner Alexander Copeland and his bride, Ellie, chatted and laughed. They were engrossed with each other and their newborn daughter tucked in the safety of Alexander's arms. One couldn't be blamed for assuming the pair had been married for years. In fact, they'd been officially together only since late November. Her husband had passed last summer, leaving Ellie pregnant and dependent on hostile in-laws. She'd gone to work for the café owner, and the rest was history.

"Is that Grant and Jessica, too?" Ben said. "What's going on?"

The former marshal and his obviously pregnant wife rode up on a wagon packed with goods. When everyone had descended on them, Ben and Isabel learned they were giving them a belated welcome to married life. There were household items and baby-related necessities.

Ben guided Isabel aside and, tugging her and the baby close, spoke in a voice husky with wonder. "I've realized something. Family isn't limited to blood relations, marriage contracts or adoption papers. Friends can become part of your family, too."

She snuggled close to his side. "Family is what you make of it."

Angling toward them, he dropped a kiss on Fran's head and caressed Isabel's cheek. "Are you happy, sugarplum?"

She smiled. "My answer hasn't changed since you asked me yesterday or the day before."

His eyes glowed with the love he felt for her. "I'm going to ask you tomorrow and the next day and the one after that. I'm going to ask you every day for the rest of our lives."

* * * * *

If you enjoyed A LAWMAN FOR CHRISTMAS,
look for the other books in the
SMOKY MOUNTAIN MATCHES *series,*
including RECLAIMING HIS PAST,
THE BACHELOR'S HOMECOMING,
FROM BOSS TO BRIDEGROOM
and WED BY NECESSITY.

Dear Reader,

This book is the final installment of my Smoky Mountain Matches series. I count myself blessed to have been able to create a fictional world centered around a place near and dear to my heart. I hope you've enjoyed these characters and their stories. While I'm looking forward to new projects, I admit I'll miss the O'Malleys and their friends. When I planned the first book, *The Reluctant Outlaw*, I had no idea if it would be published, much less become an entire series! I'm grateful to my editor, Emily Rodmell, for her invaluable guidance throughout this journey.

For more information on these and other books, please stop by my website, www.karenkirst.com. I'm active on Facebook and Twitter, @karenkirst, and love interacting with readers.

Blessings,
Karen Kirst

Get 2 Free Books, Plus 2 Free Gifts—

Love Inspired® HISTORICAL

Just for trying the Reader Service!

YES! Please send me 2 FREE Love Inspired® Historical novels and my 2 FREE mystery gifts (gifts are worth about $10 retail). After receiving them, if I don't wish to receive any more books, I can return the shipping statement marked "cancel." If I don't cancel, I will receive 4 brand-new novels every month and be billed just $5.24 per book in the U.S. or $5.74 per book in Canada. That's a savings of at least 13% off the cover price. It's quite a bargain! Shipping and handling is just 50¢ per book in the U.S. and 75¢ per book in Canada.* I understand that accepting the 2 free books and gifts places me under no obligation to buy anything. I can always return a shipment and cancel at any time. The free books and gifts are mine to keep no matter what I decide.

102/302 IDN GLWZ

Name	(PLEASE PRINT)	
Address		Apt. #
City	State/Prov.	Zip/Postal Code

Signature (if under 18, a parent or guardian must sign)

Mail to the **Reader Service:**
IN U.S.A.: P.O. Box 1341, Buffalo, NY 14240-8531
IN CANADA: P.O. Box 603, Fort Erie, Ontario L2A 5X3

Want to try two free books from another series?
Call 1-800-873-8635 or visit www.ReaderService.com.

* Terms and prices subject to change without notice. Prices do not include applicable taxes. Sales tax applicable in N.Y. Canadian residents will be charged applicable taxes. Offer not valid in Quebec. This offer is limited to one order per household. Books received may not be as shown. Not valid for current subscribers to Love Inspired Historical books. All orders subject to approval. Credit or debit balances in a customer's account(s) may be offset by any other outstanding balance owed by or to the customer. Please allow 4 to 6 weeks for delivery. Offer available while quantities last.

Your Privacy—The Reader Service is committed to protecting your privacy. Our Privacy Policy is available online at www.ReaderService.com or upon request from the Reader Service.

We make a portion of our mailing list available to reputable third parties that offer products we believe may interest you. If you prefer that we not exchange your name with third parties, or if you wish to clarify or modify your communication preferences, please visit us at www.ReaderService.com/consumerchoice or write to us at Reader Service Preference Service, P.O. Box 9062, Buffalo, NY 14240-9062. Include your complete name and address.

LIH17R2

Love Inspired®

Inspirational Romance to Warm Your Heart and Soul

Join our social communities to connect with other readers who share your love!

Sign up for the Love Inspired newsletter at **www.LoveInspired.com** to be the first to find out about upcoming titles, special promotions and exclusive content.

CONNECT WITH US AT:

Harlequin.com/Community

 Facebook.com/LoveInspiredBooks

Twitter.com/LoveInspiredBks